CW00506860

THEODORE TERHUNE STORIES

A Case for Solomon

A THEODORE TERHUNE MYSTERY

BRUCE GRAEME

With an introduction by J. F. Norris

 Moonstone Press

This edition published in 2021 by Moonstone Press
www.moonstonepress.co.uk

Introduction © 2021 J F Norris
Originally published in 1943 by Hutchinson & Co Ltd
A Case for Solomon © the Estate of Graham Montague Jeffries,
writing as Bruce Graeme

ISBN 978-1-899000-30-2
eISBN 978-1-899000-31-9

A CIP catalogue record for this book is available from the British Library

Text designed and typeset by Tetragon, London
Cover illustration by Jason Anscomb
Printed and bound by CPI Group (UK) Ltd, Croydon, CRO 4YY

Contents

INTRODUCTION

Cherchez le Livre!

In *A Case for Solomon* (1943), the third novel featuring bookseller and accidental detective Theodore I. Terhune, Bruce Graeme continues to experiment with detective-novel conventions, subgenres and narrative structure. As the title suggests, there will be a legal conundrum requiring the wisdom of the Old Testament king known for solving squabbles and disputes by applying a keen insight into human nature. Once again the novel defies categorization and is an amalgam of several subgenres. Opening as a traditional detective novel when Theo and his sometime girlfriend Helena Armstrong find a dead body in the woods, the story transforms into a courtroom drama as Terhune reviews a transcript from a past murder case. The mystery of the murdered man found in the forested pathway at the edge of Bray-in-the-Marsh leads to some detective work focusing on the clue of a book left behind near the body. And the final chapters take us once again to courtroom for a finale filled with unexpected turns of events.

What of that book? Perhaps this would be the time to discuss the "bibliomystery" as a subgenre of detective fiction. All of the Terhune mystery novels feature rare books and manuscripts in the plot. As many devotees of crime fiction know, the bibliomystery is one of the most treasured of detective-fiction subgenres, dealing as it does with books (often extremely obscure or rare books) and book-collecting. In *A Case for Solomon* Terhune discovers a leaf-covered copy of *Rosamund*, one of Algernon Swinburne's verse plays, a short distance from a dead body. Examination of the book proves that it came from his own shop— Terhune vaguely recalls having sold it only a few days ago. Terhune then devotes much of his time in detective work trying to prove that a set of initials written in pencil on the flyleaf is that of the purchaser and owner of the book. This copy of *Rosamund* serves as a keystone in the murder investigation as it will ultimately lead to identifying the culprit. Rather than the standard detective mantra "*Cherchez la femme!*", Terhune and his policeman colleague Detective Sergeant Murphy adopt "*Cherchez le livre!*" as their motto. A better bit of advice could not have been penned by sometime author Terhune himself as we follow the two sleuths on the trail of the book from purchaser to various owners and readers, until we finally end our search literally on the doorstep of the murderer.

Elsewhere in the Terhune series, books and manuscripts are featured as prominent pieces of evidence that are instrumental in unravelling the various mysteries. As readers may have already discovered, the search for missing pages from a manuscript about heraldry and a genealogy of the MacMunn relations sets in motion an international adventure in *Seven Clues in Search of a Crime* (1941). The research into completing a manuscript on the history of House-on-the-Hill leads Terhune and Julia MacMunn to the ghastly secrets of long-forgotten crimes committed in the mansion known as *House with Crooked Walls* (1942). Later, readers will learn of the odd short stories encoded with clues about the murder of a vagrant in *Twelve Trails to Tyburn* (1944), and an exciting book auction that will be a highlight of *A Case of Books* (1946), in which Terhune's bookshop business takes centre stage and his inventory becomes the focus of yet another tale of theft and murder.

Graeme continually found inventive ways to incorporate books and manuscripts into the plots of the Theodore Terhune mystery series, never once repeating himself. His contemporaries may have created detectives who read voraciously and often quoted "great works" (Gervase Fen, Lord Peter Wimsey, Sir John Appleby, among many others), or were involved in the book trade themselves (Elizabeth Daly's Henry Gamadge, Joel and Garda Glass in *Fast Company* by Marco Page), but Graeme's bookseller detective displayed his knowledge of books in a fashion that is intrinsic to solving the mystery. Of all the bibliomystery detectives created by Graeme's contemporaries, Henry Gamadge comes closest to Terhune, yet of the fifteen books in which he appears as the central detective only five of them are remotely about books or manuscripts—and in two of those five the book aspect is so negligible that it could have been eliminated altogether without affecting the story. What makes the Terhune books stand out as some of the most innovative bibliomysteries of the Golden Age is that the stories could not exist without the presence of unusual books or manuscripts. Not only are they essential clues, but these books become additional characters that dominate the action, never far from discussion, never ignored by Terhune. That the biggest clue in *A Case for Solomon* turns out to be a book is a noteworthy achievement—and in contrast to dozens of mystery novels that claim to be genuine bibliomysteries.

Intriguingly, the courtroom transcript in the first third of *A Case for Solomon* also becomes an element of the bibliomystery. A transcript is of course a record of a trial, but for Theodore Terhune it is a literary work that reveals the character and personality of the witnesses. Had he been present at the trial Terhune and everyone else in the court would have had the luxury of seeing each witness, would have been able to take note of manner of dress, behaviour, facial expressions and vocal infection. All of this helps in determining personality and ultimately whether or not the lawyers, judge and jury believe a witness. A transcript, however, is not a screenplay and cannot record anything other than actual speech. Terhune is left only with words, as he would be with any of his books. As he reads each bit of testimony his book sense takes over and he begins to take note of language as a revelation of character. He has an epiphany after reading the crucial testimony of Patricia Webb, the supposed fiancée of Charles Cockburn, the defendant, who is accused of murdering a man Patricia was flirting with while they were on a weekend trip aboard a boat:

Now that he had had the opportunity of reading the rest of Patricia Webb's evidence, Terhune considered that she was more real to him than she had been at first. He felt sorry not to have had the chance of watching her answer the questions put to her by counsel for the defence. The bald, printed words conveyed no hint of her real feelings [unlike the other witnesses]. For instance: her "I do", in answer to counsel's "Do you still love [the defendant]?" Had she breathed the two words with all the embarrassment, yet all the fervour of a person genuinely in love; or with the emotionless defiance of a woman making the best of a bad job, or as a woman unwilling to admit a mistake, or as a woman putting loyalty before conviction?

Two simple words can carry so much weight, in Terhune's estimation. He goes on to judge her relatively simple answers to all the questions while on the stand as probable "proof of their sincerity". Having spent some time in courts, he recognizes that the rambling, overly detailed testimony of some witnesses is often a tactic to distract from the truth, a mechanism of deceitful characters who are trying to withhold information or cover up the actual truth. Graeme's treatment of a courtroom transcript as if it were a literary work is only one of many unusual ways in which he manages to transmute detective fiction conventions into something more artful than mere narrative gimmickry.

Graham Montague Jeffries (1900–1982), better known as Bruce Graeme, was married and had two children: Roderic and Guillaine. Both his son and daughter went on to write books and interestingly also used their father's alter ego surname for their own pen names. Guillaine Jeffries, as "Linda Graeme", wrote a brief series of books published between 1955 and 1964 about a girl named Helen who was a ballet dancer in theatre and on TV. Roderic Jeffries followed in his father's footsteps and turned to writing crime fiction, using his own name and the pseudonyms Roderic Graeme (continuing his father's series about the thief turned crime novelist Blackshirt), Peter Alding, Jeffrey Ashford and Graham Hastings. In addition to more than sixty crime, detective and espionage novels, Roderic wrote a number of non-fiction works on criminal investigation and Grand Prix racing.

Late in life Graeme gave his Elizabethan farmhouse in Kent to Roderic and his wife. Graeme moved up the road to a bungalow and would have lunch with his son and daughter-in-law once a week. According to Xanthe Jeffries, Bruce Graeme's granddaughter, he remained in Kent while his son's family moved to Majorca in 1972. They remained close even while apart, and Graeme would visit in May every year, on his birthday.

When I asked for any family stories she might share with Moonstone Press readers, Xanthe very politely complied with an anecdote-filled email. I learned that her grandfather kept a couple of marmosets as pets and had inherited a Land Rover from his son when Roderic moved away. She also wrote of his annual visits to Majorca: "If the weather was not to his liking," she reported, "we never heard the end of it. On his last trip to us he became very worried about having to travel back to the U.K. via Barcelona." Apparently he was concerned about Spanish customs law. "When asked why he told my parents that his walking stick was in fact a swordstick!" Clearly, Graeme was something of an adventurer himself.

Books, manuscripts, even courtroom transcripts are the signposts for Theodore I. Terhune in his many adventures as detective in Bray-in-the-Marsh. *A Case for Solomon* is unique in the Terhune series for its treatment of all three types of the written word and is as innovative as any of Bruce Graeme's crime fiction. Readers will have much to enjoy in this compelling and insightful book, as they will with the remaining four volumes, soon come from Moonstone Press.

J. F. NORRIS
Chicago, IL
March 2021

A NOTE FROM THE PUBLISHER

While a reader does not need to have read the earlier novels to enjoy this one, *A Case for Solomon* is the third book in the Theodore Terhune series and as such contains some spoilers for earlier books in the series, particularly *Seven Clues in Search of a Crime*.

Chapter One

The day was Wednesday—early closing day at Bray-in-the-Marsh. The hour was 12.50 p.m. In Bray's one and only bookshop, Theodore I. Terhune—known to some as Tommy, to Julia MacMunn as Theo, and to Lady Kylstone as Theodore—was trying to conceal his impatience at being forced to listen to one of Sir George Brereton's fishing stories for the fifteenth time in the past nine months. Or was it the fiftieth? Terhune was sure he could recite the details by heart.

"—and no sooner had we reached this tree I was talking about, Terhune, than William turned round to me and said: 'George, old fellow, if you think it is any use fishing this stretch on a day like this, you are a worse angler than I have always said.' Poor old William! He considers himself the best angler south of the Tweed—"

Simultaneously with the word Tweed the telephone began to ring. Sir George ignored the interruption.

"—and in reality, of course, I know nobody who knows less of the subtleties of the sport than he does. Why, bless my soul, I have known him use a February Red when any schoolboy would have selected an August Dun."

Terhune made a tentative move towards the telephone. "If you will excuse me, Sir George—"

Brereton remained insensible of the interruption. "Naturally, I ignored William's rudeness. You and I both know our William, do we not, Terhune, my dear chap? Well, the moment he said that, which was precisely what I was expecting him to say—"

"I am wanted on the telephone, Sir George."

"—I turned to him and remarked: 'William, you are an obstinate old fool who is too blinded by his own conceit to recognize a really first-class stretch of water when you see one. I'll wager you five pounds that I land something better than a nine-inch fish in less than two hours from this minute—'"

Terhune became desperate. "You must excuse me, Sir George. I really must answer the telephone," he insisted firmly.

"The telephone! Ah! It's ringing. You must answer it at once, my dear fellow." He glanced at his watch. "Good Heavens! Nearly one o'clock. I must hurry home, or I shall hear what's what from Olive. I shall finish the story some other time. Remind me when I see you on Saturday."

As Sir George hurried from the shop, Terhune made his way to the telephone and lifted the receiver.

"Hullo."

"Hullo, Tommy, how is the proof-reading proceeding?"

He recognized the warm voice of Helena Armstrong, Lady Kylstone's secretary and companion.

"It isn't. I finished last night, and posted the proofs back to the publishers this morning."

"Oh; Tommy, I am glad. Did you have to make many alterations?"

"Not so many as I should have liked. It is a strange experience, seeing one's first novel in print for the first time. All the good passages seem so much cleverer, all the bad ones more terrible than one could have believed possible. If I had had a free hand I should have re-written at least three chapters."

"Then why didn't you?"

"Because the alterations would have cost me more than I shall receive from the publishers on account of royalties."

"Tommy, you are teasing me! Surely you would not have to pay the publishers money for making alterations in your own book?"

"Somebody has to pay the cost of the compositor's time in carrying out any corrections the author makes."

"Oh!" After a slight pause she continued: "What are you doing this afternoon, Tommy?"

"Nothing of special interest."

"Lady Kylstone wants me to visit Agnes Hamilton after luncheon. Would you care to come with me?"

"I should love to," he answered promptly. "Do we walk or cycle?" He glanced through the plate-glass window, and saw that the sleepy Market Square beyond was still bathed in the cheerful glow of mid-October sunshine. "As the weather seems to be holding up I suggest walking through the woods."

She replied in an eager voice: "That would be lovely, Tommy. Can you be ready by three o'clock?"

"I can be ready by two."

"I shall come as soon after two as possible," she said swiftly. "See you later."

He grinned cheerfully. "The sooner the better," he told her before he disconnected.

II

From the window of the dining-room upstairs above the shop Terhune saw Helena enter Market Square by way of the Ashford-Willingham road. She rode her bicycle, and as she turned to her right into the short stretch of cobbled road which bordered the east side of the square, the southerly wind swirled up her back and ruffled her loose hair into charming disorder.

His eyes twinkled as he studied her from behind the concealing curtain of the upstairs room. She wore a thick woollen jumper of pastel blue, which clung to her slim, youthful figure; a tweed skirt, of a blue check to match the jumper (or did the jumper match the skirt, perhaps?); woollen stockings uncomplimentary to her shapely legs; a pair of thick walking shoes; and woollen gloves. It was typical of Helena to study her surroundings and her requirements rather than her appearance, to choose serviceable clothes in preference to stylish; to be, more often than not, attractively wind-swept.

In this, as in mostly everything, Helena was unlike Julia MacMunn. Julia was invariably neat. Everything about her was always so precisely as it should be that one was apt to feel that she could safely venture out into the wildest gale without having a single black hair blown out of position. She, too, often wore tweeds, but always cut to her figure with an elegance which betrayed, unmistakably, the skill of a West End tailor. As for stockings, she never wore other than sheer silk. But Julia disliked life in the country, while Helena would have been miserable in any surroundings which did not consist of woods and hills and arable fields and hedge-bordered pasture land.

Terhune watched Helena until she was lost to his view as she rode out of the square proper, and along a few yards of the side-road which pursued a tortuous course past a handful of houses, cottages, and farms, only to come to an abrupt and inglorious end in front of Three Hundreds Farm. He hurried towards the stairs which led down to the private door which opened on to the side-street. He was half-way down when the bell rang.

Helena's cheerful smile greeted him as he opened the door.

"Am I too early?"

"Not by five minutes. I'm all ready." He took her bicycle from her, carried it into the small hall, and leaned it against the staircase. "Still no sign of rain about?"

"No. Old Hobby says there will be no more rain before tomorrow night."

"Those old shepherds are not often wrong with their weather forecasts. At any rate, I've never caught old Hobby out, so I'll take no overcoat." He made sure that he had money, a handkerchief, and his keys. Then he selected two walking-sticks, one of which he passed on to his companion. "Ready?"

A nod of her head confirmed that she was. They stepped out of the building, he slammed the door. Then they turned south, back towards Market Square, which they crossed, still bearing south. From her window, above Collis's the grocer's. Miss Amelia watched them making their way across the cobbled square, which, tomorrow, market day, would become animated and crowded, but which just then was empty save for a few parked cars, and a small group of people discussing the Harvest Festival with the Rector.

Miss Amelia's eyes twinkled as she saw the two walkers, but presently the twinkle was displaced by a more serious expression. "I wonder when Mr. Theodore is going to make up his mind which girl to choose," she mused. "I hope it will be Miss Helena. Miss Julia won't make a good wife for any man with that sharp tongue of hers, and her way of making people feel they are not half so clever as they have always believed. Not that she hasn't her good points, too. I must grant her that—"

Unaware of the problem that was perplexing dear Miss Amelia— and many others, not excluding Helena and Julia themselves—Terhune talked to Helena with an easy, unselfconscious camaraderie which would have discouraged Helena had she allowed herself to dwell upon it. Encouraged by her questions, he spoke of his book, his first, which he had finished a few months previously, and which had quickly found a publisher. That is to say—his first work of fiction, for his first book, an historical account of House-on-the-Hill, the House with Crooked Walls, had been published privately a short while before he had finished *The Victim Came South.*

"I am longing to read it," she commented wistfully. "I think you were very mean not allowing me to read the proofs."

"I want you to read it at its best."

"But you didn't have to make many alterations, Tommy; and, even now, it may be months before the book is published."

"You must possess your soul in patience."

"That is not easy."

"Besides, you will not care much for it. You don't like detective stories."

"Not usually, but knowing the author will make me interested in it. Oh, Tommy, I do hope it will be a success."

"You can't hope for that more than I do. But let's not talk about my book any more, Helena, or we shall wear the subject threadbare. How is Lady Kylstone's cold?"

III

They walked on and, leaving behind them the outskirts of the small market town, soon found themselves approaching a small rise from the far side of which they would be able to see the large expanse of flat countryside which lay between Bray-in-the-Marsh (a misnomer, indeed, for Bray was on a higher elevation than the reclaimed marshland) and the coast.

They reached the summit of the rise, and a lovely vista of quiet, natural beauty. The scene was not one, at first sight, to affect one's emotions, for it contained nothing that was arresting or unusual. There was little to be seen other than a chequered pattern of green fields and wooded patches, bisected by the startling straightness of a muddy, man-made canal, and the grey-blue background of a quiet sea. Only after contemplation was one able to appreciate the subtleties of the landscape, whereupon the cropping sheep, the variegated autumn shades, the wheeling gulls, the unhurried progress of a hay-piled wagon, the coruscating sheen on the water, the smudgy formlessness of a coasting tramp, merged into a timeless poem of serenity and blended colour such as few other corners of the world could equal.

The scene was a familiar one to the two walkers, so they absorbed it in passing, and enjoyed it almost automatically. While discussing Terhune's trip to the U.S.A., which subject the conversation had reached by a series of devious and untraceable divergencies, they passed over the canal and presently left the quiet, winding road in order to take a short cut, a footpath through a wood of several hundred acres known locally as Windmill Wood, no doubt because some long-forgotten windmill had once occupied a site not far away.

In mid-summer the path resembled a cool, green tunnel, but this effect was already passing, for leaves had begun to fall, turning the mossy path into a slippery, yellow-brown carpet, and the roof into a pattern of delicate tracery through which the cold blue of the sky was to be seen.

They had penetrated into the wood a matter of a hundred yards or so when Terhune, in stepping aside from the footpath to avoid a pronounced puddle, struck his right toe against a hard substance which moved forward under the impact. He glanced down at the ground, and saw beneath a partial covering of leaves a square brown object. Because of its temporary camouflage it was not easy to identify it from above, so he stooped and picked it up. His action prompted Helena to halt, and turn.

"What is the matter, Tommy?"

He chuckled. "Look at what I have just found."

She echoed his laughter. "A book! It would have to be you, of all people, to find a book. Of course it is a detective story. Let me guess. By Georges Simenon? Or Michael Innes?"

"You are hopelessly wrong, Helena. It is a copy of Swinburne's *Rosamund*. Quite a nice copy, too." He passed it over to her.

"Where did you find it?"

"By the side of the path." He pointed to the spot.

"I wonder how it came to be there," she mused aloud, as she turned over the pages. Unexpectedly, she smiled. "Here is a chance to reveal your detective skill, Mr. Theodore Terhune. Tell me everything you can about the owner of this book, how long it has been here in the wood, and why it was lying where it was."

"I can tell you how long it has been lying here, my dear Miss Watson," he informed her with simulated solemnity.

For a moment she was surprised by his apparent gravity. Then she entered into the mood of the moment. "How long, Mr. Terhune?"

"Between twenty-one and twenty-two hours."

"Indeed! By what simple process of deduction have you arrived at that period?"

"The back cover is limp with damp, isn't it?"

She examined the book. "Yes."

"The front cover, although damp, is still moderately stiff."

"Well?"

"About what time did that rainstorm stop yesterday afternoon?"

"About four-thirty. It started at four, and lasted nearly thirty minutes."

"Exactly! Therefore the book must have been dropped later than about one hour after the rain had stopped. Had it been dropped before then the front cover would also have been impregnated with damp. As it has not rained since, I conclude that the book must have been dropped here between five-thirty and six-thirty."

For the first time she realized that Terhune was not entirely joking with her. Her interest became even keener.

"Why do you place the time at five-thirty, Tommy? Could it not have been at a quarter to five?"

"I do not think so, Helena. You see, after heavy rain such as we had yesterday trees drip for some time after the rain has ceased. As the front cover does not seem to have been dripped upon, I have made allowance for the dripping to cease."

Her eyes glowed with pride and admiration. "Tommy, you really *are* a detective." Then she continued triumphantly: "Now explain why you think the book was dropped at five-thirty last night, and not at nine-thirty this morning?"

"Suppose we deal with last night first. It was dark soon after six-thirty, so I assume that the person who was carrying that volume of Swinburne about with him—or her—was not likely to have passed through these woods once the night had become really black. Therefore, I assume that it was dropped between the hours of five-thirty and six-thirty."

"But why not this morning?"

"The front cover is almost covered with damp leaves which have stuck to it. It was the high wind during the night which probably caused many of those leaves to fall. As the wind dropped with the dawn probably not many have fallen since then."

"Of course! How simple the answers become—when they are explained." A mischievous light played in her eyes. "Now tell me the name of the owner?" she challenged.

"I can tell you his initials."

"Tommy, I do not believe you."

"They are G.H."

She shook her head. "This time I know you are teasing me."

"Weren't you teasing me when you asked the question?"

She nodded her head.

"All the same, Helena, I am sure the owner of that book possesses the initials G.H."

She continued to doubt him. "How could you possibly tell the initials of its owner merely by looking at a book?"

He chuckled. "Because he has written them on the flyleaf. Look for yourself."

Her expression was rueful as she opened the book, but she persisted obstinately: "How can you be sure G.H. has not borrowed the book from its owner?"

"Because he—or she—has inked in the initials. He might have pencilled the initials in a borrowed book, but I feel sure he would not have used ink—unless, of course, he had no intention of returning it."

She made a face at him before turning back to the book again. After a few seconds' inspection she lifted her head once more; her expression was triumphant.

"There are also some initials in the upper corner of the flyleaf. To whom do they belong?"

"What are the initials?"

"D.T."

"I could make a joke about those particular letters, but I will refrain from the obvious. D.T.! You have asked a hard question this time, my girl. Are the initials pencilled or inked?"

"Pencilled. There is a downward stroke between the D and the T."

He laughed joyfully. "You cuckoo! That is the price of the book."

"The price?"

"In code. Surely you have seen goods priced with letters instead of figures. Each seller usually has his own code." He started. "Did you say D.T., Helena?"

"Yes."

"Let me have it back. I want to examine it again."

Helena passed back the book: he peered at the price code. "Well, I'll be damned!"

"What is the matter?"

"This is my own code. D stroke T stands for two shillings and threepence. I use the first initial of the French numbers—un, deux, trois, and so on. I must have sold this book to its present owner."

"That is not very strange, Tommy. You are the only person between Ashford and the coast who sells books."

He frowned in thought. "I remember buying a copy of Swinburne's *Rosamund* more than a year ago—it was one of a collection of English poets, collected by the Reverend Fergus Macdonald, of Rye, which

I purchased from his widow—but I'm hanged if I can remember selling it again."

"Perhaps Miss Amelia sold it while she was looking after the shop."

"Probably." He was silent for some seconds. "G.H. Who do we know with those initials, Helena?"

"Doctor Harris. Colonel Hamblin."

"Alec Hamblin! Can you imagine his enjoying anything by Swinburne! As for the doctor, he confines his reading exclusively to detective stories. Then there is Bram Hocking. He belongs to my lending library, but he has never bought a book within my recollection—not from me, at any rate. Besides, none of the people I have mentioned are G.H."

"How about Hilda Hughes? Her full name is Hilda Gertrude Hughes."

"Our Hilda!" He shook his head. "Now, if this were a novel by Ursula Bloom or Denise Robins one might have cause for thinking it belongs to her. But not Swinburne." He shrugged his shoulders, and slipped the book into a pocket of his jacket. "Shall we make a move? We could stay here all afternoon making wild guesses, without getting any forrader."

She stepped across the puddle which had caused him to find the book, and slipped her hand through his arm.

"Come along, impatient. You have disappointed me. You are not so clever a detective as I had hoped. Besides, you haven't deduced any reason to account for the book's being where it was. Somebody must have been——"

Her words tailed off into a choking gasp. He glanced quickly in her direction, and saw that she was staring at the foot of an old oak tree some ten yards in front of them, to their half right. His eyes followed the direction of her gaze. Protruding from what appeared to be a pile of fallen leaves was a limp, muddy hand.

Chapter Two

Terhune put an arm round Helena. "I must find out what has happened. Would you rather walk on—"

She did not allow him to finish. "I'm not scared of seeing a—a body, Tommy," she said in a voice not altogether steady. "The war cured me of that sort of nonsense. It was just the unexpectedness of seeing the hand where it is which made me cry out. Besides, I could help you. He—" She glanced at the hand, and repeated the pronoun. "He might be in a faint—" Her voice betrayed her insincerity. The rest of the man was covered by too many leaves to suggest that he had been lying there only a short while.

He did not trouble to contradict her. "I think you had better let me attend to this business on my own, Helena. *It* might have been there for some time, in which case it won't be pleasant." He purposely stressed the pronoun.

"No, I am going to stay." She disengaged her arm, and moved towards the oak. Her shoes squelched in the mud.

Together they began the unpleasant business of brushing the leaves away from the body. From the first the stiffness and coldness of the body confirmed the man's death, but presently, as they cleared the face, their self-imposed task was made still more gruesome by the sight of bloodstains. The reason for these became apparent when the forehead was exposed, for the skull was split open, and revealed a grisly mass of bruised flesh, congealed blood, and scattered brain.

Terhune caught hold of Helena's arm, and helped her to her feet. "We have done all we should. It is the business of others to finish."

"The police?"

"Yes."

"Tommy, do you think the poor man has been murdered?"

"It looks suspiciously like it." With the ferrule of his walking-stick he pointed to a tiny strip of bark which had penetrated the wound. "My guess is, that he was killed by being struck on the front part of his head with a heavy log of wood or a hefty branch."

"Might not a branch have fallen on his head during the strong wind last night?"

"Where is the branch?"

Helena glanced round about her, but there was no sufficiently large branch to be seen, nor any likely looking mound of leaves under which one might expect to find such a branch.

"Will you telephone the police?"

"Yes." He thought for some seconds. "Isn't Mrs. Chancellor on the telephone?"

"Yes. She often telephones Lady Kylstone about the affairs of the Women's Institute."

"Come along, Helena. We'll make for Mrs. Chancellor's, her house being the nearest."

"And leave—this as it is?" She glanced down at the body. "I think we ought to cover it up in case somebody coming through the woods should see it. It could easily scare a young girl, or an hysterical woman."

He had to agree with her, so before leaving the spot they re-covered the corpse with leaves as best they could, and then started off for the far side of the woods, where Mrs. Chancellor had her house.

They were not long in reaching it. Mrs. Chancellor herself opened the door to them. As she recognized them a mingled gleam of interest and triumph leaped into her eyes. Terhune guessed that she was already anticipating the enjoyment she would have at the next meeting of the Institute by retailing how: "That young man of the bookshop, Mr.

Terhune, and Helena Armstrong—Lady Kylstone's secretary, you know, my dears," called upon her one afternoon—

"Why, good afternoon, Miss Armstrong; good afternoon, Mr. Terhune. This *is* a surprise visit. It was only a few days ago when I was speaking of you both to dear Mrs. MacMunn—"

"We are very sorry to trouble you, Mrs. Chancellor—" Terhune slipped in quickly.

She was just as quick. "You are no trouble at all. On the contrary, it is a pleasure which I hope will be repeated. Do come in."

"We have only come for a moment."

"A moment!"

"To ask whether we might use your telephone on a matter of extreme urgency."

Mrs. Chancellor seemed unable to decide whether to be annoyed with the proposed shortness of the visit, or to be diverted by the suggestion of drama which Terhune, unwittingly, had infused into his voice. She chose the latter.

"Of course," she agreed eagerly. "Please come in. The telephone is just inside the hall, on the right."

He stepped into the hall, polished so industriously that everything shone and twinkled, and dialled Exchange.

In answer to the enquiry at the other end, he asked for the Ashford Police Station. Behind him he heard a gasp of gratified surprise from Mrs. Chancellor, who was trying, with pointed delicacy, to indicate that she was not listening.

The connection was quickly established. To the impersonal enquiry at the other end he replied: "Is Detective-Sergeant Murphy there?"

"Who wants him?"

"Terhune, of Bray."

"Hold the line, please; I will find out if he is in."

After a pause of twenty seconds or so a voice said: "Good afternoon, Mr. Terhune. This is Murphy speaking."

"I have just come across something that is in your line, Sergeant."

Murphy chuckled. "Don't tell me you have unearthed another murder."

"I am afraid I have—in Windmill Wood, this time."

The chuckle developed into a burst of good-humoured laughter. "Evidently you don't deal in any crime less than murder. That is the one criticism I have of you amateurs—"

"I am not joking, Sergeant."

The detective's voice sharpened. "You are not really trying to tell me you have really hit upon another murder?"

"I am."

"It isn't possible! There is a law of average—to say nothing of coincidence. Three murders in less than that number of years in a little market town like Bray—" Poor Murphy came to a choking pause. "Have a heart, Mr. Terhune. This isn't April Fool's Day."

"I wish it were. Are you likely to be coming yourself, Sergeant?"

"I am going to pinch myself first. Why do you ask?"

"I suggest your bringing an ambulance."

Murphy sighed, as if reluctant to believe the incredible truth. "Then you have found the body first, this time? At any rate, that is a change."

Now that Murphy had drawn this fact to his attention Terhune realized that the sergeant was justified in his somewhat ponderous facetiousness. Twice previously he had helped in the exposure of a murder, but in both cases he had had reason to suspect the crime before discovering the victim.

"Will you give me the details of where the body is, and how you found it?" Murphy continued more formally.

"I am close by, and can meet you, if you like."

"Excellent. Where shall I find you?"

"On the Rye road, by the footpath to Farthing Toll through Windmill Wood."

"Right. I shall be with you in twenty to thirty minutes." The detective relapsed in amazement. "Three murders, and a ruddy amateur has to find them all!" He was still muttering as he rang off.

As he turned away from the telephone Terhune found himself facing a Mrs. Chancellor who had dropped all pretence of polite reticence, and was staring at him with a curiosity which she obviously intended should be satisfied.

"I could not help overhearing your conversation, Mr. Terhune. You must tell me what has happened."

"I have to meet the police almost at once, Mrs. Chancellor," he informed her firmly. "There is not much to tell. Miss Armstrong and I were on our way to Miss Hamilton, with a message from Lady Kylstone, when we came across a body in the wood. I telephoned the police to send an ambulance. That is all."

She shook her head reprovingly. "Not quite all. You must suspect foul play or you would not have asked to speak to a *detective*-sergeant," she commented shrewdly.

He grimaced slightly at her perspicacity. "It is true," he confessed. "It looks as if the victim—a man—died as a result of a blow on the front of his skull."

Her excitement mounted. "You must tell me more—please, Mr. Terhune. This is the most exciting thing to happen since the day of Armistice."

It was with some difficulty that he was able to make her realize that there was little more that he could tell her, but at last, using his appointment with Detective-Sergeant Murphy as an excuse, he and Helena escaped. As they passed through the wood again, on their way to the Rye road, they glanced in the direction of the corpse, and were glad to see it apparently undisturbed.

In silence they continued forward to the Rye road, where they awaited Murphy's arrival. The sergeant's time estimate proved reliable, for twenty-four minutes after being told of the crime he arrived in a police car at the appointed spot. Two other men were in the car with him, the uniformed chauffeur, and another man in plain clothes. Behind the police car followed an ambulance.

Murphy alighted and approached Terhune with an outstretched hand; his face still wore an expression of incredulity.

"I shall soon begin to believe that you commit these murders yourself," he began.

Terhune laughed. "Fortunately, I have an alibi. Miss Armstrong was with me when we made the discovery. Helena, this is Detective-Sergeant Murphy. Sergeant, Miss Helena Armstrong, Lady Kylstone's secretary."

The detective acknowledged the introduction, and proceeded to introduce the man who had followed him out of the police car—Detective-Constable Jones.

"You really have found a body?" Murphy continued, as Terhune led the way back into the wood.

"You are welcome to charge me with committing a public nuisance if I haven't."

"That sounds fair enough. Tell me what happened."

In a few simple words Terhune told of the events which had led up to the discovery of the corpse. The detective listened without interrupting, nodded his head when the story was finished, and said crisply:

"Right! I suppose you have already formed an opinion of how long the body has been lying where it is?"

"About the same length of time as the book; approximately twenty-one hours."

"So you think the book is linked up with the crime?"

"Why not? Some explanation has to be found to account for the book's being found where it was. People do not, without reason, throw away books in good condition."

"I should not generalize in the case of poetry, if I were you," the detective commented dryly. "Take me, for instance. I shouldn't trouble to give a book of poetry house room." He laughed. "All the same, you are probably right, Mr. Terhune. What do you think may have happened?"

"Something like this, Sergeant. Our Mr. X was walking through the wood last night, just before dusk, when he was suddenly attacked by a man probably in hiding behind a tree—there is a large elm just in front of the spot where I found the book—"

Murphy nodded understandingly. "Go on."

"By the apparent absence of any great flow of blood I should imagine that Mr. X died immediately. As he fell to the ground the book dropped from his hand, unnoticed by the murderer, whose next act was to drag the corpse behind the oak tree, where he heaped a quantity of fallen leaves over it in the hope of its being undiscovered for some time." Terhune came to a stop. "This is the place, Sergeant. Here is the puddle I stepped over, this is where I found the book, and there is the body."

Murphy stood still, and stared at the foot of the oak tree. "I cannot see any sign of a face beneath the leaves."

"Miss Armstrong and I re-covered the body, to prevent its being seen, pending your arrival."

"You don't overlook much, Mr. Terhune," the detective complimented. "No wonder you seem to run headlong into cases of crime."

"It was Miss Armstrong's idea."

"It was a good one, whoever thought of it. But if the murderer was cunning enough to hide the body beneath those leaves, how did he come to leave the hand uncovered?"

"I do not think he did."

"What!"

"The hand projects just far enough away from the shelter of the tree-trunk for the wind to have swirled round and blown the leaves away."

Murphy still made no move towards the corpse, but stared at the ground. His gaze followed the course which the murderer might have taken in pulling the body towards the oak tree. Presently he shook his head, apparently in disappointment, and turned to the men behind him, the detective-constable and the two hospital orderlies.

"Stay where you are until I signal you."

He glanced also at Terhune, who nodded agreement. Then he moved slowly towards the corpse, meanwhile continuing to stare at the ground. After he had walked eight or nine paces he paused, stooped, and meticulously picked up every fallen leaf within an area roughly two feet square. This process he repeated farther on. At another spot he stooped and appeared to dig something out of the ground. When he stood upright and examined what he had picked up it looked to Terhune as though the detective was holding nothing more exciting than a piece of twig.

At last he reached the foot of the tree, where, instead of removing the camouflage of leaves from the dead man, as his watchers had anticipated, he returned to the group on the footpath, and spoke to Jones and Terhune collectively.

"I think your deductions are right, Mr. Terhune. Something rounded and heavy was dragged over the ground, which left its impression, and pushed this into the muddy ground." He exposed the twig which he had picked up. Then he spoke directly to the detective-constable. "We can uncover the body now."

Jones nodded.

To Terhune, Murphy continued: "Would you like to stand by?"

"Please."

"And you, Miss Armstrong?"

"I should prefer to stay here."

"I don't blame you, miss. I still dislike corpses."

The three men walked to the foot of the oak. The two detectives carefully brushed away the leaves from the head and face of the corpse.

"A nasty sight," Murphy grunted. He peered at the wound, and presently nodded. "He was killed by a branch right enough. Look! There is a slither of bark stuck deep in the skull." He looked up at Terhune. "Do you recognize him, sir?"

The wound itself, the bloodstains, mud splashes, and the moisture from the damp leaves made recognition a chancy affair. There was nothing about the face which jogged Terhune's memory.

"No, although I might if the face were to be washed."

The sergeant sighed. "A pity. In cases like this an early identification halves our work. Let's hope he is carrying papers of sorts. What would you judge his age to be? About the late forties?"

Both Terhune and the constable nodded. Murphy went on:

"Hair beginning to grey round the ears. Thin face. Ruddy complexion, which looks like the result of an outdoor life." He glanced at the hand which Jones had just uncovered. "Finger-nails chipped and uncared-for. Hands rough, and calloused. Probably those of a manual worker. Suit, dark blue serge of inferior quality, well worn. Shirt, collar, and tie all frayed." He stopped speaking, and resumed the work of uncovering the body, which Jones had meanwhile continued.

As soon as the body was completely exposed the three men were able to see that it was of a thick-set man of average height, whose trousers and boots confirmed the impression which Murphy had already formed, that the man wore the clothes of a not-too-well paid manual worker.

The sergeant began to search the pockets of the blue serge suit. The first articles he pulled out were pipe, tobacco pouch, and matches. These from the left pocket of the man's jacket—he wore no overcoat. From the right pocket a short length of tarred twine, which made Murphy exclaim his satisfaction.

"I thought so. A fisherman or seaman."

From other pockets Murphy produced a key; silver coins totalling two shillings; three coppers; a grimy, coloured handkerchief; a packet of Woodbines; a box of matches; a substantial knife; and a tin of peppermints, half full. Nothing more.

"Blast him!" Murphy swore without malice. "No papers. And probably no laundry marks that will prove of any assistance to us."

"Why do you think that?" Jones queried.

Murphy grinned. "Ask Mr. Terhune here. I'll bet a tanner he can answer a simple question like that."

"Because his washing was probably done at sea?" Terhune hazarded.

"Of course. And when at home no doubt his old woman washed for him." The sergeant took one more comprehensive glance at the corpse. "I don't think we need him here any longer." He signalled to the hospital orderlies.

"Take him away, lads; and be careful about lifting him on to the stretcher."

The orderlies were careful; lifting the corpse well into the air before lowering it on to the stretcher. The detectives, and Terhune, watched this operation carefully, lest anything fell from the corpse which might offer a clue, but all that did, in fact, drop were pieces of moss, some fallen leaves, and a short length of bramble.

The sergeant nodded to the orderlies. They raised the stretcher, and bore it away. Murphy turned to Jones.

"We will search about for the weapon, and anything else likely to be useful. You take t'other side of the footpath, while I take this."

"Can't I help?" Terhune offered.

"Gladly." Murphy indicated an area of the wood. "Will you take over that patch between that fallen trunk over there, and that copper beech? Don't overlook anything, however insignificant it might appear at first sight." He laughed unexpectedly. "But there, I am forgetting. I don't have to tell *you*, Mr. Terhune."

The three men parted, and began their search. Helena joined Terhune, though he warned her she would get her shoes in a mess if she did so. The prospect did not daunt her; perhaps she was already infected with the pernicious germ which is bred of the excitement of a man-hunt. However, they found nothing whatsoever, so they returned to the elm where they found Murphy and Jones gingerly handling and examining a thick branch, about four feet in length.

"This is it, Mr. Terhune." The sergeant pointed to the thicker end. "There are traces of blood and flesh to be seen."

"Where did you find it?"

"Jones found it. Over there behind that holly bush on the left. As you see, it's elm. Further proof that the murder was committed just here by the side of the footpath. Ten to one this branch fell from this very tree." Murphy pointed upwards. "See that stump, about twenty feet up, just on the right, above that big branch there? That looks about the same thickness as this bit. My guess is, that the murderer saw the other man coming, looked about for something to use as a weapon, saw this likely branch lying close to his feet, picked it up, took a swipe at his victim, and knocked the man down. As soon as the murderer saw that his blow had succeeded he threw the weapon as far as he could into the undergrowth, dragged the corpse to the foot of the oak tree, and covered the body with dead leaves. Then he probably left the scene as quickly as he could get going." He looked down at his muddy boots. "I think it's time we did the same."

Murphy turned, and led the way back to the Rye road.

Chapter Three

Having proceeded a few yards Murphy said: "May I look at the book which you picked up, Mr. Terhune?"

Terhune took the volume out of his pocket and passed it on to the detective. Murphy examined it carefully. "Are these the pencil marks which you made?" He pointed to the code letters inside the cover.

"Yes."

"Are you sure the writing is yours? Many people prefer to use code letters in preference to figures."

"I am positive it is mine. Besides, I remember buying a copy of Swinburne's *Rosamund* about twelve months ago."

"And it was this particular copy?"

"I would not swear to its being this copy in particular. But surely there can be little doubt—"

"There is no doubt to my mind," Murphy hastened to confirm. "I was only trying to find out how far we can go in proving that this was the copy you bought and sold. A man's life might have to depend upon the strength or otherwise of your testimony."

Terhune shook his head. "I don't think so. I cannot remember having sold it again, so I could not identify the purchaser."

"Can you give me any idea as to when you sold it?"

"Not in the slightest. I think it was possibly sold by Miss Amelia, who takes charge of the shop for me whenever I am absent."

"Then she might just as well have sold it a year ago as last week, for instance?"

"I am afraid so."

Murphy was disappointed. "If it was sold a year ago it may have passed through several hands since then. Ah, well!" He shrugged his shoulders. "I take it you found nothing of any interest in the wood?"

"No."

"Nor did we, apart from the weapon."

The detective paced on in silence for a short time. Then he began: "Returning to the subject of the book, Mr. Terhune, would you care to help us in our enquiries?"

"Naturally. What do you want me to do?"

"For one thing, try to find out from that Miss Somebody of yours— what is her name—"

"Miss Amelia." Terhune chuckled. "I think she was born with a surname, but it is so little used I cannot remember it."

"Well, ask her whether she can recollect having sold the book, and if so, to whom?"

Helena interrupted: "Poor Miss Amelia! She has a terrible memory."

Murphy grunted. "That's helpful! Another thing you can do for me, Mr. Terhune, is to supply me with a list of your clients who are interested in poetry, and who might have purchased the book from your shop. By the way, I must retain possession of *Rosamund* meanwhile, in case it has some connection with the case. Incidentally, do any of your regular clients live round about Farthing Toll and beyond?"

Terhune mentally listed the people he could remember offhand. "At least a dozen. Probably more," he volunteered presently.

"Have any of them a surname beginning with H?"

"Yes. Hunt. Thomas Hunt."

"Hunt of Whistling Farm. I know him. I'll bet he doesn't read poetry. I suppose thrillers are more in his line."

"You are wrong, Sergeant. When Hunt reads he takes a busman's holiday. He likes books about the soil and nature—A. G. Street, Sheila Kaye-Smith, Henry Williamson."

"What about those two boys of his? Young Jim, and the other—"

"Harold."

"Yes. Are they readers?"

"Only of Westerns. But why are you so particularly interested in the book, Sergeant? If you identify the body you will find out, at the same time, who owns—or owned—the book."

"*If!*" Murphy repeated emphatically. "But I think you are overlooking the fact that two men were present at the time of the crime."

"Two?"

The detective chuckled. "The murderer was also there."

"Good Lord!" Terhune's round face expressed his astonishment. "Are you suggesting that the book might have belonged to the murderer, and not the victim?"

"Why not?"

"Such an explanation would be psychologically out of harmony. Can you imagine a murderer carrying a volume of Swinburne about with him?"

"Stuff and nonsense!" Murphy exclaimed pleasantly. "This murder is a plain, brutal, human homicide, not one of those fancy crimes with yards of trimmings, like the affair of the House With Crooked Walls. Besides, for that matter do you see Swinburne being carried about by a corny, calloused hand like that of the victim's?"

Terhune grinned—that characteristic shy grin of his was part of the charm which endeared him to so many residents of Bray, especially the women, whose immediate reaction to it was a desire to mother him.

"Of course you are right, Sergeant. I suppose I was so sure that the book had fallen from the victim's hand when he was struck down that I did not stop to consider the second possibility." His voice became more serious. "If the book were being carried by the murderer, then it becomes all the more important to trace the owner of the initials?"

"Exactly," Murphy exclaimed drily. "That is why I am so keen to enlist your help."

II

Having seen the ambulance and the police car leave for Ashford, Helena and Terhune resumed their interrupted journey to Agnes Hamilton's. Once again they passed through Windmill Wood. This time they reached Farthing Toll, a tiny village of scattered cottages, centred around an old Toll House, from which the locality derived its name, an ancient church, and a blacksmith's forge. Agnes Hamilton lived in a house about one hundred yards south of the forge.

On their way to Honeysuckle House—Agnes Hamilton's—Helena and Terhune talked incessantly of the crime upon which they had stumbled, until they had exhausted every possible aspect. After this they tried genuinely to divert the conversation along more normal channels, but it was no good. It seemed that, no matter what subject was introduced, it had some bearing on the crime, so that back they were again before they had realized where the conversation was leading.

For instance, they stopped to admire a fine specimen of a British Saanen goat of the hornless variety. Upon Helena's saying that the goat must be Mrs. Stockwell's famous Patsy of Farnaby, Terhune immediately recollected that he had seen Mrs. Stockwell in Bray during the late afternoon, so might it not be possible that while she had passed through the wood on her way home she had met either the murderer or his victim? Then Terhune recognized at a distance a Mr. Hobday, and remembered that he was often in the bookshop, as a buyer of inexpensive books on a variety of subjects. Later, Helena saw a man feeding a pen of Rhode Island Reds, on a smallholding opposite the Toll House, and announced that he, too, had a name beginning with the letter H—Harrison.

"Does he buy books from you, Tommy?"

Terhune was dubious. "The face is not really familiar to me. Why? Are you still thinking of the crime, Helena? Do you think *he* might be our murderer?" His voice was, perhaps, somewhat ironical. Harrison was a frail-looking man, of average height, with bowed shoulders, and greying hair.

Her face reddened. "We are weak-minded, aren't we, Tommy, not to be capable of forgetting the murder for more than two consecutive minutes. Let's talk of—" She paused.

"Agnes Hamilton," he concluded drily. With good reason, for Miss Hamilton was approaching them.

Still later, after he had seen Helena home to Timberlands, Terhune went up to his cosy little den, which served him as a combined library, study, and occasional dining-room—for 'tray' meals—stoked up a cheerful fire of ash logs, settled into a deep, cosy but somewhat shabby armchair, lit a pipe, and again returned to the subject of the crime.

He began by trying to jog his memory into recollecting any transaction involving the copy of *Rosamund*—after all, he might easily have sold it without retaining any lasting impression of the transaction: on any Thursday morning, market day, people were constantly in and out of his shop, exchanging library books, turning over his latest acquisitions, requesting him to try and secure on their behalf a copy of this, that or t'other, or buying a book from one of the shelves marked: 'All Volumes on this Shelf, *6d.*' Or one shilling, one shilling and sixpence, two shillings, and upwards, as the case might be. It could easily have happened that, while he was busy with some other customer, a man had approached the table which served him as desk-cum-counter, passed over *2s. 3d.*, saying: "I'll take this," and left without his—Terhune's—consciously observing the title or the face of the man who had made the purchase.

Presently Terhune gave up trying to force his memory, and went downstairs to the shop where he kept a card-index of his regular clients and their usual requirements. Tidily untidy in his personal life—his study was the despair of any woman, and yet he always knew exactly where to find everything—he was meticulously orderly where his business was concerned. Having turned to the Hs, therefore, he was at once able to count the number of his regular clients under that initial. In all, twenty-four. For Murphy's benefit he copied out the list.

Hamblin came first; Alec, Colonel. Alec Hamblin was a distant relative of Lady Kylstone, first cousin, once removed. Hamblin lived in Boundary House, so called because the east half of the house was in the Parish of Willingham, and the west half in the Parish of Wickford. Boundary House was on the south side of the Ashford road—the road which ran from Ashford to nowhere in particular, via Great Hinton, Bray-in-the-Marsh, Wickford and Willingham. Alec Hamblin's reading consisted almost solely of books dealing with military campaigns — Louis XIV's, Marlborough's, Napoleon's, Wellington's, all the battles of the First and Second World Wars.

Next on the list came Doctor Arthur Harris. Harris, like his rival doctor and friend, Doctor Edwards, lived in Bray. He read intelligent detective novels—but not those of the 'thriller' variety—and occasionally a modern biography, especially those with a medical background. His wife, Vera, was also a keen reader. Her taste ran to the sophisticated novel, and she would go without reading for a week rather than open one which did not fall within this category.

Nicholas Harvey was a retired bank manager (the *Westminster* Bank, he always emphasized—nobody knew why!). He lived, with his middle-aged spinster daughter, who kept house for him, in a small cottage on the outskirts of Great Hinton. The cottage had two acres of land attached to it, so Harvey was able to indulge his one and only hobby—gardening—to his heart's content. When he was not in his garden, which was very seldom, he was reading a gardening text book, or Beverley Nichols, or Marion Cran, or Eleanour Sinclair Rohde.

George Hayward was Bray's one and only chemist. He read anything and everything. All was grist which went into his reading mill, he was fond of announcing in a loud, jovial voice. Nevertheless, Terhune noticed that Hayward's first choice usually contained a certain amount of 'spice' in varying degrees. '*Anything and everything.*' And

Hayward's first initial was G! Terhune decided to put a cross against the name of George Hayward.

Both the next two names from his card index were readers of detective novels and thrillers. The first was George Hedley, who was Mr. Justice Pemberton's chauffeur, and lived in the servants' quarters at Hinton Manor. The second, William Hemming, was a farmer. His farm, John's Close Farm, was in Willingham.

The next name was of a Farthing Toll man, Stanley Heppenstall. Heppenstall was an Ashford business man, being owner of the 'Clarendon Hotel' there, but preferring to live with his family in an old Elizabethan farmhouse in Farthing Toll. He was an occasional visitor only to Terhune's bookshop, and then as a buyer, not a borrower. He was of the 'choosey' variety, and would often spend thirty minutes in selecting a book. Sometimes he bought books from the quarterly catalogues which Terhune circulated near and far. He was, in fact, the type of reader who might well have bought Swinburne's *Rosamund*. Terhune marked a cross against the name of Heppenstall. True, he was down in the card-index as S. Heppenstall, but it might be that he had a second name beginning with G. That was something for Murphy to find out.

A woman was next on the list, Mildred Hetherington. She was a spinster, with an income just sufficient with scrupulous care for her needs. As a consequence, her one and only ambition in life was to travel widely. As she had never left the shores of England, and apparently was never likely to do so, she did the next best thing: visited the cinema frequently, and read books on foreign travel, or novels with foreign settings. She was as obstinate as Mrs. Harris in refusing books which did not fulfil her requirements.

Next, Thomas Hicks, who farmed three hundred acres just north of Bracken Hill, which village was itself due north of Bray. Hicks, perhaps because he was deeply rooted in soil which had belonged to his ancestors for centuries, steeped himself in history. Anything historical was his one demand. Fiction or biography. His favourite authors were Sabatini, Farnol and Orczy. He had a habit of reading in turn every published work by these three writers, until the list was exhausted. Then he would begin at the beginning, and read them all again.

Terhune had a second Hicks on his list: Robert Graham. There was no relationship between the two Hickses, though Robert Graham, like Thomas, was also a farmer. At least, he called himself a farmer. In reality, he was a so-called gentleman-farmer, something very different. His farm, Bray Tap Farm, was south-east of Bray, on the far side of the canal, not far from Windmill Wood. Another G.H.! And another cross from Terhune, although Robert Graham Hicks was interested only in books dealing with the stage, probably on account of his grandmother, who was reported to have had a short-lived success at Covent Garden. Every autobiography by a famous theatrical star, every book of criticism by a well-known critic, were all avidly read by him. In particular, he was a fan of James Agate.

Yet another farmer supplied the next name. Bram Hocking. But as Terhune had earlier pointed out to Helena, Hocking had never been known to buy a book. He was interested in the lending library only, and his taste in literature ran to fiction, which had to be of an exciting nature—perhaps as a contrast to his life's work. Hocking's farm, Peartree Farm, was in Willingham, just beyond the MacMunn property.

Mabel Hogben was the widow of the late curate of Bray church. She read only classical literature. She lived at 5, Sea-view Road, a neighbour of Everard Winstanley.

The two brothers Houlden, Frank and John, next came out of the index. Both were bachelors, and kept the *Hop-Picker*, at Wickford, with a first cousin, a middle-aged widow, to fulfil the double function of barmaid and housekeeper. Frank liked Westerns and thrillers, and was briskly businesslike in making his choice. John, on the other hand, made his exchanges with a shy furtiveness, as he tried to hide the titles of the borrowed books. This was due to his partiality for the type of romantic literature which is usually read by young girls in their 'teens.

Brian Howland was a dentist, who held a day surgery in Ashford every day of the week, and an evening surgery in Bray, from 6.30 to 8.0 p.m. on Tuesdays and Fridays, or on other nights by special appointment. He lived in one of a row of Georgian houses which formed the western boundary of Market Square, and visited Terhune's shop almost every other day, about 4.30 p.m., to exchange his book. Howland was a dilettante in science: he read hundreds of books on every branch of the subject, from astronomy to zoology, but Terhune was never able to discover whether or no Howland had really absorbed any genuine knowledge from his reading.

Hilda Hughes, and the Hunts—from Farthing Toll—followed Howland's name. After them came the two Huttons, Godfrey and his wife Patricia. Godfrey had inherited a fair-sized fortune from Hutton's Famous Olde Englishe Jam—*via* his deceased uncle and godfather, Godfrey Hutton—and spent an agreeable but utterly useless life playing golf in the mornings, tennis in the afternoons, and auction or poker— preferably poker—in the evenings. In between these strenuous periods of sport and pastime he made love to every passable widow within an hour's car-ride of his home—Wickford—and read French and German in the original, translations from other European languages, Virginia Woolf, Gertrude Stein and, even, James Hadley Chase. Patricia, who adored her husband, ten years older, was content to read Naomi Jacob, Frank Swinnerton and Howard Spring.

Francis Hyde was another Bray resident. He was a veterinary surgeon, and was another reader who enjoyed a good yarn irrespective of its subject, time, or locale. Lastly, Mrs. Jane Hyde-Williams, who lived opposite Willingham church. She was one of the few women readers who enjoyed thrillers, and this liking only dated from the night when Terhune had prevented the robbery in Kylstone family vault. The events of that night had so excited Mrs. Jane Hyde-Williams that, a few days later, she had timidly asked Terhune to recommend a detective novel. He chose an old one—not because of its age, but because it was one of his own favourites: A. E. W. Mason's *The House of the Arrow*. In consequence, she had become an enthusiastic fan of detective novels, and now read nothing else.

As soon as he had noted down the names and addresses of all his regular clients whose surnames began with an H, Terhune began a new list, this time of clients who lived in Farthing Toll, or beyond, irrespective of their name. These numbered seven, excluding Heppenstall and the three Hunts: Harry Beadle, farmer; Ivan Brown, an elderly retired business man from Crouch End; Captain James Forbes (R.N. retired); Henry Forrester, seedsman and market gardener; Mrs. Agatha Joy; George Binks, a local bus-driver; and Colonel Terence O'Malley (Inniskilling Dragoons, retired), Captain Forbes's neighbour, rival (in the cultivation of roses) and instinctive antagonist.

Terhune sat up and stared curiously at the two lists, wondering whether he had just written down the name of a murderer.

Chapter Four

The following morning Terhune had reason to reflect, somewhat disconsolately, that whenever he was involved in some unusual occurrence, more often than not the day was a Wednesday. As a consequence, he was compelled, the following morning, not only to cope with the usual rush of market-day clients, but also with a large number of curiosity-mongers who used the excuse of buying a book—rarely at a cost of more than sixpence—to plague him with their questions. Of course, it was all fine for business, but while the curiosity-mongers would have been welcome, more or less, on a Friday morning, when barely a dozen customers would enter the shop, their arrival on a Thursday morning created a rush of work which ruffled his normally placid temper.

From the moment of his opening the door of the shop the ordeal began. The eagle eyes of Mrs. Collis, the grocer's wife, espied the door move. Regardless of the fact that she was just gaining the upper hand in an intensive bargaining bout with Alf Bodkin, a second-hand merchant who toured the markets of Kent and East Sussex in a motor-van which undoubtedly had been among the first hundred to be manufactured by Mr. Ford—Mrs. Collis sacrificed her chance of rare victory in an effort to be the first to enter Terhune's shop.

She was the first. "Mr. Terhune," she began breathlessly, "I couldn't believe my eyes when I read the *Daily Mail* this morning. Is it *really* true that you discovered the body of a dead man in Windmill Wood yesterday afternoon? You must tell me what happened. Did you—"

Mrs. Moore, of Three Ways Farm, entered the shop. She ignored Mrs. Collis. "I have just read all about you in the *Daily Express*, Mr. Terhune. Who was the poor man? I am sure you must have recognized him."

Old Hobby was close behind Mrs. Moore—he sometimes worked for her husband, as a spare shepherd. "Good day to 'e, mister. I've been hearing as 'ow 'e has been mussed up in another crime do. In Windmill Wood, they, do say which I can't nowise believe, for I was in Windmill Wood myself, not many hours afore 'e was, and I ain't seen 'un, and me old eyes is still good fer all me seventy-five years. Aye, seventy-five come next Christmas Day, mister, and there baint be many younger men can boast of being as good as me—"

"You keep that chattering old tongue of yours still, Thomas Hobby," Mrs. Moore ordered sharply. "Mr. Terhune is speaking to me."

The old man chuckled throatily as two more women entered the shop. "Mister Terhune won't soon have no time to speak to nobody in pertickler."

As the morning began, so it continued. Presently Sir George Brereton entered, saying: "My dear fellow, if one is to believe *The Times*, you land a crime more easily than I can a fat, juicy trout."

And later, Mrs. MacMunn bustled in. "Dear boy, it isn't true. It just cannot be true. I know, there must be some mistake about that report in the morning newspapers about your having discovered *another* body."

Still later, Julia MacMunn appeared. Her fine features were marred by a furious, sulky expression.

"So you are unable to resist publicity, Theo? But of course, in these days novelists welcome publicity, do they not, darling? It helps to boost their sales."

"If you are referring to the reports of the discovery in Windmill Wood—"

"Of course I am," she snapped.

"That was none of my doing, Julia. Or, for that matter, of my choosing. I had not the slightest idea the Press had got on to the story until my telephone started ringing just after eight o'clock last night. For the next two hours I was scarcely able to get away from it."

"If you did not let the Press know in the first case that you discovered the body how did they find out?"

"Search me. I know Murphy didn't reveal the name of his informant: I asked him not to do so."

"Of course it was not Murphy," she said scornfully. "It was Helena."

"Helena? Nonsense!"

"She was with you, was she not, when you saw the body?"

"Well, yes," Terhune admitted uncomfortably—he did not like the expression in Julia's eyes. "We were on our way to Agnes Hamilton with a message from Lady Kylstone."

"And Helena thought the publicity might help the sales of your first novel if she informed the Press of your discovery."

"I am sure Helena did nothing of the kind," Terhune denied irritably. "She knows as well as you do that I am *not* fond of publicity, and that I do *not* like being advertised—and laughed at—as Bray's 'brilliant amateur detective, who has already solved two murder mysteries in the past two years'."

She laughed without humour. "The *Daily Herald*?"

"Yes."

"If neither you, nor Helena, nor Murphy told the Press of your discovery, who did?"

"I suspect Mrs. Chancellor, of Farthing Toll."

"What had she to do with the crime?"

Terhune told Julia of the telephone call he had made from Mrs. Chancellor's house, and of the scanty information which he had passed on. He continued: "Perhaps she has a relative in the Press Association, Reuter's, or one of the other agencies."

The explanation satisfied Julia, but her expression of angry annoyance remained.

"Let us not talk of the affair any more, my sweet, but of more important matters. Mother sends you an invitation to dinner Saturday night. Can you come?"

"Gladly," he replied, with sincerity—for he liked Julia except when she indulged in tantrums, or allowed her caustic tongue too much freedom.

So it was arranged. Julia's eyes smouldered with satisfaction as she left to join Jeffrey Pemberton in the smoking-room of the *Almond Tree*.

I I

As soon as he had a few minutes to spare Terhune rang up Detective-Sergeant Murphy.

"Terhune speaking, Sergeant. Have you identified the body yet?"

"No. There hasn't even been an enquiry about it except one telegram, from a Glasgow wife who asks if the body has red hair, is six feet two inches in height, and two toes missing from the left foot; if so, it is her missing husband. And a second telegram from an Ipswich mother, to ask whether we have found her son who disappeared six weeks ago, and was last seen in London. As she doesn't give a description, we are no wiser."

"What about the autopsy?"

"It's being held this afternoon. Just around now, in fact. How about you? Have you any news for me?"

"I have prepared a list of all my clients with a surname beginning with H, and another, of any clients who might have used the footpath through Windmill Wood."

Murphy was pleased. "Good. Will you be at home about seven-thirty tonight?"

"Yes."

"Then I shall call about then, if I may."

I I I

It was nearly eight when Murphy arrived. As he sank into the armchair in front of the study fire Terhune noticed that his visitor was looking weary.

"There is no news yet as to identity," Murphy said shortly, as he offered a cigarette and lighted his own. "Two more red herrings have come in, one from Hastings, the other from Chipping Norton. We have asked Scotland Yard to circularize his description tonight to all stations."

"What is his description, by the way?"

"Five feet eleven inches, blue eyes, black hair greying round the ears, hairy chested, big-boned, about forty-five years of age, bronzed complexion, dressed—well, you know how he was dressed. Incidentally, he has one very distinct identification mark: a zig-zag scar on the right shin, about two inches below the knee-cap."

"That should prove helpful."

Murphy nodded.

"What was the result of the autopsy?"

"The blow on the head killed him sure enough. And there isn't much doubt about his having been a seaman. There is evidence of salt in his hair, tar and paint under his finger-nails; his vest came from an Australian store, his shoes from a Los Angeles shop."

"In that case I suppose you have been in touch with the ports?"

"For the past two hours. Now what about those two lists, Mr. Terhune? They sound interesting."

Terhune passed over the list. Murphy examined them carefully. At last: "These crosses, I take it, are meant to indicate the most likely suspects, because they are G.H.s?"

"Yes."

"Suppose we consider them in alphabetical order. This George Hayward, for instance. What kind of books does he usually read?"

Terhune answered the question fully.

"Spicy, eh! Well, that doesn't mean much. I don't object to a spicy book myself, now and again, though I don't search 'em out. What kind of a man is he?"

"A little too much of the 'Hail, fellow, well met' type for my personal liking, but apart from that not too bad. I should not judge him to be a man likely to commit murder."

"Don't bring psychology into this," Murphy said sharply. "There isn't a truer saying than that still waters run deep. As like as not your surly, unlikeable fellow gives all his spare cash to the local hospital—anonymously—while that other chap, the prime favourite of everyone who knows him, is capable of the meanest behaviour to his unfortunate wife and family."

"Returning to Hayward, does he spend much time in his shop, or does he have an assistant?"

"His wife occasionally acts as assistant, but for the most part he is usually to be found there himself."

"Then we should be able to check up on his movements fairly easily."

"Not on a Wednesday afternoon."

"Damn!" Murphy exploded. He passed on to the next name.

One by one the two men discussed the names, while Murphy made notes. He was particularly interested in Godfrey Hutton.

"I see that this man Godfrey Hutton lives quite near Windmill Wood—near enough, at any rate, to account for his being there just before dusk. What do you know of him?"

Terhune related all he knew of Hutton.

"A man who can read French and German in the original sounds like a man who might choose to read Swinburne. And a widow chaser

into the bargain, eh! I know the type. They are as capable as anyone
I know of committing a murder when their sins find them out."

"Sins? In the form of a relative?"

"Perhaps, but I wasn't thinking of a relative in this particular
instance: I don't see an ordinary seaman being the relative of any
widow Hutton might be chasing, unless, of course, he goes a long
way outside his own circle. No, the thought occurred to me that
our seafaring man may have been indulging in a spot of blackmail,
perhaps, and that Hutton cracked him across the head in a moment
of fear or anger, or because he was prepared to commit murder,
rather than pay blackmail." Murphy shrugged. "The idea was just
a passing one, and more in your line, as a writer, than mine—the
few odd cases of murder in which I have been connected, directly
or indirectly, have turned out to be quite commonplace and sordid.
How about examining some of the names of those whom you haven't
specially noted?"

He glanced down the list once more. "This man Francis Hyde. You
say he reads books of all types. Have you ever known him read poetry?"

"Once or twice. I ordered a copy of *Hiawatha* on his behalf about
eighteen months ago. He wanted it as a birthday present for a nephew
living somewhere in Yorkshire. I forget where."

"Is he married?"

"Yes."

"Any family?"

"Two girls."

"Do you know their names?"

"Yes. Hilda and Gertrude."

"Gertrude! Gertrude Hyde! There is another G.H. for us to keep
in mind." The detective saw Terhune about to speak. "No, I'm not
suggesting that a woman killed our seaman. Far from it. But maybe
Papa Hyde was short of reading matter, and picked up the copy of
Rosamund which he had bought some time previously, and given to

his daughter." Murphy threw his cigarette butt into the fire with an irritable gesture. "But all this theorizing is rather futile. It must be your influence, Mr. Terhune."

Terhune chuckled. "I'll take the blame, Sergeant. My shoulders are broad. But in what way am I responsible?"

"Isn't that how you writers work? Don't you invent some new way of killing someone, and then spend the next few weeks thinking of the most unlikely person upon whom to pin the crime?"

"You are asking me to betray trade secrets. You will have to join the Detective Story Writers' Union before those are revealed to you."

"Then put me down as a prospective member for nineteen-sixty-five. I am due to retire about then and shall need an easy occupation to keep me busy. By the way, have you had the opportunity of speaking to your Miss—Miss—Miss Amelia?"

"Yes, an hour ago. She remembers having sold the book—"

"She does!" Murphy sat up alertly.

"To fourteen different people—in turn. By tomorrow she will probably have increased the number to thirty or more."

"Damn!" Murphy rose to his feet. "Gilbert was justified in writing the lyric of that song about a policeman's lot not being a happy one. Well, thanks, anyway, for *your* help, Mr. Terhune. These lists will give us something to work on for a start. We shall begin by checking up on them first thing in the morning." He held out his hand. "If you come across anything else of interest, will you let me know?"

"Of course."

"Thanks, again. I'll get in touch with you as soon as we identify the corpse."

IV

Nothing of interest connected with the murder occurred the next day, except that double the number of people usually entering Terhune's shop on a Friday morning came in, and spoke to him of the crime. In the afternoon the number tailed off, and life resumed its more normal aspect.

Terhune listened anxiously for the telephone bell to ring, but it remained obstinately quiet. He went to bed half an hour later than usual, just in case Murphy might ring up. But he didn't.

Saturdays were always busy days for Terhune. As busy as Thursdays, for, on Saturdays, most of his clients called in to make sure of having new reading matter for the weekend. During the day he did not have much time to ponder on the question of identification, but when he closed the shop at six o'clock he gazed at the telephone with quizzical eyes and wondered whether he dared ring Murphy up. Perhaps the sergeant had forgotten his promise. If so, he was a good-natured chap, and would not object to being reminded of it.

Terhune resisted the impulse because, in his heart, he knew that the detective was not a man to forget such a promise. Besides, he argued with himself, Murphy might have knocked off work for the weekend. Or, if he had not, he might be away from his headquarters. And even if he were there he wouldn't thank Terhune for telephoning…

Nearly an hour later the telephone bell rang. Terhune hurriedly answered the ring.

"Hullo."

"Detective-Sergeant Murphy speaking, sir. I suppose you have been cursing me for not having telephoned you before now?"

Terhune was too truthful by nature to deny the charge. "I have been wondering how you were getting on."

"Well, I haven't been getting on. I am no wiser now than I was Thursday evening about the identity of the murdered man. Of course, some facts are by now fairly well established. For instance, it seems certain that the corpse isn't that of a local man. Nor does he appear to have been staying anywhere in the district as far as we can discover."

"That theory sounds somewhat improbable."

"Why?"

"If he wasn't a local man, and had not been staying in the district, one has to conclude that he had only just arrived."

"Well?"

"It is not easy to think of the motive which would have prompted somebody local to murder a man the moment he set foot hereabouts. Unless—"

"Unless what?"

"Unless his ship had arrived back that same day from a long voyage—"

"That is a theory I am working on," Murphy interrupted "Police are checking up on all ships' crews which arrived at: southern ports from Tuesday midday to Wednesday morning. Suppose he had come off one of the ships which arrived during that period at, say, Southampton. What then?"

"If he had been paid off he might have had a substantial amount of money in his pocket. Perhaps the motive was just plain robbery."

"It's a possible theory, Mr. Terhune, but robbers and thugs do not carry volumes of Swinburne about with them. At least, I have never heard of any who do—except in novels."

"I thought presumptions based on psychology were barred? Perhaps the book had nothing to do with the crime."

"Perhaps it hadn't, but the murder took place approximately about the same time as the book was dropped. The man's clothes were soaked through to the skin at the back, but in front only the jacket was damp. His vest and pants were practically dry. His death obviously took place after the rainstorm. What is it?"

"I said nothing."

"Not you, Mr. Terhune. I was speaking to somebody at this end. Will you hold the line a minute?"

The minute proved an elastic one. Nearly ten minutes elapsed before Murphy spoke again. There was a sharp note in his voice.

"Sorry to have kept you waiting, Mr. Terhune, but some news has just come in which confirms the robbery theory. Do you know Six Oaks Farm?"

"No."

"It's a smallholding of about fifty acres or so, a mile south of Farthing Toll, on the Dymchurch road. It belongs to a farmer called Billy Robinson. He and his missus have just called here to give me some news of the corpse. Just as the storm was blowing up on Wednesday Mrs. Robinson saw our man sheltering under an oak tree just by the gate. She called out and asked him whether he would like to shelter inside the house. He said he would, and made a run for it.

"While he was there she brewed him a pot of tea, and talked to him. Apparently he didn't say much about himself, but he did let out the fact that he was walking to London, was it far to Ashford, and did she know of any place there where he could have bed and breakfast? She told him of a friend of hers in Station Road who had a spare bedroom which she let for the night to hikers. Then Mrs. Robinson told him that his quickest way to Ashford was by way of the footpath through Windmill Wood. He said he would take it. As soon as the rain stopped he started off on his journey again. Mrs. Robinson has identified the body as that of her visitor."

"Why did she wait until tonight before saying anything to the police?"

Murphy laughed derisively. "You might well ask that, sir. Believe it or not but the first Mrs. Robinson knew of the murder was tonight, when her old man brought her into Ashford to take her to the cinema. They called first at the friend in Station Road, to ask if the stranger had slept there on Wednesday night, and so learned what had happened."

"Why do you think the information apparently confirms the theory of robbery? If he were walking to London might that not prove that he was too poor to pay the fare?"

"Yes and no. Some people like walking for its own sake. If he had had only the couple of shillings in his pocket which we found it wouldn't have been much use his looking for bed and breakfast."

"The enquiry might have been meant as a hint to Mrs. Robinson to put him up for the night."

"Perhaps. But there is another fact to be kept in mind. Apparently the man had no intention of stopping in Bray—in fact he had never heard of Bray, according to Mrs. Robinson; the route he had intended taking was by way of Wickford and Bracken Hill. Therefore his encounter with his murderer in Windmill Wood must have been unpremeditated. As such, robbery seems to be—at the moment—the only reasonable motive."

Murphy hurried on: "I must ring off now, Mr. Terhune. I am wanted again. I will keep in touch with you."

V

Three days passed by, during which time Terhune heard nothing more from Murphy.

On the afternoon of the fourth day, Wednesday, Murphy 'phoned to find out whether it would be convenient for him to call in the evening. Terhune said it would be. So, just as the clocks were striking the hour of seven-thirty, Murphy called again.

"How go things?" Terhune asked lightly, as his visitor sat down in the armchair and stretched out his legs towards the warm fire. "Have you identified the body yet?"

Murphy stared into the heart of the fire. "We have," he replied in an unnatural voice. "As a last resort we took impressions of the dead man's finger-prints and sent them up to New Scotland Yard. This morning they telephoned to say that they were sending down one of their experts to check the prints."

"To check them! Why?"

"You will hear. The expert took another set of impressions, and compared them with those on a record card which he had brought with him. As soon as he had completed his examination he looked up, and said—well, have a guess, Mr. Terhune."

"That the corpse was that of a notorious criminal?"

"No."

"That the man was just a petty criminal?"

"No."

Terhune shook his head. "Then I can't guess."

"He said the finger-prints were those of Frank Hugh Smallwood."

Terhune appreciated the fact that Murphy had enunciated the name with dramatic emphasis, also that the sergeant was staring at him with gloating anticipation. But Terhune had to confess that the name conveyed nothing to him.

Murphy looked pleased, and sucked in his breath with relish. "Frank Hugh Smallwood was *first* murdered on the fifteenth of April, nineteen-twenty-seven," he announced.

Chapter Five

Terhune was sure he had not heard aright.

"Pardon?"

Murphy did not try to hide his satisfaction at the effect his words had upon his host.

"I said that Smallwood was *first* murdered on the fifteenth of April, nineteen-twenty-seven," he repeated emphatically.

Terhune felt bewildered. "Yes, I thought you said something of that sort," he muttered. His confused thoughts considered the fantastic statement, until the reason for it became clearer, and he became excited. "Is this the first case of duplicated finger-prints?"

"What do you mean by that, Mr. Terhune?"

"You say that the finger-prints of the Windmill Wood man are identical with those of Smallwood?"

"Yes."

"Then the old-established theory that no two men possess identical finger-prints has been shattered?"

"Not at all. You misunderstand me. I did not mean to convey the fact that the two sets of prints were similar, but that they were the *same*."

"But—but—you are not making fun of me, Sergeant?"

"You have my word that I am not."

"But a man cannot be *twice* murdered!"

"That is another old-established theory."

With a despairing gesture Terhune ruffled his hair. "Then Smallwood was not murdered in nineteen-twenty-seven?"

"On the sixteenth of November, nineteen-twenty-seven, Charles Cockburn was convicted at Old Bailey for Smallwood's murder, and sentenced to death."

"Good God! But, Sergeant, this is a crazy situation. As a man cannot be twice murdered, either the man who was killed in Windmill Wood is not Smallwood, despite the apparent evidence of his finger-prints, or alternatively, Smallwood was not murdered in nineteen-twenty-seven."

"I'll deal with your arguments in the same order. Do you recollect the zig-zag scar on our seaman's left shin?"

"Yes."

"Smallwood possessed a similar scar. In fact, it was the evidence of that scar which was largely responsible in influencing the jury to bring in a verdict of Guilty against the defendant, Charles Cockburn."

"Then the truth really is, that Smallwood was *not* murdered in nineteen-twenty-seven?"

"Yes," Murphy admitted regretfully, as if sorry to bring Terhune's mystification to an end. "But would you like to hear the story from the beginning? I warn you that it is a long one."

Terhune nodded. "Please. How about a whisky-and-soda to help the story along?"

"That certainly is an idea, sir."

After a short interval Murphy was ready to begin. "By the way, is it true that you dabble in legal studies?"

"Entirely as an amateur, Sergeant."

"Would you prefer to read the evidence in the trial? I have the official record in my pocket."

The idea appealed to Terhune, so the sergeant handed the papers over. Terhune settled himself as comfortably as possible in his spring-back typing chair—he glanced regretfully at his usual, commodious chair, which the detective was occupying—and began to skim through the evidence.

*

The first witness for the prosecution was Thomas Vetch. He took the oath, gave a Richmond address, and announced himself as an employee of the Thames Conservancy, as lock-keeper of the Teddington Lock.

"Were you on duty on Saturday, the twenty-fourth of September, nineteen-twenty-seven?"

"I was."

"Did you, on that day, find something on the riverbank just above the lock?"

"I did."

"What was that something?"

"The lower part of a human leg."

"Do you identify the human remains which the usher will pass up to you [produced] as those which you found?"

"I do."

"What makes you sure they are the same?"

"The scar on the upper part of the shin."

"As a consequence of finding these remains what did you do?"

"I reported to the local police, who collected them."

"Anything else?"

"Yes, sir. I searched the bank on either side of the river, above and below the lock, to see whether I could find any more bits of body."

"Did you find any?"

"No."

"Neither then, nor upon any other occasion, between the day of your discovery and today?"

"No, sir."

"Did police officers also make a search?"

"Yes, sir."

The next witness was a sergeant of police who testified to receiving human remains from the lock-keeper, which he identified as those now preserved in the jar, produced. The sergeant went on to give evidence of delivering the remains to Doctor Percy for examination.

John Percy, honorary pathologist to the Home Office, was next called. He identified the remains produced as those delivered to him by Sergeant Hopkins.

"Did you examine the remains, Doctor Percy?"

"I did."

"Will you tell the Court of your findings?"

The pathologist identified and named the different parts of the leg and foot.

"Are the remains those of a human being?"

"Of course."

"Male or female?"

"Before I answer that question may I be allowed to point out that the remains are in an advanced state of decomposition as a result of having been immersed in water for a considerable length of time."

"I see. Did the state of decomposition render your examination more difficult?"

"It did."

"Nevertheless, you did arrive at a conclusion respecting the gender of the remains?"

"Yes. The number of hairs, and the development of the muscles, indicated the probability of the remains being those of an adult man."

"The remains are not those of an entire leg, are they, Doctor?"

"Unfortunately no. The leg had been crudely severed in two, just below the knee-cap, by means of a wide, sharp instrument, probably an axe or meat-chopper, used by a person unskilled in anatomical dissection."

"Why do you think the dissection was performed by an unskilled person?"

"Because a skilled person would have dissected the limb by severing it at the knee joint, and not below, where the shin-bone offers resistance to an operation of that nature. The severance is jagged, and bears evidence of having been made by at least four distinct chopping blows."

"Would you say that the severance was deliberate, and not the result of an accident, say, the wheels of a train passing over the limb?"

"Emphatically."

"Did you take measurements of the remains, Doctor?"

"I did."

"Did those measurements help you to arrive at any conclusions?"

"Again making allowance for the state of the remains, the measurements were consistent with those of a man of medium height, probably five feet eleven inches."

Counsel for the prosecution asked a few immaterial questions which Terhune skimmed over. This time examination-in-chief was followed by cross-examination.

"Doctor, in the course of your long—and may I add, esteemed—career first as a medical man, then as honorary pathologist to the Home Office, you must often have taken measurements of human bodies."

"Alive or dead?"

"Both."

"The answer is yes, in both instances."

"Are you prepared to state, categorically, that the measurement of a foot is invariably consistent with the height and build of its owner?"

"Of course I am not. Such an assertion would be incorrect and ridiculous."

"Ah! Then you agree that it is possible for small-sized men to have unusually large feet, and for big men to have disproportionately small feet?"

"Naturally."

"You cannot, therefore, ask the Court and members of the jury to accept your estimate of the original height of the owner of the remains as being indisputable?"

"No. I said that the remains were those of a man *probably* five feet eleven inches in height. My estimate was based on averages."

"But the living man could have been no more than five feet seven inches in height?"

"It is possible."

"Alternatively, the height of the living man could have been six feet two inches?"

"Yes."

The next witness was also a doctor, Edward Barry, of Putney. During the preliminary questions, Barry confirmed that he was in practice at Hammersmith, as general practitioner, and that one of his patients had been Frank Hugh Smallwood, of 27, Crescent Drive, Hammersmith.

"When did Smallwood first become a patient of yours, Doctor Barry?"

"I cannot say for certain. Possibly in nineteen-thirteen or nineteen-fourteen."

"The exact date has no significance, but can you assure the Court that Smallwood became your patient either just before or just after the outbreak of the Great War?"

"I can. I know it was previous to the Christmas of nineteen-fifteen. My daughter, Mary, died from double pneumonia on the twenty-eighth of December that year. Her illness was a result of a severe drenching, while cycling to Leatherhead with three other friends, one of whom was Frank Smallwood. Frank and Mary met as a result of Frank's becoming a patient of mine."

"How old was Smallwood at the time of your daughter's death?"

"Between fifteen and sixteen."

"You have already testified that Smallwood remained your patient until approximately a year ago. During the intervening years, did he often come under your care for medical treatment?"

"There were probably about nine occasions, or ten, or even twelve. I cannot remember the exact number."

"Can you remember the reason for your being called in on some or any of those occasions?"

"I think so. Yes."

"Can you describe them?"

"Once for jaundice. I think that was when he first became my patient. He had recently moved, with his widowed mother, to Hammersmith, Another occasion I remember was early in nineteen-seventeen. He asked me to make a thorough medical examination, as he proposed to volunteer for the Royal Flying Corps."

"Did you examine him?"

"I did. I think I found him A One. Indeed, I must have done so, for he entered the Royal Flying Corps without any difficulty."

"And the other occasions, Doctor?"

"Yes, the time when he had his motor-cycle accident."

"Tell the Court about that accident, if you please, Doctor."

"One Sunday morning, just after surgery, a young girl brought a verbal message to ask whether I would visit Crescent Drive immediately, as Mr. Smallwood had just had an accident. I went—"

"One moment, Doctor. What year was this?"

"Nineteen-twenty-one, I think."

"Thank you. You visited Smallwood's house?"

"I did, to find that he was suffering from slight shock, lacerated face and hands, and a deep cut in the upper third of his left leg. I put several stitches in the leg wound, then treated those of the face and hands, which were only superficial."

"Do you know how the accident occurred?"

"Yes. Frank was starting off on a motor-cycle ride. He had

proceeded about twenty yards or so when the machine skidded, and threw him on to the road."

"When the shin wound healed, did it leave a scar?"

"Yes, a very pronounced scar."

"Can you describe it?"

"I think so. It was in the form of a crudely drawn Z."

"After the treatment for the accident was at an end, did you ever see the scar again?"

"Yes, two years later. Frank came to me for a medical examination, and to be vaccinated against smallpox."

"Why, Doctor?"

"Because he was proposing to emigrate to the United States of America. He told me that all immigrants to the States were subject to a medical examination, and had to produce evidence of having been vaccinated within the past few years—five, I think, but I have forgotten."

"And you saw the scar again during the course of examination?"

"I did. I made a weak joke about the immigration officials mistaking it for the mark of a secret society."

"Why did Smallwood want to emigrate to the States? Was he unable to obtain work in this country?"

"His mother, and only relative, had recently died. Being highly emotional, impulsive, and upset by his mother's death; being, also, naturally a rolling stone, and of an unsettled nature, Frank decided to leave England for ever, and start a new life in the New World."

"Was that the last time you saw him, Doctor?"

"Dear me, no. In less than two years he was back again. He returned to Hammersmith, where he remained in lodgings for two years or so, until his death. During that time he became a motor-bicycle casualty for a second time, I had to treat him for an arm broken in three places. The right arm."

"Could you identify the scar if you were to see it apart from its possessor?"

"I believe so." (Exhibit produced.)

"Now that you have had the opportunity of examining the exhibit, Doctor, do you identify the scar with that on the left leg of Frank Hugh Smallwood?"

"It bears a strong resemblance to Smallwood's scar."

"Thank you. Now, Doctor, when did you last see Smallwood?"

"In the early hours of the last Sunday in October, last year, I was summoned by Smallwood to the local police-station, to examine my patient and declare him sober."

"Were you able to do so?"

"No, sir, I regret to say that I could not do so."

"Your patient was violent, was he not, Doctor?"

"He was."

"One last question. From your personal knowledge of Frank Hugh Smallwood, can you say that he was suffering from schizophrenia?"

"In its mildest form, yes."

"Would you explain the meaning of the complaint to members of the jury, please, Doctor?"

"Schizophrenia is the medical term for a split personality. In common language, Smallwood was a man of extreme and contrary natures. Sometimes he was charming and kind; at such times nobody could have wished for a better friend or a more cheerful companion. Unfortunately, this split personality sometimes—indeed, often— caused him to be wilful and cruel. To people who opposed him, or for whom he had a dislike, Frank Smallwood was a tyrannical bully."

Counsel for the defence had only a few questions to ask.

"You are aware, I believe, Doctor, that Smallwood had served terms of imprisonment?"

"I am. He was twice convicted of embezzlement, but in my opinion he stole the money not for the purpose of gain, but solely for the purpose of hurting the interests of the employers concerned."

"Referring to Exhibit One—the human remains—you said, in answer to my learned friend's question as to whether you could identify the scar, that it bears a strong resemblance to Smallwood's scar. Your answer does not satisfy me, Doctor Barry. I am going to put the same question to you, but I want you to answer only Yes or No. Do you identify the scar exhibited with that on the left leg of Frank Hugh Smallwood?"

"The question is not one which I can answer so simply."

"Ah! Then you are not prepared to state positively that, in your considered opinion, the remains produced are those of Smallwood?"

"There are certain infinitesimal differences between the exhibit, and Smallwood's scar, as it remains in my memory, but I am prepared to say that such apparent differences might have resulted from long immersion in water."

"What are those differences?"

"The downward stroke of the Z in the exhibit could be a shade longer, and a shade nearer to the perpendicular, to resemble exactly the scar on Smallwood's leg—as I remember it."

On that point cross-examination wisely stopped, but counsel for the prosecution re-examined the witness.

"How many years have elapsed since you last saw the living scar, Doctor Barry?"

"Approximately two. To be more precise, I saw the scar last in the August of nineteen-twenty-five, when I was examining my patient for signs of further injuries after his second motor-bicycle crash."

"Was that when Smallwood broke his arm in three places?"

"Yes."

"No doubt you will admit, Doctor, that after a period of two years and three months, the picture in your memory might not be, shall we say, as sharply etched as if the period were days and hours instead of years and months?"

"I suppose that is so."

"On the other hand, Doctor, what would you estimate the chances to be of two different scars being as similar as the exhibit before you, and the one in your memory?"

"I am not a betting man, sir, but I should say—a million to one against."

"Thank you, Doctor."

Chapter Six

Turning aside for a moment from the evidence in Rex v. Cockburn, Terhune realized that his cigarette, barely started, had burned itself out in the ashtray, that Murphy's glass was empty, and that Murphy was gazing sleepily into the fire.

Terhune was apologetic. "I'm terribly sorry, Sergeant. This evidence is absorbing, I have been reading it line by line—"

The detective stirred slightly. "That's all right, sir. Take as long as you like," he muttered dreamily.

"But you must be bored. May I find you something to read? There's the latest copy of the *Saturday Evening Post* on the corner of the table, close to your right hand."

"If you want the truth, Mr. Terhune, I'm enjoying myself no end. Home's a fine place, especially when you have three kids pestering you all the time to play games with them, or help them with their homework, or make something for them. But now and again a spot of quietness isn't to be sniffed at. I'm feeling warm and lazy, so if you're in no hurry yourself read what you like of the evidence. In the light of what we now know it's darned interesting."

Having refilled Murphy's glass, offered his visitor another cigarette, and lighted one for himself, Terhune resumed his reading of the trial.

The next witness was one Joseph Morgan, a retired schoolmaster living at Brighton.

"Were you once a schoolmaster at Southall County School, Mr. Morgan?"

"I was."

"Between the years nineteen-hundred-and-seven and nineteen-hundred-and-seventeen?"

"Nineteen-hundred-and-eighteen. I left the school after the summer term of that year."

"Among the pupils of that school do you remember a boy by the name of Frank Hugh Smallwood?"

"I do."

"I think he was a scholar there from the school's opening in nineteen-hundred-and-seven to nineteen-fourteen?"

"I do not know the exact date of his leaving, but I remember the boy well."

"Why?"

"Because he was always being brought prominently to my notice, sometimes by his good work, and sometimes because of his wayward nature. I was never able to decide what kind of a lad he was: one of the worst of us in whom there was good, or one of the best of us in whom there was bad."

"Then you will not be surprised to learn that he was suffering from a mental disease known as 'split personality'?"

"Indeed I should not. In fact he was as near to being a modified Jekyll and Hyde as anyone I have met."

"Now, Mr. Morgan, do you also remember another pupil of yours, by the name of Charles Cockburn?"

"It would be impossible for me to remember Smallwood without remembering Cockburn at the same time."

"Indeed! Why?"

"Because there sprang up between the two lads one of those instinctive antagonisms for which there is no apparent explanation." (Interruption from the prisoner. In answer to the judge:) "Yes, my lord, perhaps, unwittingly, I have been unfair to the accused."

His Lordship: "Please explain."

"May I describe the character of the accused, as I knew it?"

His Lordship: "Yes."

"My lord, Charles Cockburn had what I can only describe as a sweet nature. He was honest and forthright, he was kindly and considerate, and he was industrious, though backward. Unfortunately, he was also a natural victim for a bully. I was present at what I believe was the first meeting between the two lads—in class. At that time Smallwood had been in my class for one term. On the first day of Smallwood's second term, Cockburn was a new pupil to the school, and to my form. It was always my habit to question new members of my class, to ascertain their names and ages, to gain some idea of their scholastic knowledge, and to try and put them at their ease. Cockburn had a gentle voice, and a gentle manner. As soon as he began to answer my questions I saw Smallwood's eyes light up with a gloating expression. That I was not mistaken was proved a few minutes later, when I turned my back to the class. I heard a sharp cry. When I turned round Cockburn was rubbing his face. Upon my questioning him he replied that something had struck him in the face—"

His Lordship: "This is a very lengthy explanation, Mr. Morgan. Can you compress it?"

"I am sorry, my lord. The point I desire to stress is this: Smallwood both despised and disliked Cockburn, and took every opportunity to cause the gentler lad distress. I knew this from personal knowledge, and had persistently to punish Smallwood for his bullying tricks. On the other hand, I never had reason to believe that Cockburn reciprocated Smallwood's dislike. On the contrary, I believe his feelings were almost of admiration, and a regret that Smallwood was not his friend."

His Lordship: "Thank you, Mr. Morgan. Will you continue, Sir Charles?"

Sir Charles Stewart: "I thank your lordship. Now, Mr. Morgan, you have told us of what Smallwood did to Cockburn, but did Cockburn never retaliate in any way?"

"On two occasions I caught the lads fighting each other, but Cockburn, I believe, was the loser in each case. He was a slighter lad physically, and no match for his tormentor."

"That is no answer to my question. I asked if, at any time to your knowledge, Cockburn retaliated upon Smallwood?"

"Yes. Once Cockburn picked up a stone and threw it at the back of Smallwood's head."

"How do you know of this incident?"

"I saw it from the classroom window. When I first looked out Smallwood and two other boys were bumping Cockburn. As soon as they had finished with their victim the three boys walked away. Cockburn then rose to his feet and threw the stone, as I have described."

"It was a case of the worm turning?"

"I suppose you might so describe it."

"After being hit by the stone, what did Smallwood do to Cockburn?"

"He did not have a chance of doing much at that time. Cockburn wisely ran away as quickly as he could."

There was further evidence from Morgan of Smallwood's treatment of Cockburn, also from a witness who had been a classmate of both boys for three and a half years. There was no cross-examination of any consequence. Next came a witness named Philip Shakespeare, who described himself as a clerk, and said he was an employee of the Royal Insurance Co., Ltd.

"At which office do you work, Mr. Shakespeare?"

"At the Head Office, in Lombard Street."

"In which department?"

"Employers' Liability."

"Do you know the accused?"

"I do."

"At the time of his arrest for the alleged homicide of Frank Hugh Smallwood, was the accused employed by the Royal Insurance Company?"

"He was."

"In the same department as yourself?"

"Yes."

"Did you become friendly with him?"

"I did. He was best man at my wedding in nineteen-twenty-five."

"Previous to marriage your wife, also, was employed by the same company, was she not?"

"Yes, as stenographer. We met through both being in the same firm."

"Do you know a Miss Patricia Webb?"

"Yes."

"Does she, also, work as stenographer at the same office?"

"Yes."

"Was she friendly with your wife, previous to your marriage?"

"She still is. Patricia is Eileen's best friend."

"Quite. Was Patricia Webb one of your wedding guests?"

"Yes."

"Did it appear to you that Patricia Webb and Charles Cockburn became friendly as a result of meeting at the wedding ceremony?"

"Yes."

"Soon after your return from your honeymoon did you and your wife form a quartette of friends, as it were, with Patricia Webb and Charles Cockburn?"

"Yes. We often met, sometimes at our house, sometimes at Patricia's."

"Did you never meet at the house of the accused?"

"No. Charles lived in rooms near South Kensington station, so that it was not convenient for us to visit him. He used to repay our hospitality by taking the three of us out to one or another of the Soho restaurants."

"Do you recall, in particular, one evening about the middle of November, last year, when you were dining at the Chanticleer Restaurant?"

"Clearly."

"Who was present on that occasion?"

"Eileen, Patricia, Charlie and me."

"Would you tell the Court and members of the jury what happened?"

"Soon after we had sat down at table I noticed that a man who was dining across the far side of the restaurant was staring at Patricia. I did not say anything, but whenever I glanced across the room I saw that he was still looking in our direction. Towards the end of our meal, after we had finished eating, and were waiting for coffee to be served, I saw the man rise from his chair and approach our table. As soon as he was near enough he clapped Charlie on the shoulder and said loudly: 'Well, well, well, fancy meeting my old school friend, Charles Cockburn, after all these years!'"

"What did the accused do?"

"He looked up and said: 'Frank Smallwood!' Then Charlie introduced Smallwood to the rest of us, and after some pointed hints from Smallwood, asked him whether he would like to join us for coffee and a drink."

"Did Smallwood accept?"

"Like a shot. He sat down between Charlie and Patricia, and remained with us for the rest of the time we were in the restaurant."

"As a result of the encounter with Smallwood, did you receive any impression of anything?"

"Yes. I was sure that Smallwood was attracted by Patricia, and that he had used his recognition of Cockburn only as an excuse for obtaining the opportunity to speak to her. As he said good-bye to her, I heard him ask for her address."

"Did she give it?"

"Yes."

"Had the encounter any other consequences?"

"Yes, although whether those consequences were direct or indirect I cannot say. A week later Charlie informed me that he had proposed marriage to Patricia, and had been accepted."

"Did the four of you continue to meet, as in the past?"

"Yes."

"Frank Smallwood never joined you?"

"No."

"We shall hear later from your wife that, early in January of this year, she saw Miss Webb and Smallwood entering the Stoll Picture Theatre. When she returned home that night she told you of what she had seen, I believe?"

"Yes."

"Were you surprised?"

"Yes and no."

"Would you explain your answer, Mr. Shakespeare?"

"Well, I didn't know that Patricia was seeing Smallwood. I did not even suspect that she was in contact with him. But it had seemed to me that, following her engagement, after the first flush of happiness had worn off, her manner towards Charlie changed."

"Did it grow cold?"

"No. I shouldn't care to describe it as cold. I should say, perplexed, and sometimes absent-minded, as though she were wondering whether she had done the right thing in becoming engaged to Charlie."

"Did you mention to the accused that your wife had seen Miss Webb going about with Smallwood?"

"No. It was none of my business."

"Did the accused ever find out by any other means?"

"Yes, Patricia herself told Charlie."

"Was he upset?"

"For a time, I think, but it all blew over."

"Did Miss Webb and Smallwood go out together again?"

"Not to my knowledge."

"I propose now to touch upon more recent events, Mr. Shakespeare. Some time in February, did the accused inform you that he intended leaving his rooms in South Kensington?"

"Yes: He told me that he proposed to live during the summer months on a houseboat which he had hired for the season."

"Anything else?"

"Yes. He said he was planning a house-warming party for the Easter holiday, and would Eileen and I be his guests?"

"Did you accept?"

"Gladly."

"Did he say whether there were to be other guests?"

"Only Patricia."

"Was anything said of Frank Smallwood?"

"Not a word."

"Did you and your wife, in fact, spend the Easter holiday aboard the houseboat?"

"Yes."

"And Miss Webb?"

"Yes."

"Where was the houseboat situated?"

"On the Thames, opposite Hampton Court Palace."

"Upon which day did you travel to the houseboat?"

"On the Thursday, after office hours. Patricia, Charlie, and I went to Waterloo, where we met my wife. The four of us went together to the houseboat."

"How many bedrooms did the houseboat have?"

"Four. Two at one end of the boat, and two at the other."

"Did the bedrooms communicate in pairs?"

"Yes."

"And were the two pairs separated by a large dining-sitting-room?"

"Yes."

"Who occupied the bedrooms on the first night of your visit?"

"Patricia occupied the end bedroom, nearest the bridge. My wife and I slept in the accompanying room."

"And Cockburn?"

"The bedroom at the far end of the houseboat."

"Was that downstream?"

"Yes."

"Where was the kitchen?"

"Opposite Cockburn's bedroom."

"Who cooked the meals?"

"Charlie. He is a good cook."

"Did any of you help him?"

"He wouldn't allow us to do any work other than tidying up and washing and drying the dirty crockery."

"Did anything unusual occur during the remaining hours of Thursday, the fourteenth of April?"

"No. We were all very happy together."

"Can you say the same of Good Friday?"

"No. Everything went well until some time between four and five p.m."

"What happened then?"

"Frank Smallwood arrived. The afternoon was warm and sunny. We were sitting on the verandah feeding some swans and watching the boats passing by, when somebody waved to us from a punt, and came towards us from downstream. The man was Smallwood. He came alongside, climbed aboard the houseboat, and made fast the punt. Then he announced that he was spending a punting holiday, adding pointedly that spending a holiday by oneself wasn't much fun. We all realized that he was hinting very broadly that he should join our party. Charlie couldn't do anything else but ask him to stay. After pretending to protest, Smallwood quickly accepted the invitation. Charlie transferred Smallwood's bag from the punt to the vacant bedroom."

"Did your party remain a happy one?"

"Not so far as the remainder of Good Friday was concerned. Smallwood openly flirted with Patricia."

"What was the prisoner's reaction to that situation?"

"Must I answer that question, my lord? Charlie is my friend."

His Lordship: "You must answer counsel's questions, Mr. Shakespeare. We all appreciate your feelings at being called here today to give evidence against your friend, but you must remember that this is a Court of Justice. The members of the jury will give equal attention to anything you may say in favour of the accused."

"Thank you, my lord."

Sir Charles Stewart: "Well, Mr. Shakespeare?"

"Charlie became extremely morose. By dinner-time he would scarcely speak to any of us. After the meal he said he had a headache, and was going off by himself to walk it off. Patricia wanted to go with him, but he refused. He left us just before nine o'clock."

"How would you describe Smallwood's behaviour?"

"It was rotten. He kept on taunting Charlie about their schooldays, and of the number of fights they had had, and how, he, Smallwood, had always come out best."

"What was Cockburn's reply to these taunts?"

"He said nothing, but merely became more and more moody until, as I have said, he announced his intention of going for a walk."

"At what hour did the accused return that night?"

"I don't know."

"Why was that?"

"As he had not returned by eleven o'clock, we all went to bed."

"All of you?"

"Yes, sir."

"Did you hear him return?"

"No."

"Did you wake up during the night?"

"Yes. About twelve-thirty a.m. I heard a low murmur of voices from the other end of the houseboat."

"Male or female voices? Or both?"

"Only male voices."

"Could you recognize them?"

"No, but I concluded that they were the voices of Charlie and Smallwood."

"What did you do?"

"Nothing. I turned over and fell asleep again."

"Did you hear no other noises during the night?"

"No."

"When did you wake up?"

"At five-thirty a.m. I felt my wife pulling at my arm. When I asked her if anything was wrong she said that she had been worrying on and off all night about Patricia and Charlie, and now had a brute of a head, so would I be an angel and make her a cup of tea so that she could take some aspirins?"

"What did you say?"

"I said I would. I got up from bed, slipped on slippers and dressing-gown, and crept along to the kitchen."

"And did you see anything unusual upon opening the kitchen door?"

"Yes. A meat-chopper under the sink."

"Did you examine it?"

"Yes."

"Was it clean?"

"No. It was bloodstained."

"Were you startled?"

"No."

"Why not?"

"Well, one expects to find bloodstains on a meat-chopper."

"I see. Did you see signs of blood elsewhere?"

"There were some brown stains on the floor which I thought might be bloodstains."

"Were you still not startled?"

"No. I thought to myself that maybe Charlie would serve up a juicy steak later on that day."

"What did you do then?"

"Made a small pot of tea, and took it back to the bedroom, together with two cups and saucers, and some milk I had found. Eileen and I both had a cup of tea. Then I got back into bed again, and fell asleep. The next time I woke up Eileen was again pulling my arm, but this time to say that Charlie had just knocked on the door to say that breakfast would be ready in thirty minutes' time. I washed, shaved, dressed, and went off to give Charlie a hand while Eileen and Patricia occupied the bathroom, which was opposite Patricia's bedroom, and corresponded with the kitchen at the other end."

"I see. And did you give the accused a hand with breakfast?"

"Yes."

"Did you see the meat-chopper again?"

"Yes."

"Was it still bloodstained?"

"No."

"It had been cleaned?"

"I presume so."

"Were the other bloodstains to be seen?"

"No."

"They, too, had been cleaned up?"

"They were not to be seen, so they must have been."

"What was Cockburn's demeanour?"

"Cheerful."

"Did either of you speak of the events of the previous night?"

"Not until I had glanced out of the kitchen window and noticed that Smallwood's punt had gone. Then I said something about Smallwood's energy in going for a punt before breakfast."

"What did the accused say?"

"He told me that Smallwood had gone for good, and not that morning, but the previous night. He went on to explain that he had told Smallwood exactly what he, Charlie, thought of Smallwood for inviting himself to a party at which he was not wanted."

"Shortly, Mr. Shakespeare, what did the accused lead you to infer?"

"That Smallwood had left the houseboat of his own accord."

"Did you see Smallwood again during the Easter holiday?"

"No."

"Have you seen him since?"

"No."

"Thank you, Mr. Shakespeare."

Chapter Seven

Terhune glanced at Murphy. The detective's eyes were closed. This, and the expression of sublime peace and contentment on his face, led Terhune to believe that his visitor had dozed off. He turned back to the evidence.

Cockburn's counsel cross-examined Shakespeare, but at no great length: perhaps because he considered that Shakespeare's evidence on its own was not sufficiently damning against the accused to warrant prejudicing the jury against the defence, by attacking an honest, sincere witness. He asked a few perfunctory questions which did no more than establish that Shakespeare had not entered the kitchen between the hours of two p.m. Friday and five a.m. Saturday, and an admission that, as far as he knew, the meat-chopper could have been bloodstained before the departure of Smallwood from the houseboat. The witness further admitted that Cockburn had served lamb chops for luncheon on the Saturday, and a leg of lamb for dinner on the Sunday.

"If I were to say that the chops which you had on the Saturday were cut from the hindquarter, the leg of which you had on the Sunday, would you be surprised?"

"No."

"If I were to add that Charles Cockburn himself severed the chops from the hindquarter, would that surprise you?"

"No."

"If I were to conclude by saying that Cockburn performed that operation upon his return to the houseboat after his solitary promenade on Friday night, would you have any reason for contradicting me?"

"No."

"One last question. Did you notice, on the Saturday morning, that Cockburn was wearing a bandage about his left wrist?"

"Yes."

Shakespeare's wife, Eileen, followed her husband. Most of the earlier questions she was asked were merely to confirm, or enlarge, upon Philip Shakespeare's evidence. Presently, counsel touched upon the friendship between Patricia Webb and Frank Smallwood.

"You were in Miss Webb's confidence, were you not, Mrs. Shakespeare?"

"I believe so."

"Did she ever speak to you of Frank Smallwood?"

"Now and again."

"Did you, at that time, believe that she was attracted by Smallwood?"

"I never gave the matter a thought."

"Is it a fact that, in January of this year, you saw Miss Webb and Smallwood together in town?"

"It is."

"What were the circumstances, please?"

"On the night in question my husband did not return home as usual to the evening meal because he was going to a Masonic meeting in town. We had previously arranged that I should amuse myself in town, and meet him after, so that we could come home together. I am not sure of the exact time, but I think it must have been between seven and half past. I was passing by the Stoll Picture Theatre, in Kingsway, when I saw the back of Patricia Webb. She was walking up the steps of the theatre towards the vestibule."

"Was she alone?"

"When I first saw her, she was. I hurried up the steps after her, but just as I pushed open one of the doors I saw a man, who had been buying tickets from the right-hand box-office, join her. I recognized Frank Smallwood."

"Were you surprised?"

(Witness remained silent.)

"Come, come, Mrs. Shakespeare, you must answer my questions. I repeat: Were you surprised?"

"I suppose I must have been."

"Did you speak to your friends?"

"No. I watched them go towards the stalls and then I left the theatre."

"Do you think that Miss Webb was in love with Charles Cockburn when she accepted his hand in marriage?"

"She wouldn't have said Yes if she hadn't been in love with him."

"That is no answer to my question."

"I think she was very much in love with Charlie."

"Within a few weeks of the engagement, did you notice any change in Miss Webb's attitude towards the accused?"

"Yes. She seemed to become easily irritated by his—his—"

"His what?"

"He was always cuddling and kissing her—"

"I see. At first, Miss Webb enjoyed his kisses, but after a few weeks, was she—shall I say?—less receptive to her fiancé's physical manifestations?"

"Yes. At least, that was my impression."

"Did you tell Miss Webb you had seen her at the Stoll Picture Theatre with Frank Smallwood?"

"No."

"Did she ever mention to you that she had been out with him?"

"No."

"Do you recollect how you and your husband spent the Easter holiday this year?"

"Yes. We spent them aboard a houseboat which Charlie had rented for the season."

"We have heard from your husband that Smallwood joined you on the Friday afternoon. Did you expect him?"

"Certainly not."

"Can you say whether or no his appearance was a surprise to Miss Webb?"

"I cannot."

"Did Miss Webb ever discuss Smallwood's call with you, either before or after the event?"

"She did. The next morning, Saturday morning, she told me that—"

"We must not hear what Miss Webb told you, Mrs. Shakespeare. Was Smallwood's departure as much of a surprise to you as his unexpected appearance?"

"Yes."

"Why?"

"When he said good night to us, he said nothing of leaving within the next hour or so."

"Were you astonished when you heard the explanation from the accused the following morning?"

"No."

"Why not?"

"I was rather pleased with Charlie for having been man enough to insist upon Frank Smallwood leaving. Usually he has such a kind, gentle nature—"

"Quite, Mrs. Shakespeare. From your remark I take it that you, for one, were glad to hear that he had gone."

"I was."

"Didn't you like him?"

"It wasn't that I didn't like him for his own sake, but for Patricia's and Charlie's sake I hated to see the way he made up to Patricia."

"Exactly! You feared that his continued friendship with Miss Webb might possibly result in ruining the romance between Miss Webb and the accused?"

"Oh! I didn't think that."

"What did you think, Mrs. Shakespeare? You must have had some reason for being glad to hear that Smallwood was not to spend the rest of the holidays aboard the houseboat."

"I suppose something of that sort must have been at the back of my mind."

"Reverting to the events of Friday, what was Smallwood's attitude to you all?"

"He was very mean to Charlie, and kept on taunting him about his schooldays. To Philip and me he was quite affable."

"And to Miss Webb?"

"He seemed to be trying to impress Patricia."

"Did he succeed?"

"I don't know."

"I will put the question in another form. What was Miss Webb's attitude towards Smallwood? Disagreeable? Or friendly?"

"Friendly."

"Very friendly?"

"I suppose you could say that it was very friendly."

"Do you think that the accused saw the *very friendly* attitude of his fiancée towards Smallwood?"

"I couldn't say."

"Come, Mrs. Shakespeare, we cannot be satisfied with that answer. You seem to be an intelligent woman. You have a pair of sound eyes. Surely you must have noticed whether or no the accused was affected by the sight of an uninvited and unwanted visitor trying to steal his girl from under his nose."

Mr. Barclay Keyes: "My lord, there is no evidence to suggest that Smallwood was trying to steal Cockburn's fiancée."

Sir Charles Stewart: "My learned friend is evidently very broad-minded. However, I will rephrase the question. Mrs. Shakespeare, how did the accused react to Smallwood's behaviour towards Miss Webb?"

Mr. Barclay Keyes: "The witness's husband has already testified that Cockburn turned morose and sulky."

Sir Charles Stewart: "Mrs. Shakespeare might prefer to use more emphatic words. Well, Mrs. Shakespeare?"

"Morose is the right word, I think."

"Very well. On Friday evening the accused was morose. What was he like on Saturday?"

"Very happy and cheerful."

"As though a weight had been lifted from his mind?"

"Yes."

"And was Miss Webb similarly happy and cheerful?"

"She was very quiet."

"Somewhat *triste*?"

"*Triste?*"

"A little sad and unhappy?"

"Yes."

"At any time during the holidays did you see the accused wearing a bandage?"

"Yes."

"When?"

"Saturday and onwards. Patricia dressed it for him."

"You did not see it before the Saturday?"

"No."

"Speaking of the events of Friday night, we have heard that you spent a restless night. Were you awake at any period?"

"I seemed to be waking on and off the whole night through."

"Did you hear any unusual sounds during any of those wakeful periods?"

"Yes. Once I heard a number of people singing and shouting from the bank opposite."

"I was referring more specifically to sounds aboard the houseboat. Did you hear the prisoner returning to the houseboat, for instance?"

"Yes."

"How was that? Was he noisy?"

"No, but one end of the gangway was close to our bedroom door."

"Are you a light sleeper?"

"Very."

"Did you hear any more footsteps, on that night, of people passing up or down the gangway?"

"No."

"You did not hear Smallwood leave the houseboat?"

"No."

"Thank you."

Cross-examination followed. "Did you hear any other sounds, of which no mention has yet been made?"

"I did hear the noise of muffled hammering."

"What was the hammering like? This?"

"No. The pauses were longer in between each bang."

"Like this?"

"Something like that."

"Might those sounds have been caused by a meat-chopper severing chops from a hindquarter of lamb?"

"I couldn't say."

"Have you never heard a butcher separating chops from a joint?"

"Oh, yes!"

"Did the sounds you heard during the night resemble those which you have heard in a butcher's shop?"

"Now that you come to mention it, they did."

"My learned friend has asked you a question concerning the bandage which Cockburn wore round his wrist from Saturday morning onwards. At any time did Cockburn offer an explanation to account for the wound beneath?"

"Yes. He said that he had sliced a strip of flesh from his arm with the meat-chopper."

"Did he say when this accident had happened?"

"No, but I took it for granted that it must have happened between him leaving the houseboat in a paddy, and the next morning, when I first saw the bandage."

"That is all, Mrs. Shakespeare."

A short re-examination followed.

"Did you say that the accused had left the houseboat in a *paddy?*"

"It wasn't exactly a paddy, it was—"

"But you said paddy, did you not?"

"Yes."

"So that must have been the word which was in your thoughts at the moment of speaking?"

His lordship: "You must answer the question."

"Yes."

I I

Terhune placed the evidence down upon his knees while he lighted a cigarette. In his imagination he saw the Old Bailey Court, as it must have been on that bleak November day, nearly twenty years ago. He pictured the impassive face of the judge as his lordship studied the faces of the witnesses, or entered in his notebook a précis of the pertinent parts of their testimony. He saw, vaguely, the unhappy expressions on the faces of Eileen and Philip Shakespeare as they stood in the witness-box, not daring to defy the famous K.C. who was prosecuting, not caring deliberately to perjure themselves, and yet striving desperately, but futilely, not to say anything which might help to convict their friend in the dock, and yet, at the same time, slipping in any little word or hint which might be of assistance to the defence.

He saw, too, the Clerk of the Court, the soft-footed ushers, the rows of counsel, solicitors and solicitors' clerks, the bright-eyed, excited public. And last of all, the prisoner in the dock, stunned, despairing, white.

Terhune picked up the volume of evidence, and glanced quickly at the name of the next witness. Miss Patricia Webb! As he had expected. He paused, before reading on. What sort of a girl had this Patricia been? Flighty? A coquette? Or just a thoughtless girl to whom Smallwood had meant no more than an evening's amusement?

Patricia gave an address in Richmond, and announced that she lived there, with her parents, and a younger, unmarried sister. For the first ten minutes or so she amplified evidence which had already been given in Court. Then Sir Charles said:

"Do you remember dining with Mr. and Mrs. Shakespeare and the accused at the Chanticleer Restaurant, in Soho, about the middle of last November?"

"Yes."

"On that occasion a man joined you, whom the accused: introduced as Frank Smallwood."

"I remember perfectly."

"Had you ever met him previous to that night?"

"No."

"Did you like him?"

"I don't know. I suppose so. I didn't dislike him."

"The fact is, that you got on well with each other, is it: not? So well, indeed, that as you were all parting company, he asked for your address, I believe."

"He did."

"And you gave it to him?"

"There was no reason why I should not do so."

"Quite, Miss Webb. At that time you were not engaged to the accused, I believe?"

"No."

"A few nights after your first meeting with Smallwood, did the prisoner propose marriage to you?"

"Yes."

"And you accepted him?"

"Yes."

"Were you in love with him?"

"Of course I was."

"How soon after you had given your address to Smallwood did he get into communication with you?"

"What bearing has a question like that on this case?"

"Perhaps you will be good enough to allow his lordship to be the judge of the relevance or otherwise of my interrogation. Now, Miss Webb?"

"He telephoned me two nights later. That would have been on a Monday night."

"Did he have any special reason for telephoning?"

"No. He said he merely wanted to talk to me again."

"Did you tell the prisoner of the conversation?"

"No. I did not think it necessary."

"Why not?"

"At that time I was not engaged to Charlie, and my private life was still my own affair."

"When did you become engaged to the prisoner?"

"On the following Wednesday night."

"How soon after your engagement did you next hear from Smallwood?"

"Two nights later. That would have been a Friday night."

"Did he still only desire an opportunity of talking with you?"

"No, he asked me to go out with him."

"Did you accept?"

"No. I told him of my engagement, and said I could not go out with him alone, either on the night suggested, or any other night, and begged him not to ring me up any more."

"Did you tell the prisoner of this second telephone call?"

"I did."

"What was the effect upon him?"

"He was not very pleased."

"Would you say that the knowledge made him jealous?"

"Only a little."

"Only a *little* jealous! Well, now, Miss Webb, did Smallwood forbear from telephoning any more?"

"No. He telephoned again the following week, to ask whether I couldn't spare him just one hour of my time."

"Did you say that he might?"

"I said very definitely that he could not."

"Were you angry with him?"

"Not really. Usually a woman is too flattered to become really angry with a man for being attracted by her."

"I see. Did you tell your fiancé of Smallwood's third telephone call?"

"No."

"Why not? Because you didn't want him to become a *lot* jealous?"

"Perhaps."

"Did Smallwood, by any chance, continue to flatter you by telephoning at intervals?"

"He telephoned."

"And you continued to keep that knowledge to yourself?"

"Yes."

"What effect did Smallwood's persistence have upon you?"

"No effect whatever."

"Are you quite sure?"

"I do not understand what you mean."

"Are you not aware that your friends observed a change in your customary demeanour?"

"Oh!"

"Is it not so, Miss Webb, that within a few weeks of your engagement, you were beginning to express irritation with the prisoner because he wished to confirm his love for you by physical manifestations?"

"I did not do so consciously."

"Perhaps not, but I am sure you will agree with me that if your friends—your very dear friends—observed a change in you, the prisoner cannot have remained unaware of those same symptoms?"

"I never thought—I didn't realize—he didn't say anything—"

"It is too late to be distressed now, Miss Webb."

Mr. Barclay Keyes: "It is also unnecessary. There is nothing in the depositions to justify my learned friend's assertion that Cockburn was aware of any change in his fiancée's attitude towards him."

Sir Charles Stewart: "Very well. Perhaps you will answer this question instead: Did Smallwood continue to pester you to go out with him?"

"Yes."

"And did you eventually agree?"

"I thought it might satisfy him if I did so."

"Acting on the theory, no doubt, that the best way of combating temptation is to give way to it! However, did you keep the meeting, when it came off, secret from your fiancé?"

"I told him of it two nights later."

"After the telephone call or after the meeting?"

"After the meeting."

"Did the information make the prisoner just a little jealous? Or perhaps a lot jealous?"

"He was cross with me, but I promised I would never again go out with Smallwood alone."

"Did you keep that promise?"

"I did."

"Did Smallwood continue to telephone?"

"Yes."

"Was it from you that Smallwood heard of your invitation to spend Easter holidays aboard the prisoner's houseboat?"

"I am afraid it was."

"How did that come about?"

"The week previous he telephoned to ask if I couldn't, as a very special favour, meet him one morning during the holidays and have a cocktail with him. I replied that it would be impossible for me to do as he suggested, because I was spending the holidays with the Shakespeares and Charlie, aboard his houseboat."

"Did he ask you where the houseboat was situated?"

"Yes."

"Did you tell him?"

"Yes."

"When you gave him the address did you anticipate that he would invite himself to the party?"

The witness's answer was on the next page. Before turning over, Terhune asked himself: Had Patricia given the address intentionally or foolishly?

Chapter Eight

For some reason Patricia Webb, from the first, had been, for Terhune, a less 'visionable' person than the other witnesses who had preceded her. Their character, and something of their personalities, had revealed itself in their brief replies to counsel's interrogation. The doctor's obvious confidence in himself and his own judgment. The schoolmaster's pedantic language, his half-shamed admiration for an obvious bully contending with a kindly, rather patronizing regard for the too gentle-natured Cockburn. Shakespeare's suburbanism, and stubborn loyalty to a friend accused of murder. Eileen's vague disapproval, and even vaguer envy, of her friend's friendship with Frank Smallwood.

But Patricia Webb was different. So far he saw her, not as a human being, with human frailties and human qualities, but rather as a cardboard puppet dangling at the end of strings attached to the fingers of fate. A person of no character, and no dimensions. A person whose eye was flattered by the unscrupulous attentions of an ostentatious bully. If anyone more than the murderer himself was indirectly responsible for the murder of Frank Hugh Smallwood, Patricia was that person.

This subconscious reflection caused Terhune to experience a mild shock. Immersed by the rather gruesome fascination of watching the manner in which the case against the accused was being built up, item by item, fact by fact, inference by inference, he realized suddenly that he was overlooking one vital point—that in the light of his own discovery of the previous week, it was obvious that the man in the dock was innocent of the murder of Frank Smallwood.

Terhune experienced a queasy spasm: a feeling very much like that which had affected him as a boy, when he entered Tussaud's Chamber of Horrors for the first time. For him there could be no distraction in the exciting speculation as to whether Cockburn would be acquitted for Murphy had said that the prisoner had been convicted of the crime. He had suffered for a crime he had not committed. The poor devil! As he turned over the page Terhune began to hate the girl who had hesitated to make a definite choice between two men.

He read on:

"I—I suppose—"

"You suppose what?"

"I—I didn't give the matter real thought."

"But you must have guessed that Smallwood had some reason for asking whereabouts the houseboat was situated?"

"I suppose I did. Yes, I did gather from what he said that he intended to visit the houseboat, but I swear I did not anticipate his staying overnight. I believed he was merely proposing to drop in and have a drink with us."

"Do you think it was fair to your fiancé to have encourage Smallwood to visit the houseboat?"

"I did not foresee any—any harm in just a brief visit."

"You knew that the prisoner disliked Smallwood?"

Mr. Barclay Keyes: "My lord, I must again protest at my learned friend's inferences. There is no evidence to suggest that Cockburn disliked Smallwood. On the contrary, one witness, Mr. Joseph Morgan, has testified that Cockburn's feeling towards Smallwood were—I have the witness's words before me, my lord—Cockburn's 'feelings were almost of admiration and a regret that Smallwood was not his friend'."

Sir Charles Stewart: "The attitude of the prisoner toward Smallwood on the occasion of the latter's visit to the houseboat was scarcely consistent with admiration, and a desire for friendship."

His lordship: "I think, Mr. Keyes, that Sir Charles is justified in assuming that the witness should have realized that a visit by Smallwood to the houseboat would not be welcomed, to say the least, by the accused."

Mr. Barclay Keyes: "As it please your lordship."

Sir Charles Stewart: "I shall rephrase the question in the light of his lordship's observation. Did you think that a visit by Smallwood to the houseboat would be welcomed by the prisoner?"

"No."

"Then why did you encourage it? To make the prisoner jealous? Or because you wanted to see Smallwood?"

"That is an unfair question. Neither of those alternatives influenced me."

"Are you quite sure?"

"Quite."

"You were not anxious to make the prisoner jealous?"

"Certainly not."

"Nor were you particularly anxious to see Smallwood again?"

Mr. Barclay Keyes: "My lord, I cannot comprehend the relevance of my learned friend's present interrogation. Surely the witness's motive in giving or withholding the whereabouts of the houseboat is immaterial?"

Sir Charles Stewart: "My learned friend is begging the question. If it be established that the witness was attracted by Smallwood, that fact contributes to the establishment of jealousy as the motive for the crime."

Mr, Barclay Keyes: "Then it would be more to the point if you were to try and prove, not that the witness was, or was not, attracted by Smallwood, but that my client knew or believed that she was."

Sir Charles Stewart: "I shall hope to oblige my learned friend with that evidence in the course of the next few minutes." (To the witness): "Well, Miss Webb?"

"I suppose I did not object to seeing him again. But just because I didn't mind seeing him did not make him attractive to me. Such a statement is nonsense. I loved Charlie. I still do. I always shall."

"It is a pity such admirable sentiments did not influence your actions last April. Had they done so your fiancé might not be facing the present charge of homicide. Reverting to Smallwood's telephone request for the address of the houseboat, you have admitted that you thought Smallwood intended to call at the houseboat over the holidays. Did you inform the prisoner of that probability?"

"No."

"Why not?"

"I don't know."

"I suggest to you that you know very well why you said nothing. I suggest to you that you remained silent because you knew that the prisoner was jealous of Smallwood."

"No! No!"

"Then why did you not warn the prisoner of the proposed visit?"

"I don't know. I don't know. I have told you, I don't know."

"Very well, we will leave your answer at that, Miss Webb. You do not know why you remained silent. We have been told by previous witnesses that Smallwood arrived at the houseboat towards late afternoon of Good Friday. What was your attitude towards the visitor during the next few hours?"

"Just friendly, I suppose."

"Come, Miss Webb, surely you are not asking the Court to believe that a mere *friendly* attitude towards Smallwood would have been sufficient to make your fiancé leave the houseboat in a temper? Did you flirt with Smallwood?"

"No! No! No! Why are you trying to make me out as something despicable?"

"*Qui s'excuse s'accuse!* Neither I, nor anyone else in Court, is sitting in judgment upon *your* ideas or acts. I want merely to ascertain the reason for the prisoner's strange behaviour on the evening of Friday, the fifteenth of April. Come, I will put the question differently. Was your attitude towards Smallwood, though quite innocent on your part, such as to tempt the prisoner into feeling jealous?"

"Perhaps I—"

"Speak up, please, so that his lordship and members of the jury can hear."

"Perhaps that might have been so, but not intentionally. I did not want Charlie to go for a walk by himself. I wanted to go with him, to keep him company. I really did love Charlie. You must believe me. Please."

"He refused your offer, did he not?"

"Yes. He was too—"

"Well, Miss Webb, what were you going to say?"

"Nothing."

"I insist upon your finishing that sentence. The prisoner was too—what?"

"Too—too angry."

"Ah! Now, Miss Webb, did you see the prisoner again that night?"

"No. I was awake when I heard him coming up the gangway. At first I thought of getting up to ask whether he was feeling better, but I changed my mind."

"Why?"

"I was still cross with him for having acted as he did."

"Were you able to hear from his movements what he did upon his return to the houseboat?"

"I think he went into his bedroom."

"And afterwards?"

"I could not say. I fell asleep."

"Did you wake up again before the morning?"

"No."

"Did you hear nothing extraordinary happen during the night?"

"No."

"No more sounds of people moving about the houseboat?"

"No."

"No more footsteps passing up or down the gangway?"

"No."

"Would you please look at a plan of the houseboat?" [Produced.] "Can you recognize your bedroom?"

"I think so. Isn't this my bedroom?"

"Yes. There are two windows marked, are there not? A and B."

"Yes."

"The window marked A overlooks the bank; that marked B faces roughly upstream. On the night of Good Friday, were either of those two windows open?"

"Both were open."

"Speaking of the window A, would you agree that the chart is correct in showing the distance from the middle of the window to the nearer side of the gangway to be fifteen feet?"

"I couldn't say. I think it might be about that."

"In fact, the gangway was near enough to your open window for you to have heard the sound of feet passing along the gangway?"

"If I were awake, yes. But not if I were asleep. I am a sound sleeper."

"Do you maintain that you heard no noise of any kind, between falling asleep soon after the return of the accused and waking up the next morning?"

"Yes."

"Very well, we will now deal with the events of the next morning, Saturday. Did you wake up, or were you awakened?"

"I woke up about eight-twenty, and day-dreamed for about ten minutes. I was just about to get up and go into the bathroom when I heard Charlie knock on the door of the Shakespeares' room to say that breakfast would be ready in half an hour's time. Then Charlie knocked on my door, and said the same thing. Before I could reach the bathroom I heard Philip enter it, so I waited until he had finished, and shared it with Eileen."

"When did you first hear of Smallwood's alleged departure?"

"As Eileen and I entered the dining-room. Both Charlie and Philip were there, waiting for us. Philip said to Eileen: 'What do you think has happened since last night, darling? Smallwood has slung his hook.'"

"Inferring that Smallwood had departed?"

"Yes. Philip often uses slangy expressions."

"Did the news surprise you?"

"Yes."

"Because Smallwood had gone, or because he had gone without saying good-bye to you?"

"For both reasons, I think."

"Did you ever ask the accused for an explanation of Smallwood's unexpected departure?"

"Yes. Charlie told me that, on his return to the houseboat, he had had it out with Smallwood, and asked him to leave."

"By 'having it out' with Smallwood, I suppose that the accused inferred that he had accused the other man of flirting with you?"

"I couldn't say. I did not ask him to explain further."

"You accepted the story, without feeling any doubt in its veracity?"

"Charlie is not a liar."

"But think, Miss Webb. This Smallwood possessed an aggressive, bullying nature. We have heard evidence that he persistently taunted your fiancé for having lost every fight in which the two men had engaged. Moreover, he was obviously doing his best to alienate your affections. Are you prepared to swear to his lordship, and to the members of the jury, that you accepted, without the slightest mental reservation, a story—I go so far as to say, an amazing story—to the effect that Smallwood, this same Smallwood who had practically invited himself aboard, was content tamely to leave the houseboat, in the middle of the night, when asked to do so by a man whom he had despised from their first meeting, and of whom he was frankly contemptuous?"

"I am afraid I do not follow you, Sir Charles."

His lordship: "I think the question is merely an elaboration of the previous question, Sir Charles, to which the witness replied that she accepted the prisoner's story without experiencing any doubts."

Sir Charles Stewart: "Quite so, my lord, but I find it hard to believe that, the circumstances being what they were, anyone could be so trusting, or so simple-minded."

His lordship: "We males are not supposed to be adept at solving the riddle of a woman's trust in her chosen mate, Sir Charles." (To the witness): "'Let us be quite clear on this point, Miss Webb: when you were told that Smallwood had left the houseboat after, apparently, having retired for the night, you did not even reflect that midnight, or thereabouts, was an unusual time for a guest to leave?"

Miss Webb: "No."

His lordship: "You were not even mentally hurt by his apparent discourtesy in not waiting until the morning so that he could bid you good-bye?"

Miss Webb: "No. I—I expected to have the explanation from him by letter or telephone."

His lordship: "Go on, Sir Charles."

Sir Charles Stewart: "I thank your lordship. Now, Miss Webb, please inform the Court as to whether you did, in fact, receive an explanation from Smallwood, either by telephone or by letter?"

"No."

"Or by any other means of communication?"

"No."

"From the moment of saying good night to Smallwood, on the night of Good Friday last, have you ever seen or heard from Frank Smallwood?"

"No."

"Have you had any indirect news of him?"

"No."

"Have you not, subsequently, felt surprised by his silence?"

"I have been a little surprised."

"Have you ever remarked upon Smallwood's silence to the accused?"

"No."

"Has he ever asked you, since the Easter holidays, whether Smallwood had communicated with you?"

"No."

"Or whether you had seen him again?"

"No."

"In fact, have you ever discussed Smallwood with your fiancé since the Easter holidays?"

"No."

"Thank you, Miss Webb."

Keyes's cross-examination of Patricia Webb was short, but skilful.

"Did your friendship with Smallwood result in your contemplating breaking your engagement with Charles Cockburn?"

"Never."

"Did you fall in love with Frank Smallwood?"

"No."

"Did you ever give Cockburn reason for believing that you had fallen in love with Smallwood?"

"No."

"Or that you might do so in the future?"

"No."

"Are you still engaged to Cockburn?"

"I am."

"Do you still love him?"

"I do."

"That will be all, thank you, Miss Webb."

*

Now that he had had the opportunity of reading the rest of Patricia Webb's evidence, Terhune considered that she was more real to him than she had been at first. He felt sorry not to have had the chance of watching her answer the questions put to her by counsel for the defence. The bald, printed words conveyed no hint of her real feelings. For instance: her "I do", in answer to counsel's "Do you still love him?" Had she breathed the two words with all the embarrassment, yet all the fervour of a person genuinely in love; or with the emotionless defiance of a woman making the best of a bad job, or as a woman unwilling to admit a mistake, or as a woman putting loyalty before conviction?

The simplicity of her answers was, he felt, probably proof of their sincerity. Had she tried to elaborate he would have been less willing to believe in her, for having spent spare hours in the Law Courts, and Old Bailey, he realized that the majority of witnesses having something to conceal did so by adding rambling and unnecessary details, in the hope of diverting their questioner. Only the extremely direct, and—paradoxically—the habitual criminal made ideal witnesses.

The part of her evidence which he frankly did not believe was that relating to her reaction to Smallwood's departure from the houseboat. He was convinced that she had lied; it was not natural for anyone not to feel astonished by such behaviour. At the same time, he felt that her perjury was almost excusable: she had obviously done her best not to give evidence of anything which could be used against the man in the dock.

For the rest, Terhune believed her to be no more and no less than a rather nice, suburban girl who, not from any vicious motive, had behaved foolishly. Without any justification, he pictured her with carefully waved blonde hair, blue eyes, a round, pink and white china shepherdess face, very slim, and fashionably flat-chested.

*

The next person to give evidence was a Mrs. Smith. She, it appeared, had rented the room to Smallwood in which he had been living for six months prior to the Easter holidays. A short time before the beginning of the holidays he had announced his intention of spending the time punting on the river. From that holiday he had never returned. She had neither seen him, nor heard from him from the moment of his leaving her house early on the Good Friday morning.

No, he had not said anything about leaving for good. On the contrary, he had arranged to have some friends come to his room on the last Saturday of the month for a game of cards. Yes, he often played cards. No, he did not owe her any money for rent, he paid her on the Friday morning for that week. No, he did not usually pay her on Fridays, but on Mondays, for the past week. Yes, he had left his personal belongings behind; she still possessed them, put away in an old trunk. Yes, she had let the room to another gentleman.

Mr. Harold Grigg, general manager of a firm of tea importers, testified that Frank Hugh Smallwood had been in the firm's employment for three months and two weeks previous to his disappearance over the Easter holidays. Yes, he had been employed in a clerical position. No, he had not returned to the office since the holidays. No, he had not communicated with anyone in the office since his departure on the Thursday afternoon. No, he, Grigg, knew of no explanation to account for Smallwood's absence. (In cross-examination: No, Smallwood was not an ideal employee—he had too restless a nature to be entirely reliable.)

George Barker, boatman, gave evidence of having rented a punt to a Mr. Smallwood for the Easter holidays. Yes, he had paid in advance, and left a deposit. No, Smallwood had never returned the punt. Yes, the punt had been returned to him by a friendly boatman who had found it floating downstream early Saturday morning. No, he had not reported the matter to the police, because he didn't like sticking his nose into matters which didn't concern him. No, Smallwood had never claimed the deposit. No, he had not seen Smallwood since Good Friday morning.

Two other men, friends of Smallwood, gave evidence to prove that it was his intention to return to Mrs. Smith's house. They, too, confirmed that they had neither seen nor heard of Smallwood subsequent to the Easter holidays.

The case for the prosecution came to an end. Mr. Barclay Keyes made his opening speech for the defence, which he concluded by calling upon Charles Cockburn to enter the witness-stand.

Chapter Nine

Terhune skimmed over the first part of Cockburn's evidence, which, for the most part, merely confirmed or enlarged upon facts which had been touched upon during evidence already given. The accused testified that he lived on his own because he had no relations closer than three first cousins, one aunt and one uncle. He admitted having been the butt of Smallwood's bullying propensities, and having fought—and lost—upon several occasions. He vigorously denied having reciprocated Smallwood's antagonism.

Presently his counsel began to question him on more recent happenings.

"Do you recollect the occasion when Mr. and Mrs. Shakespeare and Miss Webb were your guests at the Chanticleer Restaurant?"

"I have taken them there on several occasions."

"I refer specifically to the night, last November, when you were joined by Frank Smallwood?"

"I remember that night only too well."

"Is the account, which you have heard given by witnesses for the prosecution, substantially true?"

"Yes."

"Had you met Smallwood in between the period when you attended the same school, and the night just referred to?"

"I had neither met him, nor heard of him."

"Is it true that, after Smallwood had joined your party, he seemed to pay more attention to Miss Webb than to anyone else?"

"I did not like the way he looked at her."

"Was Miss Webb equally interested in Smallwood?"

"Oh, no!"

"Is there any significance in the fact that you proposed marriage to Miss Webb within a few days of this dinner-party?"

"Yes. I had been wanting for some time past to ask Miss Webb to marry me, but I was not sure whether she loved me, so I hadn't had the pluck to propose."

"What gave you the necessary courage?"

"When I saw how Frank—Smallwood—was looking at Miss Webb I realized that, as long as she remained free, other men were at liberty to show interest in her. I became afraid she might return that interest, so I determined to ask her to marry me before it was too late."

"Would it be true, then, to say that Smallwood's attitude towards Miss Webb did not make you jealous of him in particular, but of all other men in general?"

"Yes, sir, that would be a true statement."

"We have heard that Miss Webb accepted you, and that you both were, shall I say, deliriously happy for the next week or so. You have also heard Mr. and Mrs. Shakespeare say that, later, Miss Webb's attitude became rather more casual. Do you agree that such was the case?"

"I was not aware of any change."

"Do you deny that Miss Webb later expressed a distaste for your embraces?"

"May I answer that question in my own way?"

"Please do."

"It is not correct to say that, after the first two weeks or so of our engagement, my fiancée expressed a distaste for my embraces. What happened was, that she limited my caresses, on the grounds that she did not want familiarity to turn into contempt, as it were. Whenever I did kiss her, however, she returned my kisses with quite as much warmth as previously."

"Did it occur to you that a growing interest in Smallwood might have been the indirect cause of that limitation?"

"It did not. I still do not think Smallwood had anything to do with Miss Webb's request. In my opinion, it was the natural reticence of her sex."

"Were you aware that Smallwood had taken your fiancée to the Stoll Picture Theatre?"

"I was. Miss Webb herself told me of her visit with Smallwood to the theatre."

"Was that before or after the night in question?"

"Afterwards."

"How did the information affect you?"

"I was not pleased. No man likes to realize that his fiancée can even think of another man. But I was not really angry with her."

"Were you jealous?"

"No, I was not."

"Miss Webb has said that you were a little jealous when she told you of Smallwood's second 'phone call to her."

"I was not really jealous. I might have pretended to be, but in my heart I wasn't jealous."

"Why were you not really jealous?"

"Because I was sure of Miss Webb's love for me, and I was convinced that Smallwood was not the type of man to appeal to her."

"If you were not genuinely jealous of the call, why did you pretend to be?"

"To flatter her natural vanity. She would have been disappointed if I remained unaffected by the information that another man was pestering her. At least, that is what I thought at the time."

"In between that occasion and yesterday, when you heard Miss Webb's evidence, did you know that Smallwood continued to telephone your fiancée?"

"No."

"Did you have any reason to suspect him of doing so?"

"No."

"Did you see anything of him, or hear from him, during the period from the night he joined your party at the Chanticleer, and his visit to the houseboat?"

"I did not."

"Were you surprised when he hailed you and your friends, and boarded the houseboat?"

"Yes."

"Disagreeably surprised?"

"No."

"We have heard that, in response to his pointed hints, you invited him to stay with you for the rest of the holidays. Have you any criticism of that statement?"

"No. I was not anxious to have him as a guest, partly because it made our party uneven, but my objections were not sufficiently pronounced for me to ignore his hints. When he wished, Smallwood could make any party a jolly affair. I decided to ignore my own feelings for the benefit of my guests."

"Was any pressure put upon you, directly or indirectly, to ask him?"

"Definitely not."

"In that case, your subsequent attitude is all the more curious."

"I am not proud of my pettish behaviour."

"That is a matter with which we are not concerned. Can you explain why, having asked Smallwood to stay, you subsequently left your guests on their own?"

"I will try. I think it was because I could not bear to see the way in which he stared at Miss Webb."

"How did he stare?"

"Gloatingly."

"How did Miss Webb react to Smallwood's offensiveness?"

"Offensive is not the word, sir, to describe his behaviour. His behaviour was—well, too over-bold to please me. But I do not think Miss Webb was conscious of the fact; she acted towards him as though he were a good friend."

"Then why did you leave the houseboat, Mr. Cockburn?"

"I have tried to explain. It is not easy. What I want to emphasize is, that Miss Webb did nothing to upset me. It was my own foolishness which prompted me to go off on my own."

"I understand. In simpler language, Miss Webb did nothing to give you cause for feeling jealous of Frank Smallwood?"

Sir Charles Stewart: "I appreciate my learned friend's partiality for simplicity, but not at the expense of translating simplicity into a leading question."

Mr. Barclay Keyes: "I did not lead the witness. The witness already has said that Miss Webb did nothing to upset him."

Sir Charles Stewart: "Surely no statement ever less demanded simplifying!"

His lordship: "Perhaps Mr. Keyes is an exponent of Basic English." (Laughter.)

Mr. Barclay Keyes (to the witness): "Did you have a drink at any time during your absence from the houseboat?"

"No."

"What did you do during your absence?"

"I walked the entire time."

"At what time did you return to the houseboat?"

"A few minutes after eleven-thirty."

"Will you please tell us what happened subsequent to your return?"

"I went first of all to my bedroom, where I pottered about, tidying up, drawing back the bedclothes, pulling my pyjamas out of their case, and so on. Then I—"

"One moment. Had you any particular reason—as you put it—for pottering about?"

"Yes. The exercise had refreshed me. Instead of feeling sleepy, I was so alert that I felt fidgety."

"I see. Continue."

"Presently I left the bedroom, and went into the kitchen with the idea of getting the breakfast things ready for the next morning. While I was doing so, I remembered the hindquarter of lamb, and decided to cut off the chops for Saturday's lunch. I took the joint out of the meat safe and put it on the table. Then I took a sharp knife and a meat-chopper out of a drawer and proceeded to separate the chops from the joint."

"Go on."

"Just as I had finished this job Smallwood walked into the kitchen. He said to me: 'What the hell are you doing at this hour of the night, Charlie?' I told him. He said: 'You might damned well have remembered that everyone is asleep.' I replied: 'The little noise I made couldn't have been heard at the other end of the boat.' He said: 'What about me?'

"Well, we sparred about like that for a minute or two until I began to feel angry. I said to him: 'As you are here I have something I want to say to you, Frank. I don't like the way you look at Miss Webb.' He laughed. 'Beginning to feel jealous?' I replied: 'It would take a better man than you to make me jealous. Miss Webb wouldn't look at you if you offered her a fortune.'

"I can't remember all the things we said to each other, but I admit that they were rude. At last I said: 'Look here, Frank, I only asked you to join my party when you forced yourself upon us this afternoon. Nobody here really wants you, so you can damn' well take yourself off, here and now.'"

"What did Smallwood say?"

"He began to threaten me, saying that he had beaten me up in the past, and was capable of doing it again. With those words he advanced towards me. Without thinking what I was doing I picked up the meat-chopper, and told him that he had better remain where he was, if he didn't want to get hurt."

"And then?"

"I saw that I had shaken him, and that he was suddenly frightened of me. At the same moment I realized that I had a wonderful opportunity of getting rid of him. I simulated a show of temper, waved the chopper about fiercely, and made him back a pace. 'Get out now, while you are still safe,' I told him. 'Get out, blast you!'"

"And did he?"

"Yes. He almost ran back into his bedroom, and threw all his belongings into the small case he had brought with him. Then I ordered him to get into the punt, which he did. After that I undid the painter, and gave the punt a push with my foot. The last I saw of Frank Smallwood was his face staring at me with astonishment as he disappeared into the darkness."

"And then?"

"I turned quickly to re-enter the door into the houseboat. In doing so I hit my right hand against the lintel of the door, the force of which swung the chopper towards my left wrist, and caused the edge to slice the flesh."

"Is that the complete story of Smallwood's departure from the houseboat?"

"Yes."

"After Smallwood's departure, what did you do?"

"Went back into the kitchen, placed the chopper on the table, and tried to bind up my wrist."

"Was that an easy matter?"

"Not very. But I managed it in the end. Afterwards, I went back into the bedroom, undressed, and got into bed. I was so pleased with myself at having got rid of Smallwood that I fell asleep almost at once. I woke up about six-fifteen, dressed, washed, shaved, and went into the kitchen to get breakfast. I noticed that the meat-chopper was a little bloodstained, also the table and floor, the blood splashes apparently having dropped from my wrist while I was trying to bind it up. I cleaned away the bloodstains, and prepared breakfast."

"Then the story of Smallwood's departure which you passed on to your guests was not entirely true?"

"It was true in essence. The only part of the truth which I omitted was the fact of my having pretended to threaten Smallwood with the chopper."

"You have heard that the prosecution accuses you of having murdered Frank Smallwood, of having dissected his alleged corpse by dismembering it, and of disposing of the alleged mutilated parts of the corpse by throwing them into the river. I put it to you formally, Mr. Cockburn: Did you kill Frank Hugh Smallwood?"

"I did not."

"Did you dismember his corpse?"

"No."

"Did you throw any part or parts of Smallwood's corpse into the river, either on the night of the fifteenth-sixteenth of April, of this year, or at any other time?"

"I did not."

"Do you know anything of the alleged death of Frank Hugh Smallwood?"

"I know nothing whatsoever."

"Thank you, Mr. Cockburn."

II

Terhune glanced at Murphy. The sergeant's eyes were open; he was looking at his host with eyes that expressed part content, and part amusement.

"The case interests you, Mr. Terhune?"

"Immensely."

"I thought so. I have been watching you for the past few minutes. Judging from your expression I should guess that you are reading Cockburn's evidence."

"So I am, but how—"

"You looked pitying."

"That is how I feel. It was ridiculous of Cockburn to hope to make a level-headed jury believe such a story. It is the weakest, most preposterous defence I have ever read."

Murphy nodded. "It is. It was a piece of cake for the Crown. You haven't read the cross-examination yet?"

"No."

"Sir Charles Stewart tore Cockburn's evidence into rags. The tragedy is, that we know now that it must have been true."

"I wonder!"

"What! But there is no doubt about the identity of our corpse—"

"I wasn't referring to Smallwood's death. If Smallwood was still alive nearly twenty years after his supposed murder, it is obvious that he wasn't killed. But there are many loose ends which need tying up."

"The scarred leg, for instance?"

"No, I wasn't thinking of that piece of leg. The similarity of the two scars was a ghastly, damnable coincidence which might not happen again for a million years. The first point which does not satisfy me is connected with Cockburn's story of his quarrel with Smallwood.

"If one can accept all the evidence given in Cockburn's trial, it is apparent that Smallwood was a mean, unscrupulous bully who had gained the ascendancy of Cockburn, had retained it throughout the years they had remained at school together, and who still retained it to some extent after a period of more than ten years. Do you agree?"

"That was my impression of the two men."

"Very well. That being so, was it likely that Smallwood would have submitted so tamely to his victim's orders to leave the houseboat there and then?"

"A meat-chopper can lend considerable authority to such an order," Murphy commented dryly. "Besides, don't forget that a bully is more easily overawed than an ordinary man once the bubble of his superiority has been pricked."

"I am not overlooking either point, Sergeant. I am willing to agree that a braver man than Smallwood might have been temporarily frightened of a man who had been brewing over his troubles for the previous few hours, and who had probably worked himself into a state of insane anger. Smallwood might have had good reason to believe that Cockburn would kill him if he didn't take himself off fairly quickly. But from what we know of Smallwood's character do you believe that he would have been content to have remained away from Patricia Webb afterwards?"

"I hesitate to give too decided an opinion, Mr. Terhune. People are funny animals, and their pride sometimes makes them do funny things. Smallwood might have been so ashamed of himself at having been bested by a man whom he had always despised, that he decided to keep away, not only from Cockburn, but from Patricia Webb as well."

"And his friends, his place of employment, his room, and his personal belongings as well? That would be carrying a sense of shame to extreme limits. Even so, such a course of action might have been taken by an ultra-sensitive person—perhaps by Cockburn, indeed—but surely not by Smallwood."

"I have seen too many people act in most unpredictable ways in a crisis to have much faith in explanations based on psychology. Otherwise, I should agree with you."

"Then what do you think happened, Sergeant? That Smallwood was so flabbergasted at being driven away from the houseboat by an unusually aggressive Cockburn that he cleared out of the country there and then?"

Murphy chuckled. "I haven't given much thought to what did happen. I am merely trying to keep an open mind on the subject. The facts are, that Smallwood did disappear, and that he possessed an impulsive, unsettled nature which had previously taken him abroad."

Terhune frowned. "That explanation doesn't sound reasonable to me. Where did he get the money from, to pay his passage abroad? And surely his feeling of hurt pride was not so intense that it wouldn't even allow him to return the punt, and reclaim the deposit? What happened to the poor devil who was supposed to have killed Smallwood? Was he hanged?"

"No. The judge's summing-up was unbiased, and the jury, had they wished, could have brought in a verdict of Not Guilty without being accused of being contrary. But I think Cockburn must have made a bad impression upon them, for they brought in the verdict of Guilty.

"Keyes appealed, but he had no real grounds for doing so, and the appeal failed. Nevertheless, the public, with that uncanny instinct which manifests itself every now and again, clamoured for a reprieve. Many declared their faith in Cockburn's complete innocence; others believed he really had killed Smallwood, but only in self-defence. Others, again, argued that Smallwood only got what he was asking for, and that the verdict should have been reduced to one of Manslaughter.

"The upshot of the agitation was, that the death sentence was commuted to one of life imprisonment, which, as an amateur lawyer, you probably know is the equivalent of twenty years, the maximum sentence any man is called upon to serve. Cockburn was a model prisoner, and earned the maximum remission of one quarter. As soon as he was released he joined NAAFI, and was sent to the Middle East. He had been there three months only when he was killed during an enemy air-raid while driving his canteen well up towards the front line."

"Poor devil!" Terhune muttered feelingly.

Chapter Ten

T he news which Murphy had passed on to Terhune, 'broke' the following morning in the daily Press. The more popular among the morning newspapers made the most of it, as well they might, for the unexpected *dénouement* was the most sensational happening since the end of the Second World War. In bold headlines the public were told:

WINDMILL WOOD VICTIM
TWICE 'MURDERED'!
GRAVE MISCARRIAGE OF JUSTICE EXPOSED
'DEAD' MAN COMES TO LIFE
STARTLING DEVELOPMENT IN TWENTY-YEAR-
OLD MURDER TRIAL
WHOSE LEG CONVICTED ACCUSED IN 1927
'HOUSEBOAT CRIME'?
MAN CONVICTED OF MURDER PROVED
INNOCENT NINETEEN YEARS LATER

The number of newspapers allocating less than one column to the Windmill Wood Crime could have been counted on one hand—almost on one finger indeed. Even *The Times* gave unusual prominence to the case, dwelling particularly on the legal aspect of the circumstantial evidence which had wrongly convicted an innocent man. Of the London papers the *Telegraph* gave the news a double column spread; the *Daily Express* used five columns for its headlines; the *Daily Mail* the same. Nor were the *News-Chronicle* and the *Daily Herald* less generous. The

Daily Sketch and the *Daily Mirror* both used the entire front page for headlines, pictures, and a brief *résumé* of the *Houseboat Crime*, leaving inner pages free for a fuller account of the two crimes. The provincial newspapers were equally lavish.

Some of the papers reprinted high-lights of the evidence given in the proceedings against Charles Cockburn. Others printed short commentaries by *Our Legal Correspondent*. At least two mentioned the trial in leading articles: "Miscarriages of justice in British Courts of Law are happily rare, but the positive and indisputable identification of the man found recently murdered in a Kentish wood with the victim in a notorious, twenty-year-old trial for murder, will give renewed heart to the anti-death-sentence, and the anti-circumstantial-evidence fanatics who are for ever tilting lances at our ancient and well-tested legal system. While no level-headed person would desire to give undue prominence to the miscarriage of justice which twenty years ago sentenced the accused to a term of life imprisonment for the alleged murder of a man who was still alive not two weeks ago, even the most sober-minded among us will be asking himself whether it is not possible to devise some alteration in our present legal system by which a similar miscarriage could be avoided in the future. It is not enough to speak blithely of the inexorable law of averages, or to maintain that so grave a human error is not likely to happen again in this century." And so on, in that same strain.

The interest of the public in the Windmill Wood Crime was heightened by the first editions of the evening papers. Having ascertained the circumstances of Cockburn's death—CONVICTED 'MURDERER' DIES A HERO'S DEATH—some astute member of the *Star's* editorial staff had conceived the brilliant idea of tracing out the subsequent history of many of the other principal characters in the drama.

Several of them had died. Mr. Justice Street, in 1934, and Sir Charles Stewart, in 1943. Barclay Keyes, now Sir Barclay Keyes, had become

Recorder of London. Interviewed by a Special Correspondent, Sir Barclay said that he was glad that Cockburn's innocence had been proved. "Against my better judgment I always remained convinced of his innocence," he admitted. "It is true that I was unable to believe entirely in his version of the events of that night aboard the houseboat, but I was intuitively conscious of his guiltlessness in the matter of homicide." Commenting on this interview the *Star* reminded its readers that it had been Sir Barclay's untiring efforts which had played so large a part in having the death sentence commuted to life imprisonment.

Of the witnesses, Doctor Barry was dead. So was Joseph Morgan, the schoolmaster. Morgan had, in fact, died within three months of the trial. Philip Shakespeare was still alive, and prospering, having been promoted to the managership of one of the insurance company's smaller branch offices. He was, however, a widower, his wife Eileen, and his younger son, having been killed in the December of 1940, during a German air-raid on London.

Patricia Webb was still alive, still employed at the company's Head Office in Lombard Street, and still a spinster. Interviewed as she entered the office building, she said, in answer to a question touching upon what effect the news of Cockburn's innocence had upon her:

"I feel happier this morning than I have been since Charlie's trial."

"During the past twenty years, have you believed in your ex-fiancé's innocence?"

"Always. My faith in him has never faltered. Charlie was incapable of committing murder, or any other crime."

"Did you correspond with him while he was in prison?"

"As frequently as the regulations allowed."

"Did he reply?"

"Of course."

"Did you remain in love with him?"

"Yes."

"Were you engaged to him at the time of his death in Africa?"

"No. Charlie broke off the engagement in the very first letter he wrote to me after the trial."

"Why did he do that?"

"He refused to let me remain tied to a convicted murderer. He begged me to forget him, and marry someone else."

"What did you say in reply to that request?"

"I said that if it made him happier to feel we were no longer engaged, then I would willingly break off the official engagement, but that, for my part, I should always consider myself as being engaged to him. I told him that I should be waiting for him when he came out of prison."

"And were you?"

"Yes."

"Did he ask you to marry him?"

"No. I asked him to marry me, but he refused. He said that he still would not let me marry a convicted murderer. I said I was willing to take the risk of what anyone might say, or to go with him anywhere in the world, where we might not have been known, or recognized."

"What did he reply to that offer?"

"That he was not thinking of me or of himself, but of any children we might have; that it would be wicked to have children who might one day learn that their father had been declared a murderer; and that he didn't want to enter into a marriage from which children would be prohibited."

"Did you agree with those views?"

"I wanted Charlie too much to agree. But I respected them, and loved him all the more because of them. Then I returned the engagement ring to him which I had kept throughout the intervening years."

"Why?"

"He announced his intention of joining NAAFI to go overseas, and wanted to wear the ring so that it might bring me nearer to him. He was wearing it when he was killed. It was returned to me, because he had left a letter of instruction to that effect. I have worn the ring ever since. Here it is."

The identification of Smallwood continued to supply newspaper headlines. On the following day the two illustrated newspapers published a selection of photographs dealing with the principal characters in the *Cockburn Trial*, also the *Windmill Wood Crime*, as the two cases soon came to be called. Photographs of Sir Barclay Keyes, both as K.C. and as judge; of Patricia Webb; of the murdered man; of the houseboat—which still existed—of Windmill Wood (the lower x marking the spot where the crime had been committed, the upper x the place where the body had lain concealed); of Detective-Sergeant Murphy; and, of course, of Terhune (looking more than ever like an overgrown schoolboy caught in the act of committing a mischievous practical joke); of his bookshop (both of these from the photographic 'morgues' in which the newspapers had stored them after taking and publishing at the time of the House with Crooked Walls affair), of Market Square, and of Helena Armstrong.

Very soon one of the newspapers awakened to the fact that, amid all the excitement of discovering that one man had been unjustly convicted of 'murdering' another man who had not even died at that time, no information had come from the police as to who, this time, had murdered Frank Smallwood. On the following morning, therefore, it appeared with large headlines:

NO TRACE OF WINDMILL WOOD KILLER
WHAT ARE THE KENT POLICE DOING?

On the Sunday the *Empire News* scooped its rivals with:

LIFE STORY OF WINDMILL WOOD VICTIM

From the window of his front room Terhune saw the placard outside the newspaper shop on the far side of the square. He hurried out into the street, crossed the square and entered the shop.

Behind the counter stood old Joshua Higgins. Higgins was a short, pale-faced little man, with bowed shoulders, a drooping wisp of hair for a moustache, a fringe of grey hair round a bald patch, and a pair of steel spectacles through which he peered, near-sightedly.

"Good morning, Mr. Terhune. A nice morning. Bit sharpish, though."

Terhune nodded. "As long as it keeps dry..." he murmured. "The *Empire News*, please."

"The *Empire News!*" Higgins chuckled. "I shouldn't have thought there were anything in any of the newspapers what was news to you, Mr. Terhune, you being in with the police, so to speak. Here's your copy, and you're lucky to get one, for it's the last I have. There's been a fair run on the *Empire News* today. It's that there placard outside what's done it, I don't doubt. But there, them reporting fellows seems to find out all they wants to. More'n the police sometimes, I always say."

Terhune took his copy of the newspaper back to his flat, and ignoring the *Observer* and the *Sunday Times*, which were his usual Sunday breakfast literature, he propped the *Empire News* up against the marmalade jar, and began to read the contribution by *Our Special Crime Investigator*.

The reporter had made an efficient job of his assignment. It seemed that Frank Hugh Smallwood was the younger of two sons born to Jennie, the wife of George Stanley Smallwood, a shop assistant. Between the date of their marriage, and six months after the birth of Frank, the Smallwoods had lived at Kennington. During that period the father had succeeded in achieving local notoriety for drunkenness and cruelty, this latter to his wife, his children and animals impartially. In the January of 1900 the Smallwoods left Kennington, and moved to Hayes, Middlesex, where Smallwood had bought a small grocer's shop.

Two months later Smallwood's drunkenness led to tragedy. Returning home one Saturday night, the worse for drink, he accidentally set alight the back part of the shop, above which his two children were sleeping. As a result of the fire the elder child suffered injuries from which he died, twenty-four hours later. The younger, Frank, suffered only superficial injuries, and soon recovered.

The fire and its consequences so affected Smallwood that he became a changed man, and thereafter, until his death, he led an exemplary life. As a result of hard work he prospered to some extent, and in 1907 he sent his son to Southall County School, which opened for the first time that year. There, in his second term, Frank met Charles Cockburn.

Frank remained at that school until the early days of 1914. In the first week of February of that year George Smallwood was killed by a butcher's cart drawn by a runaway horse. Two months later his widow disposed of the goodwill and stock of the grocer's shop, and moved, with her son, to Hammersmith, where Jennie's spinster sister lived in a small house of her own. Within three weeks of his moving to Hammersmith, Frank began work as an apprentice in a newly established garage not far from the Earl's Court Exhibition.

In 1917 he volunteered for the Royal Flying Corps, was accepted, and, after training, eventually arrived in France, where he served on the Western Front. There he achieved a name for fearlessness and recklessness as a fighter which quickly brought his total of 'kills' to double figures, and would, no doubt, have earned him a decoration but for the fact that he was equally reckless with his off-duty hours, and was thus frequently involved in trouble with his commanding officers. To such an extent, apparently, that only his record as a fighter, and the need for his dash and example, saved the young man from being cashiered. Despite his record, however, Smallwood was not a favourite among the fellow members of his squadron, chiefly on account of his scornful and overbearing treatment of more cautious fighters, and of his troublesome belligerence whenever he was the worse for drink.

Upon demobilization from the Royal Air Force Smallwood resumed his employment with the garage at which he had been employed previ-ous to his war service, but soon afterwards he was convicted of embez-zlement. In 1922 he went to prison for a second time. In the following year, following his mother's death in April, he emigrated to the United States of America, but returned to Hammersmith in December, 1924, where he took lodgings with a Mrs. Brownlee, of 27, Oakapple Road, Hammersmith. In January, 1925, he sought and obtained employment, as a clerk, with Kensington Garages, Ltd. In November of the same year he left that firm, to become a commercial traveller for Messrs. Benedex & Benedex, manufacturers of automobile accessories.

October, 1926, proved an unfortunate month for him. In the first week he was discharged from his firm for undisclosed reasons; two nights later he was arrested for drunkenness and violence; the day after his appearance at the police court Mrs. Brownlee ordered him to find lodgings elsewhere. The following week he moved to 13, Beech Road, where he lodged with a Mrs. Smith. From October to the end of the year he remained unemployed, but in the first week of January, 1927, he was offered a clerical position with The Oriental Tea Import Company, Ltd., of Mincing Lane. This position he retained until the 14th April, which was the day before his disappearance from the houseboat.

"Most readers will have read in the daily press what happened now in the life of this strange character. Between 11 p.m. Good Friday and dawn the following day, Smallwood disappeared in mysterious circumstances which led eventually to the trial of Charles Cockburn for murder.

"What really took place at that strange midnight meeting aboard the houseboat, between Smallwood and Cockburn? We can only surmise what happened from studying the evidence given by the defendant at his trial, but it is doubtful whether our wildest guesses can approach the truth, for the fact remains that Frank Hugh Smallwood, as such, was never heard of again until his body was discovered recently in a small Kentish wood.

"*As such!* The two words are significant, for it is now known that twenty-four hours previous to his death Smallwood was serving as a seaman aboard the Cunard Company's s.s. *Cilicia*, homeward bound from Montreal, not in his baptismal name of Smallwood, but under the false name of Thomas Wheeler.

"Enquiries have elicited from the Cunard Company that this was Wheeler's third voyage aboard the s.s. *Cilicia*. His employment with this company began a few months ago when the s.s. *Cilicia* arrived in Canada with a short crew, three men having been swept overboard during a violent gale which had overtaken the ship three days out from England. Smallwood, or Wheeler, as he called himself, was taken on as a member of the crew after presenting discharge papers purporting to belong to Thomas Wheeler, Canadian citizen, of 3, Calgary Avenue, Quebec.

"As a consequence of further enquiries among other British shipping companies, it is now possible to bridge the gap in Smallwood's life between the 25th February, 1930, and the morning of his death. On the 25th February, 1930, Thomas Wheeler was signed on, in Sydney, Australia, to serve as ordinary seaman aboard one of the Blue Funnel Line cargo vessels calling at that port. For the next twenty months Wheeler served on one or another of the Blue Funnel ships, but in October, 1931, he signed on, in London, with the New Zealand Shipping Co. In 1933 he transferred to the Furness Lines. In 1935 he was once more with the Blue Funnel Line. In 1937 he served six months with the General Steam Navigation Co.; in 1938 he was with the Ellerman Lines.

"During the Second World War he was torpedoed at least three times. After the war, when the shipping companies resumed their separate entities, Wheeler signed on with one of the Elders

& Fyffes ships. Being discharged at Jamaica, on account of an injury, he subsequently joined one of the United Fruit Company's ships, from which he later took his discharge in New York. His next ship was the Cunard s.s. *Cilicia*, as already related.

"That Smallwood and Wheeler are, and always have been, the same man is established beyond any doubt by seamen who have been his shipmates as long ago as 1930. All testify to his bullying nature, and to his hard drinking. He was by no means a favourite among his fellow seamen, and was often involved in fights with them, or in dockside brawls.

"What happened to Smallwood between the 15th April, 1927, and the 25th February, 1930? What caused him to change his name from Frank Hugh Smallwood to Thomas Wheeler? How did he come to be in Australia in 1930? When, and how, did he leave England? Why did he not appear at the trial of Charles Cockburn for murder? Was he even aware of the trial at the time it took place? Or, if not then, did he learn of it subsequently? Why did he never attempt to see, or to communicate with Patricia Webb?

"All these problems could be solved by the application of one simple explanation—that something happened, on the night of the 15–16th April, 1927, to cause Smallwood to lose his memory—if it were not for the fact that such a theory not only has no evidence to substantiate it, but is actually disproved by several seafaring men who, on different occasions, have heard him hint, when his tongue had been loosened by alcohol, that many people in England knew him by a different name from Wheeler.

"Whatever the explanation may be of Smallwood's strange behaviour during life, the manner of his death adds still one more question to the list enumerated above. Who killed Frank Smallwood? And why? At the time of his death he had been in England little more than twelve hours. But this last question is one to which the police authorities will be expected to supply the answer. It is to be hoped that that answer will not be long in forthcoming. Already this year there have been three cases in the British Isles in which the criminal murderers have gone unpunished. Is the Windmill Wood Crime to become the fourth on this already too-long list?"

Chapter Eleven

When Murphy dropped in that night Terhune was not taken by surprise. All day long he had had a feeling that the sergeant might do so. As his visitor entered the building by the side door Terhune noticed a newspaper which was tucked beneath Murphy's left armpit—it looked suspiciously like a copy of the *Empire News*. This newspaper the sergeant carried with him into the study. As he settled into the comfortable chair he held it out, still folded so that its name was invisible.

"Have you seen this paper today, Mr. Terhune?"

"The *Empire News?*"

Murphy nodded, and threw the newspaper on to Terhune's table-desk. "That means you have read it?"

"Yes. I saw a placard from my front window, and rushed across the square to buy a copy even before I had had breakfast. Even so, my copy was the last old Higgins had."

"I am not surprised. This business of Smallwood's death is a newspaperman's El Dorado. I wish some place could have a whacking great earthquake or something of that sort, to take the damned Windmill Wood Crime off the front pages. And by the way, Mr. Terhune, the next time you uncover a nice juicy murder will you, as a personal favour to me, identify the murderer at the same time?"

Terhune grinned. "Would you like me to tell you the name of the murderer before he commits the crime?"

"That would suit me."

"A whisky-and-soda, Sergeant?"

Murphy looked grateful for the suggestion. "I shouldn't say no. Begod! What a week! I'm fagged out. If you don't prod me now and again I shall fall asleep as I did the last time I visited you."

The ceremony of pouring out whiskies-and-sodas was not a long one. Presently Terhune raised his glass.

"Here's to an early arrest, Sergeant."

"I drink to that!" Murphy did so. In fact, he drained the glass, then sighed contentedly. "That was good, though I don't know why I didn't have one on the way here instead of sponging on you—" He thrust his hands deep into his trousers pockets, and his long legs towards the fire. "I don't know what you must think of my manners, settling myself comfortably like this, but your room here just makes a man forget he's not at home. If I was you, I shouldn't be in too much of a hurry to get married."

"I haven't given the idea a thought. I'll wait until I meet the right girl—"

Murphy laughed. "I thought you had met two, and didn't know which to choose. Leastwise, that's what the old tabbies round about here say." He glanced at Terhune's face. "Or shouldn't I have mentioned the fact?" he went on anxiously.

"I know the two to whom they are referring," Terhune murmured, staring at the crackling log which he had just put on the fire. "They are two jolly nice girls—good pals, both of them—but marriage— Damn it! Can't a man be friendly with a girl without having the neighbourhood marry them off?"

The sergeant was genuinely distressed. "Don't take any notice of what I said, Mr. Terhune. I—I was only pulling your leg, you being so nice and cosy here."

Terhune knew his visitor was prevaricating, but as it was useless to pursue the subject he asked: "Is there any truth in that article on Smallwood's life?"

"Every word of it. As a matter of fact it was based on information collected by Scotland Yard and ourselves. I have been trying to get over here for the past three days, to let you know what was happening, but I haven't had a chance. And all the thanks we got from that reporter bloke was to be ticked-off for not having arrested Smallwood's murderer. Ah, well! They are all the same, those newspapermen. All they worry about is serving up news red-hot to the public. I suppose I don't really blame 'em. It's the public's fault for wanting the news dished up that way."

"Is it true that the *Cilicia* had only berthed in Southampton about twelve hours before Smallwood was killed?"

"Yes."

"Was Smallwood paid off?"

"Are you wondering what happened to his money?"

"Yes."

"I can tell you. He received his pay with one hand and paid it out with the other. He was in debt to his shipmates for nearly every stiver he had earned."

"Is that why he was walking to London?"

"I imagine so."

"Rather out of his way, wasn't it, to proceed from Southampton to London *via* Ashford?"

"It was, but I can explain why. He scrounged a ride in a lorry which was transporting some goods from Southampton to Lewes. At Lewes he succeeded in persuading a private motorist to give him a lift to New Romney. Maybe he wasn't in any particular hurry. Anyway, at New Romney he was not so lucky, so he started off walking to Ashford. You know the result."

"Was he long at New Romney?"

"Approximately thirty minutes. Why?"

"I was wondering whether he got into any sort of mischief while he was there."

"Can you imagine what sort of mischief a man could get into, in thirty minutes, that would cause another man to follow him in the hope of committing a murder?"

"New Romney not being in Spain, the answer is in the negative."

Murphy chuckled. "I see what you mean, sir. But as it happens his movements are more or less known to us. As long as we didn't know who the murdered man was, or where he had been, nobody volunteered to tell us anything about him, but as soon as we started making direct enquiries all sorts of people developed a memory."

"Do you mean that some people deliberately withheld information—"

"Bless your heart! sir, not deliberately. Just careless like. Can't-be-bothered-thinking sort of attitude. But when a man in plain clothes appears and says: 'Do you remember, on such-and-such a day, seeing such-and-such a man?' why then the replies come willingly enough. But to get back to our muttons. Roughly speaking, this is what happened to Smallwood on the day of his death.

"Arrived at Southampton about dawn. Paid off just after nine. Paid out one minute later. Left Southampton in lorry about nine-fifteen. Arrived in Lewes about twelve-twenty. Left there again twenty minutes later. Arrived in New Romney at two-ten. Started walking towards Ashford about two-thirty-five. Arrived at Billy Robinson's farm just as the rainstorm broke, which was round about four o'clock. He stayed at the farm the best part of an hour, then resumed his walk to Ashford. From the Robinson farm to the spot where he was killed is a little more than a mile and a half. That distance would have taken him, say, thirty minutes to walk, which confirms your deductions as to the time the book was dropped in the wood—between five-thirty and six-thirty I think you estimated?"

Terhune nodded. "So he walked into the wood, somebody saw him coming, and killed him. Just like that! He wasn't even robbed. The story doesn't make sense."

"Don't I know it?"

"What of Mrs. Robinson's story of his asking about bed and breakfast in Ashford? He didn't have enough money to pay."

"I think your original theory must have been right—he was hinting to be put up at the Robinson farm for the night. When Mrs. Robinson failed to bite, possibly he hoped to find someone here in Bray who would give him a shake-down."

"If robbery wasn't the motive for Smallwood's murder, what was?"

Murphy's face became lined with worry. "I can't tell you, Mr. Terhune. We haven't the faintest idea why the man was killed."

"Does that mean you still haven't any clues as to the murderer's identity?"

"Other than that copy of *Rosamund*, not one. Not a damned clue of any kind. Not even a sniff of one. And for all we know that book has nothing to do with the crime. It might have been coincidence that it was dropped round about that part of the wood, just before or just after Smallwood's murder."

Before Terhune could comment on this suggestion the sergeant continued:

"I know! I know! You don't need to say it! People don't drop books so easily without being aware of the fact. And even so, if any innocent person had dropped it, wouldn't he, or she, have retraced his, or her, steps in the hope of finding it? No, I am willing to bet a month's salary that that book has some connection with the murder. That is why I am hoping that you—" He peered hopefully at Terhune.

"I should have telephoned you had there been anything new to report."

"I know that, but there was just a hope. Meanwhile, I don't mind admitting to you, Mr. Terhune, that we have practically exhausted every possible avenue of investigation without coming across a damn' hint of anything promising. If that Swinburne book doesn't eventually turn up a trump, we're sunk."

II

In view of Murphy's remarks Terhune devoted much of his spare time during the next few days trying to discover some sort of clue which might identify the purchaser of *Rosamund*. Of course, it was old ground over which he travelled, but he went over it again just in case he had overlooked something of importance on the first occasion.

For instance, the following morning, just after eight-forty-five, he crossed Market Square to call upon Miss Amelia. She had finished breakfast, and was dusting and tidying up the three rooms which she occupied. It made no difference to her task that all three rooms were already spotless: with meticulous care she did not carelessly dust round the base of the many ornaments which resided permanently on the mantelpiece of the sitting-room, or in the glass-panelled display cabinet which occupied more than a fair share of the wall opposite the fireplace. No, she carefully lifted every separate piece—with the exception of the marble clock which was too heavy to be lifted, save rarely—first passed the duster across that surface of the mantelpiece or the cabinet, on which the ornament usually stood, and then went on to dust, also, the base, the interior, and lastly the outside of the ornament. This she did every morning, without exception, so Terhune was not surprised to find her clad in overalls and mob-cap, flourishing a duster in one hand.

"Mr. Terhune!" She glanced at him a little reproachfully. "I did not expect you at this early hour."

He hastened to apologize. "I knew you were to be busy all this week, Miss Amelia. This is my only opportunity. I would like ten minutes' conversation with you, if you can spare me the time."

"I am due at Mrs. Stewart Lawson's house at a quarter to ten." She looked regretfully at her duster. "I can leave the dusting until later." She indicated a door to her left. "We can go in the sitting-room, Mr. Terhune. Fortunately, I dusted that room first this morning." As Terhune entered the sitting-room she surreptitiously slipped off the overall and cap, so it was the usual, prim, fragile Miss Amelia who sat down opposite him on a small, upright chair.

Behind her steel spectacles her pale, watery eyes were alight with barely suppressed excitement.

"Has something exciting taken place?" she questioned with fluttering eagerness.

"Nothing exciting, Miss Amelia. I am wondering whether you have remembered anything more with regard to that copy of Swinburne's *Rosamund*, about which I spoke to you two weeks ago?"

"Oh!" She tried to conceal her disappointment, but the effort was not very successful. Still, she was a loyal, willing soul, and tried to remain interested.

"No—o," she admitted regretfully. "Every night, lying in bed, I have tried to remember that title, but each time I am really sure that I sold it to so-and-so, the next moment I recollect that it was some other book. Now, if you had asked me what happened to *Astrophel*, by Swinburne, I could tell you at once—"

"I am sure you could, Miss Amelia, but it is the copy of *Rosamund* which I must trace."

She sighed. "Dear Father always told me I should grow up with a bad memory. Do you think perhaps, in the future, I should make a note of every book I sell—"

"Good heavens, no! It is only this one book in particular." He dared not give his reasons, for Murphy had insisted upon all mention of the discovery of the book being kept a secret, in the hope that its purchaser might sooner or later pay another visit to Terhune, and in the course of buying another book accidentally make some mention of his previous purchase of *Rosamund*.

"You are quite sure that it was I who sold the book?" Miss Amelia enquired disconsolately.

Terhune had several times reassured her that he was sure of nothing of the sort, but it seemed that her conscientious soul remained unsatisfied.

"I'm beginning to think that it must have been I—" he began in yet one more attempt.

"But *you* have such a good memory," she interrupted naively. "If you really cannot remember having sold the book, then it must have been I who did so. Oh! I do wish I could be of more help to you in this matter." She clasped her thin hands together in determination. "Do you not think it might have been Mr. Bigland..."

Presently Terhune returned to his rooms and had breakfast. The time taken in visiting Miss Amelia had been utterly wasted, but happily he had a nature upon which the minor pin-pricks of life made no impression, so he was able to read the newspaper without having his enjoyment tempered by nagging impatience.

Later in the morning, during convenient moments when the shop was empty—which seldom happened on Monday mornings, for after a weekend's reading many of his nearer clients had a book or so which needed changing—he resorted to his carefully filed written records. He had been through these once before, and had found nothing, but considering that his excitement might have made him careless in overlooking something of significance, he now went through them again with painstaking and conscientious care. Consequently he did, in fact, come across a mention of the book, though this was not before late afternoon. On turning up a list of books purchased from the executors of Dr. William Knight of Willesborough, on the tenth day of February of that year, he came across the title, *Rosamund*, by Swinburne, A. C., price 1s.

So his memory was faulty! His memory had supplied the name of the widow of the Rev. Fergus Macdonald, of Rye, as the probable seller of the book, and the period of the transaction, last August twelvemonth. Apparently, however, the book had come from the executors of an Ashford doctor, and not fourteen but eight months ago. From whom he had bought the volume mattered not, but the date might possibly help to narrow down the period of resale.

Encouraged by his discovery he spent the rest of the afternoon and evening in a diligent search of his postal sale records. These, too, he had previously combed. However, his second search proved as fruitless as his first, and he went to bed that night, just before 11.30 p.m., not only tired, but disconsolate into the bargain. Since Murphy's last visit, he had felt very keen to succeed where the detective had failed, but without any further information upon which to work the prospect looked far from bright.

Tuesday passed without bringing with it anything exciting or enlightening, although he continued his self-appointed task of searching through his files. On Wednesday, just before lunch, Julia telephoned him, to enquire whether he would care to go with her that afternoon in the car to Dover. Where Julia was concerned an enquiry was somewhat in the nature of a command—that is, if one wanted to keep in her good books—so Terhune was forced to answer that he would be delighted—as, indeed, he was, for one could never feel bored when in her company. Angry, perhaps, or exasperated, or even embarrassed, for Julia had a cynical wit, and, when she wished, a vitriolic tongue. But bored; never! And as far as Terhune was concerned, she never angered, or exasperated or embarrassed him, for he had a strange knack of handling Julia, and keeping her in a good humour. To such a degree, indeed, that Mrs. MacMunn had—unknown to Terhune—fallen into the habit of ending most of the rather constant arguments with her daughter by saying, slyly: "Why don't you ask that nice Mr. Terhune to come over to dinner tonight?" or "If you insist upon going, Julia, ask that young man in Bray to accompany you. He is always *so* comforting. And *so* accommodating. If I were a *younger* woman I think I should feel most interested in him. *If* he were something just a *leetle* better than a bookseller, of course. But there, my dear, there is no reason why you should not enjoy his company for the time being."

So Terhune accompanied Julia, in her high-powered coupé, to Dover, where they spent several enjoyable hours, for when she had executed two errands in Dover—an aunt of hers lived there—she suggested a *thé-dansant*, and they returned as far as Folkestone, where they danced to the hotel band, drank an excessive quantity of tea, and consumed an irrational number of cream pastries.

Afterwards they returned to Willingham Manor for the evening meal. As soon as Alicia MacMunn saw Julia's glowing cheeks and sparkling eyes, she mentally congratulated herself on having invented the errand in Dover, was especially charming to Terhune, and fussed around him like a hen with a lost chick. Julia, who knew precisely what her mother was thinking, smiled sardonically, and made Alicia drink more sherry than usual, so that Alicia giggled a lot for the next hour, and retailed local gossip which would have brought blushes to Terhune's cheeks had he not been aware of the reception Julia would have given such blushes.

The following morning—market day—brought the usual rush of customers into Terhune's shop.

They arrived in a constant stream, for on a bright morning—which it was—everybody from miles around visited Bray, even if the excuse for doing so was no stronger than that of changing a book, or having a cocktail at the *Almond Tree*, which was the rendezvous of the county folk.

Half-way through the morning a man entered the shop whose face was vaguely familiar to Terhune, but whose name was not. This man did not enter to change a library book—he was not, in fact, a member of the library—nor, it seemed, to buy any book in particular, for he did not approach any particular shelf, or make an enquiry of Terhune. Instead, he wandered from shelf to shelf, examining a book here, and a book there, and looking most contented.

Terhune paid no special attention to the stranger, for it was nothing, on market day, to have people unknown to him browse among his books for an hour or so. Indeed, it pleased him to be surrounded by 'browsers', for he sympathized with their love of books. In fact, he considered that the pleasantest hours of his work were those of an evening, after the shop was closed, when he could himself browse among his recently purchased libraries and collections.

Presently the man selected a book from one of the shelves on the far side of the shop, which, at a convenient moment, he placed before Terhune.

"How much is this, please?"

Terhune opened the book. On the inside of the front cover was his code price: D/Z= *deux/zéro*.

"Two shillings."

"Two shillings!" The man reflected. "Would you take less?" he asked wistfully.

It was not Terhune's habit to bargain, save in cases where the purchase price amounted to more than £5, for he priced his books fairly according to their market value. In this instance, he did not refuse; perhaps because his client was so obviously anxious to have the book. He examined the volume with more care, and found it was a copy of Browning's *Pacchiarotto*.

"I could make it one shilling and ninepence."

The other man nodded as he thrust his hand into his trousers' pocket. "Thank you. I will take it." He passed over a two-shilling piece.

Terhune delayed his search for change. "The price is high, for this volume is one of the special luxury edition," he explained. "Nowadays, there is very little demand for a book of poems." He paused, and fumbled in his cash drawer for coppers. "Are you fond of poetry?"

The man smiled. "You ought to know. You have sold me nearly a dozen books of poems in the last two years."

"Of course, your face is familiar to me," Terhune murmured diplomatically.

"I visit Bray at least once a month, so I usually drop in and see whether I can find something to attract me. You see, your prices are less than most places," he explained naïvely. The next moment he became embarrassed as he realized that he had just bargained for an even lesser price. "I haven't much to spare for books," he finished up awkwardly.

Terhune glanced down to hide his increasing excitement. "I do not usually reduce my prices, but being a booklover myself I can sympathize. If there are any titles you particularly want I shall be very happy to watch out for them."

The other man smiled. "I am not a specialist."

"But you must prefer one poet to another?"

"Naturally. I suppose I should place Keats at the head of my list. Then Shelley. Or perhaps, Swinburne."

"Swinburne!" Terhune exclaimed hoarsely.

"Yes." A trifle defiantly. "Yes. I like Swinburne. As a matter of fact I bought one of Swinburne's dramas in blank verse from you some months ago. Don't you remember?"

"*Rosamund?*"

"Yes, *Rosamund*," the other man echoed with a gratified smile.

Chapter Twelve

A s soon as he had mastered his excitement Terhune cautiously inspected the man on the other side of the desk-table. He was tall, and thin; his shoulders stooped somewhat; he wore horn-rimmed spectacles on the bridge of a rather prominent nose—he had thinning, brown hair—a mousy brown, and scurfy, Terhune noticed automatically. He wore a suit of navy blue with a grey pin-stripe; his shirt was clean, but had been mended just behind the tie; his boots were polished, but cracked.

So this was the man who had bought *Rosamund*! This was the man who possibly knew something about the murder of Frank Hugh Smallwood! Possibly! Terhune reflected ruefully, for if appearances were to be accepted as a criterion, he was no murderer. He might be a bank clerk, or a shop-keeper (a chemist, perhaps?), or a small, not too prosperous baker. But not a murderer!

Terhune did not allow himself to be swayed by appearances. Again and again had his friend at New Scotland Yard—Detective-Inspector Sampson—instructed him never to be influenced by appearances. With good reason, for if any face could be said to be truly villainous, the scarred, saturnine face of Sampson himself would have been foremost in that category. Yet Sampson was certainly neither villain nor criminal, but a remarkably efficient detective, a cheerful companion and a loyal friend.

Terhune looked behind the other man. Two people were waiting patiently to let him record the books they had just selected.

"Are you in any hurry?" he asked the man.

The question seemed to surprise the stranger, but he shook his head. "No."

"I should like to talk to you about *Rosamund*." Terhune glanced at the first of the waiting women. "Good morning, Mrs. Carter. Did you enjoy that book by Ralph Straus?"

"Indeed I did, Mr. Terhune, and thank you for recommending it. I have another of his, on George Augustus Sala."

"Ah! That is an older one, but it is very good. I had put another book aside for you, by Philip Guedalla, but I will keep it until you come again…"

He carried on the conversation with Mrs. Carter, and with Arnold Blye next, with but half a mind, for the other half was preoccupied with the problem of learning more about the purchaser of *Rosamund*. If the fortunate appearance in the shop of the other man was to bear results, it was necessary to learn, if possible, what his name was, where he lived, and the date of his purchase. And this without making him suspicious; no easy matter if he had taken any part in the killing of Smallwood.

At last Terhune was able to give all his attention once more to the stranger.

"Do you care only for poetry, sir?"

Unwittingly his voice must have been tinged with excitement, for the stranger answered sharply: "I do not restrict my reading to poetry."

"I thought perhaps you were making a collection—"

"Well?"

"I am always buying collections containing volumes of poetry, and periodically send out lists of books for resale. May I have the privilege of adding your name to my mailing list?"

"Ah!" For a moment the man's eyes glowed with eagerness, but the expression was quickly superseded by another which baffled Terhune. "I do not think it would be worth your while to waste postage on me. I buy too few books, and then—" He hesitated. "Then not for high prices."

"I have many clients who only buy one or two books a year from me," Terhune explained, without adding that such clients paid high prices for the few books they did buy. "It would put you under no obligation to buy."

The offer tempted the man. "If you can assure me that you would not object to my buying only one now and again—"

"Of course." With purposeful formality he produced a pad of notepaper. "Your name, if you please."

"Lloyd—Francis Lloyd."

Terhune felt disappointed. Francis Lloyd! F.L., not G.H.

"And your address?"

"Twenty-seven, Kingsmere Avenue, Hythe."

Hythe! Worse and worse, for Windmill Wood was on one of the roads leading to Rye, which was to the south-west of Bray. Hythe was to the south-east. Only someone desiring to make a fantastic detour would want to proceed from Bray to Hythe by way of Windmill Wood. Besides, it was not likely that Lloyd was in the habit of walking from one town to another. No doubt he used the local omnibus service, or perhaps cycled, or even motored, but even if he cycled there would be no reason for him to walk through Windmill Wood.

Terhune tore off the slip of paper from its pad and pushed it into a drawer.

"I shall see that you get a copy of my next list. Probably in about five weeks' time." He paused, but seeing Mrs. Edwards—the doctor's wife, and an inveterate gossip—bearing down upon his table he hastened to add, recklessly: "Let me see, Mr. Lloyd, when did you buy that copy of *Rosamund* from me?"

"In the last week of June, I think. But I did not buy it from you, but from an elderly lady—"

"Miss Amelia! Ah!"

Perhaps Lloyd felt that Mrs. Edwards was glaring at him behind his back. "I must go now. Thank you, Mr. Terhune, for your kindness."

He tapped the book he had just bought. "I shall look forward to having your next list."

He hurried away as Mrs. Edwards began: "This book by Louis Golding—"

Terhune felt ridiculously pleased as he listened receptively to Mrs. Edwards' criticism—unjustified, and distorted by personal bias, though it was. Lloyd's testimony that he had bought the book from Miss Amelia proved that his, Terhune's, memory had not, after all, been at fault. So Miss Amelia had sold it, and in the last week of June. That meant the sale had taken place on a Tuesday, for he always visited London on the last Tuesday of the month, leaving Miss Amelia in charge of the shop.

"—so don't you agree with me, Mr. Terhune, that I have a right to criticize the author in this instance?"

"Of course," he agreed with a friendly smile, not having consciously absorbed more than about one word in six of what she had been saying.

I I

Later in the day he telephoned Murphy, and was lucky enough to find the despondent detective in.

"Hullo, Sergeant. Any news?"

"Any news!" The next few words were unintelligible, but Terhune imagined their purport. "The Chief Constable is raising hell."

"Well, cheer up. I have some for you."

The sergeant's voice became loud, eager. "Go on, sir. Spill it," he shouted.

Terhune grimaced, and held the telephone farther away from his ear.

"The man who bought *Rosamund* came into the shop again today."

"Fine! Fine!" Pleased laughter, a pause, and then: "Are you sure?"

"Quite. He admitted the fact."

"You mean you asked him the question outright?" The sergeant's annoyance was unmistakable. "You should have been more careful. You may have put him on his guard."

"I was careful, and I did *not* put him on his guard. In my opinion he is not our man."

"What makes you think so?"

"Because he lives at Hythe, because he bought the book as long ago as last June, and because his initials are F.L., not G.H."

"You know his name then?"

"Yes, and address."

"One moment. I'll take it down," Murphy snapped. "Now."

Terhune repeated the name and address.

"Good. Tomorrow I'll pay Mr. Lloyd a visit."

"Sergeant?"

"Yes, Mr. Terhune?"

"Could I accompany you?"

There was a long pause. "I am afraid that isn't possible. Official regulations——"

"You need my presence to identify Lloyd. He might say you were talking rot."

Murphy laughed shortly. "I'll speak to the Old Man, but I can't promise a thing. If it leaked out——"

"It won't from me."

"Nor from me, but what about Lloyd?"

"I could turn up my coat-collar, and take *off* my spectacles ——"

"I'll see what I can do, and ring you back."

With that Terhune had to be content, but in due course Murphy rang through. The Old Man couldn't think of giving his permission—officially—but in the peculiar circumstances—and seeing that Mr. Terhune had helped the Kent police now and again—and if he, Murphy, acted upon his own responsibility—and if Mr. Terhune could make himself unrecognizable—

"In short, I go."

"You go, Mr. Terhune."

III

Terhune went—the following afternoon. Murphy called, found him ready, and had to admit that, as long as Terhune remained as he was—coat-collar up to his chin, hat down to his eyebrows, no horn-rimmed spectacles—and did not draw particular attention to himself, he might pass as a detective-constable.

The two men found Kingsmere Avenue consisted of a row of small, tidy but obviously inexpensive bungalows, on the fringe of the town farthest from the sea. Murphy brought the car to a stop outside Lloyd's house; together they walked up the few yards of imitation crazy-paving to the front door. Murphy rang the electric bell. Presently the door was opened by a middle-aged woman with thin lips, and light blue eyes.

"Yes?" she asked in a voice harsh and metallic.

"Mr. Francis Lloyd?"

"He's at work."

"What time will he be home?"

"'Bout thirty minutes' time, he should be."

"We'll call back later on."

"All right!" She closed the door in their faces, so the two men turned away, and began to walk back to the pavement, but before they were half-way there the door opened again. "And don't be coming back too late. We have our meal at six-thirty, and I don't want it spoiled." The door slammed again.

"A pleasant woman!" Terhune murmured.

Murphy nodded. "Now if *she* had been the victim, we shouldn't have to search for the motive!"

They left the car outside Lloyd's house, and walked to the promenade. There Murphy came to a halt, stood still, gazed at the rough sea which was breaking high up the shingle in thunderous, grey clouds of hissing spume, and drew in deep gulps of the crisp, salty air.

"So near and yet so far! A few miles from the sea, and yet the only times I see it are on holidays, about four Sundays in the year, or when business brings me to the coast. The average human being is a fool, isn't he?"

They walked along the promenade almost to Sandgate before turning to retrace their steps. Meanwhile, the horizon slowly disappeared as the grey sea merged into the blackness of dusk. By the time they were once more outside Lloyd's bungalow the night was quite dark.

This time they found Lloyd in—he opened the door to them. He wore no jacket, and his face was shiny as though he had just washed.

"Mr. Francis Lloyd?"

"Yes. Are you the two gentleman who called earlier on?"

"We are."

"What do you want?"

"A few minutes conversation with you. We are police officers from Ashford."

"Police! What do you want to speak to me about?" There was a note of alarm in his voice and attitude, but Murphy ignored it; he had long since learned that most people experienced a feeling of alarm upon being visited by the police, never mind how clear their consciences.

"It would be more convenient if we could talk in private." With a gesture Murphy indicated the street.

Lloyd's eyes wavered as he stepped back and opened the door wider. "Will you come inside?" he suggested hoarsely. Then, in a whisper, as they entered the tiny hall: "The wife is in the kitchen. I don't want her to hear."

Followed by Lloyd, Murphy and Terhune entered a small, but scrupulously neat and tidy sitting-room. It smelled of furniture and metal polish, and looked as though it was only used on rare occasions. The atmosphere within was chill, so Lloyd, with an apprehensive glance at the door, turned on one-half of a small electric stove.

"What do you want with me?" he demanded shakily, forgetting to ask his visitors to sit down.

Murphy sat down, nevertheless, so Terhune followed his example. "Do you know Bray-in-the-Marsh, Mr. Lloyd?"

"Yes, of course I do."

"Do you ever visit Bray?"

"Sometimes. On business. I'm in insurance—"

"Do you know the bookshop in Market Square?"

Puzzlement began to displace alarm. "Yes. Yes, I do."

"Have you ever bought any books from there?"

The question brought about the return of apprehension, but his panicky eyes glanced, not at his visitors, but at the door which he had carefully closed behind him. Terhune wondered why.

"Ye—es," he admitted in a low whisper. "Now and again. Just— just one, now and again."

"Do you recollect buying a copy of *Rosamund*, by Swinburne, a few months ago?"

Lloyd nodded his head without transferring his gaze from the door. "Please do not speak too loudly."

"Why not?"

The man's mouth twitched. "I—I don't want the wife to hear—to know that you are—are policemen."

"Are you frightened of the police?"

"No," Lloyd replied sharply, and, Terhune thought, sincerely.

"Is your wife?"

"Of course not."

"Then what are you frightened of?"

"I—I—" Lloyd became distressed. "What do you want to know about *Rosamund*?"

"Do you admit buying a book of that title from a shop in Bray?"

"Yes, yes. I have already done so."

"Not in words, but never mind. Have you still got it?"

Lloyd started. "No."

"No!" Murphy's voice became sharper. "Then where is it?"

"That's—that's my business."

"Oh! Is it?" The sergeant frowned. "Do you refuse to answer the question?"

Once again Lloyd glanced apprehensively at the door. He paused before answering, as though he were listening for something. "I'm not bound to answer that or any other question," he replied sullenly.

Murphy glanced angrily at Terhune; his lips became hard and obstinate. "So you think you know something about legal and police procedure, do you, Mr. Lloyd?"

"A little. I've picked it up in the course of business. I know my rights, and I'm sticking to them."

"If you've picked up legal procedure you know the penalty for obstructing the police in the execution of their duty," the sergeant bluffed.

The inference behind this remark appeared to startle Lloyd. "What's the execution of duty to do with a book of poetry?"

"That is our affair."

"But I don't see—Do you mean the book is connected with a crime? Was it stolen?"

"I cannot tell you that, Mr. Lloyd. What I want to know is what you did with the book after you bought it from the shop in Bray?"

Unexpectedly Lloyd moved a small chair, so that it was next to Murphy's, and sat down upon it. "I don't want to obstruct the police," he said in a low voice. "I sold the book."

"To whom?" Murphy snapped.

"To the—the second-hand bookshop round the corner."

The sergeant glared angrily at Lloyd; obviously he did not believe the answer.

"When did you sell it?"

"A week after I had bought it in Bray."

"You sold it—For how much?"

"One shilling."

"How much did you pay for it?"

"Two shillings and threepence."

Murphy pursed his lips. "Are you trying to make us believe that you bought a book for two and threepence one week, and sold it the next for a bob?"

"Yes, but I read it in between."

"You paid one and three for the privilege of reading a book of blank verse?"

Lloyd made a helpless gesture, and leaned still nearer to the detective. When next he spoke Terhune could scarcely hear what was said.

"The wife hates me to—to read poetry." He became shamefaced. "If she was to find a book of poetry about the house…"

Soon the whole pitiable story was out. The wife was a shrew and a virago, who would have nagged him for a week had she caught him 'mooning about' with poetry, and made his life a misery for longer than that time if ever she were to learn that he had squandered his hard-earned money *buying* books. Books! When the kitchen needed a new square of linoleum! *Books!* When the bathroom needed repainting! *BOOKS!* When she had not bought herself a stitch of clothing for the last two months…

Murphy believed, sympathized and did his best to help Lloyd conclude the whispered, unhappy recital.

"Never mind the other books, Mr. Lloyd. We are only interested in the copy of *Rosamund* which you bought last June. Are you sure you kept it no longer than a week?"

"A week or ten days."

"To whom did you sell it?"

"The bookshop round the corner, in Knight's Road. Jenkinson's."

"Would the shop still be open?"

Lloyd shook his head. "I don't think so. Jenkinson likes to close early. But he lives above the shop. If you ring the bell at the side door you will be able to get hold of him. If he's in. He often goes out of an evening to play billiards."

A few more minutes with Lloyd sufficed Murphy. He rose from his chair. So did the two other men.

"You won't let the wife know about my buying books of poetry?" Lloyd enquired anxiously.

"Not if I can keep the matter quiet," Murphy replied. "But I cannot make any promises."

Terhune knew that the detective was thinking of the trial which, no doubt, he was hoping would result from his enquiries.

Chapter Thirteen

The two men went on foot to Jenkinson's shop, which Lloyd had assured them was no more than three minutes' walk from the house. Nor was it, so Murphy was soon pressing the button of the electric bell at the side of the private door to the rooms above the shop—which, as Lloyd had forecast, was closed.

Evidently they had arrived only just in time, for scarcely had the sergeant placed his thumb on the bell-push than the door opened, and in the rosy light of a red-shaded electric lamp they saw on the threshold a short, tubby man clad in overcoat, scarf, hat, and woollen gloves.

"Mr. Jenkinson?"

"That's me."

"We are police officers. We are making enquiries with regard to a certain book which we understand you purchased from a client a few months ago."

"What's this! What's this! A book! What book?" Jenkinson was no exception to the general rule; but his nervousness took the form of an indignant, staccato way of speaking. "Come inside! I can't see you properly. Come inside!"

They entered the cheerless, narrow hallway, which terminated in a short staircase leading to the rooms above, but Jenkinson did not suggest taking his visitors up.

"What's all this about?"

"Do you know a Mr. Francis Lloyd?"

"Of Kingsmere Avenue? Yes. I know him."

"Does he sometimes sell you second-hand books?"

"Yes. Books of poetry. Pah! No use to me. Can't sell 'em again. Not round about here. Now, if he read Westerns or thrillers—"

"Quite! Do you keep a record of your transactions?"

"What! Spend all me time scribbling in books! Not me. If I has to pay a bob or two out of me pocket I pays it, and that's that. But I've a good memory for what I does in business hours."

"Then perhaps you remember buying a book from Lloyd called *Rosamund*, by Swinburne?"

"*Rosamund! Rosamund!*" Jenkinson nodded his head. "That'll be the book I bought from him about three months ago, say in July. Half a dollar I gave him for it. All of half a dollar, me being a generous buyer like the blooming fool I am."

Murphy ignored the difference in price. "Have you resold the volume, or is it still in your stock?"

"Resold it! Haven't I told you there's as much hope of selling a volume of poetry in these parts as of making ice cream in hell?"

"Then you still have the book?"

"Bless you, no! What would I be wanting with a book like that on me shelves?"

The sergeant began to lose patience. "If you haven't sold the book on the one hand, and haven't got it on the other, what have you done with it?" he asked sharply.

"Given it away, same as I've given all them books of poetry I've bought from Lloyd."

Murphy stared at the plump, little man with sly eyes, and a perpetual grin. He had not the appearance of a man who was in the habit of giving anything away, much less stock-in-trade. "Who did you give them to?"

"What do you want to know for? I don't see why I should tell you. There's nothing wrong in giving away books, is there?"

"There is not, but it is necessary for us to know where that book went to, after leaving your hands."

"Then find out some other way. I'm blooming well not going to tell you."

"I suppose you realize the consequences of your present attitude?"

"Consequences, me foot! We're not in court, and you're not a blooming judge."

Murphy glared at the man before him. Jenkinson still wore a grin which the sergeant would have given much to wipe away, but there was no humour in his eyes; only dogged obstinacy, a frame of mind which his thrust-out lower lip appeared to confirm. His general attitude was that of a man who was not going to be browbeaten into doing something against his will. Curiously, he no longer appeared in any way nervous, or afraid.

The detective suddenly experienced an intense dislike for the cocky little bookseller, but he carefully concealed his feelings, and patiently tried to coerce Jenkinson into talking.

"Listen, Mr. Jenkinson," he began, with an utterly false, friendly smile, "have you any reason to be afraid of the police?"

For the first time the grin vanished, as Jenkinson scowled. "I ain't, and I ain't going to have anyone say I have, not even a blooming policeman. I have a solicitor, I have—"

"All right, all right! Nobody is suggesting that you have done anything wrong. I merely asked a simple question. And you have answered it. You are not afraid of the police."

"No, I blooming well ain't—"

"Very well, then, if you have nothing to fear on your own account why are you so unwilling to tell us what you did with those books of poetry?"

"That's my business."

Murphy swallowed. His voice hardened. "I am going to give you one more chance—"

"Thank you for nothing."

"Either you answer my question, or—"

The grin returned. "Or what, mate? Making threats, are you? What'll the judge say when I tells him that you tried to get information from me by making threats?"

The sergeant realized the uselessness of remaining. He turned towards Terhune, and the door. "Come on," he ordered harshly.

Jenkinson laughed jeeringly as Murphy opened the door, and the two men passed out into the street.

II

"Do you think Jenkinson knows something about the crime?" Terhune asked, as they walked back towards the corner of Kingsmere Avenue.

"No," the sergeant replied bluntly. "He was too saucy. Besides, I was watching his eyes. After the first embarrassment there wasn't a flicker of fear in his then."

"Then why his obstructive attitude? Just cussedness?"

"I don't think so. Admittedly, he looks the type of man to take the opportunity of obstructing the police just for the pleasure of being saucy, but in this instance I have a feeling that he is shielding the person to whom he gave—if he did give—the books. Mind you; I repeat, I do not think he knows anything about the murder of Smallwood, but he realizes that the police do not usually make enquiries about anything unless it has a bearing on some crime or other, so just in case the person who had the books of poems has done something for which the police want him, Jenkinson has decided to keep his mouth shut."

"And you can't do anything to make him speak?"

"Not unless we get him in the witness-stand. Then, if he refuses to answer, we can charge him with contempt of court. By that time his information would be too late to help us in our enquiries, even if it might be useful to the prosecution."

"I believe that he spoke the truth in saying that he gave the books away," Terhune suggested abruptly.

"Why?"

"I should not be surprised to learn that he had passed them on to a relative of some sort."

"Ah!" the sergeant exclaimed softly. "You may be right, sir. That explanation would not only fit in with his assertion of having given the books away, but it would also explain why he is so cagey about revealing the name." Upon reaching the corner Murphy placed his hand on Terhune's arm, then turned back to look in the direction of Jenkinson's shop.

For some seconds they stood still in silence. Then: "What's your next move, Sergeant?"

"Put yourself in Jenkinson's place, Mr. Terhune. What would you do, if you had given the books to a relative?"

"Tell him that the police were making enquiries about one of them, and warn him to take care of himself."

"Exactly! And that is what I believe Jenkinson will do. Do you know he hasn't come out yet?"

"Well?"

"When he opened the door to us he was about to leave the building. Why didn't he do so immediately we had left? Because he has changed his mind and gone upstairs. Why? In my opinion, to do one of two things. Either to telephone the other man, or if one of them isn't on the telephone, then to write a letter. Do you agree?"

"Absolutely."

"Would you like to do something to help?"

"Of course."

Murphy spoke quickly. "Just along the road there is a telephone booth. I am going over there to ask Exchange if Jenkinson is on the telephone, and if he is, to request Exchange either to tap any call he may make during the next few hours, or, if he has already made one, to check back for the number he called. While I am gone would you mind remaining hereabouts, to keep an eye on his door?"

"Willingly. But what am I to do if he comes out while you are still on the telephone?"

"I was coming to that. If he should come out, would you trail him to his destination? Or, if he posts a letter, note where, and telephone the information to the police-station. I shall go straight to the station if I find you gone from here, and wait there until I hear from you."

Terhune laughed with boyish enthusiasm at the prospect of becoming a shadower: despite his mature—or should-be-mature—years, he was experiencing much the same pleasure as in the distant past when he had smuggled the latest Sexton Blake story into bed with him.

"I'll do what I can," he assured Murphy, who thereupon hurried off towards the telephone booth.

No sooner had the sergeant entered the booth and lifted the receiver than Jenkinson emerged from the door which led up to his rooms. Terhune laughed again, partly at Fate, because she was living up to her reputation for contrariness, and partly because he was selfishly pleased at the chance of playing the role of trailer.

Jenkinson slammed the door behind him, turned to his right, and began walking away from Terhune at some speed. At least, his pace appeared to be fast, so Terhune also moved forward at speed. In next to no time, however, he found himself catching up with the man in front, and soon realized that Jenkinson's assumed speed was more or less an optical illusion, brought about by his short, fat legs having to take six paces to the ordinary man's five.

The chase, such as it was, continued for the best part of a quarter of a mile. Then it ceased: unexpectedly, for just after Jenkinson had turned into a small shopping centre, he first stopped to post a letter in a street letter-box, then turned into the saloon door of an over-ornate public-house: *The Pig's Ears*.

Terhune was vaguely disappointed that his shadowing had come to an end so quickly, and even so tamely, but wasting no time on vain regrets he looked around for a public telephone, and presently saw one, a hundred yards farther down the street.

He reached it, lifted the receiver, and obtained the police-station.

"Is Detective-Sergeant Murphy, of Ashford, there?"

"Hold the line, please."

There was a slight pause, then: "Is that you, Mr. Terhune?"

"Yes. Our man has just posted a letter."

"Where are you?"

"I don't know the name of the street, but the box is just opposite a pub—*The Pig's Ears.*"

"Hold on a moment..."

Terhune heard the echo of Murphy's voice asking somebody at the station about *The Pig's Ears.* Then: "Okay! What about our man?"

"Inside the pub."

"Good. He'll probably remain there. We'll be with you as soon as we have arranged matters with the local postal authorities."

Murphy rang off, so Terhune left the booth, and began strolling slowly back towards the letter-box. As he did so he saw a postman approaching the box, with the object, Terhune guessed, of collecting the letters. He sprinted forward, but only arrived at the box as the postman inserted his key in the door.

"Wait a minute," he gasped, as he placed his hand on the door to prevent the postman opening it.

"All right, sir, you can drop your letter in. It'll go in with the others."

"I don't mean that. You mustn't collect the letters."

"What the—" The postman stared at Terhune. "What's the game?" he demanded truculently.

"You mustn't collect the letters from this box. The police want to do so."

"The police!" The postman rubbed his chin reflectively. "Are you a policeman?" he asked abruptly.

Terhune stammered uncertainly: "Er—no, but I—I am giving them a helping hand—temporarily—"

"You're nuts!" the postman exclaimed bluntly. "Take your hand away from this box."

"I tell you the police are on their way here—"

"Then you'd better hop it before they gets here. For the last time, are you going to take your hand off this here door?"

With unmistakable deliberation Terhune moved closer to the box. After all, Murphy couldn't be long in arriving!

"No."

The postman grinned. The ominous grin of a man who likes a rough house, and takes every opportunity of joining in. "You've asked for it—"

Before he could act, however, two interested observers from the other side of the street began to cross the road.

"What's the matter, mate? Something wrong?"

"Yes." The postman nodded at Terhune. "This barmy idiot is trying to stop me collecting the post."

"He is, is he?" The speaker quickened his pace. "My football coupons is in that box, with a postal order." He and his companion reached the box. "Move aside, you, and let the postman get on with his job, or we'll ruddy well cosh you."

Terhune felt himself losing his temper. "You mind your own, business," he snapped. "This is a police matter."

"Police!" The word made the two newcomers pause uncertainly.

"Police, me foot!" the postman exclaimed. "He ain't no more a policeman than what I am."

"In that case—" The more belligerent of the newcomers aimed a wild blow at Terhune. It brushed harmlessly by his shoulder, but by now Terhune's own dander was up. He returned the blow, but with more skill. His fist landed neatly on the other man's nose, and produced a gasp of pain.

The next moment the scrimmage began in earnest. Eagerly, the postman, backed up by his two supporters, aimed a series of unskilful blows at Terhune. Some of them landed, but only a small proportion, for Terhune had once played Rugby football, and was therefore accustomed to a scrummage. He had also boxed as a lightweight, with some success. Though the odds were three to one, the honours went to neither side. He received a real stinger on his left ear, but one of the other side danced with agony as a hard fist closed an eye. Then it was Terhune's turn to grunt, as a hairy fist landed on his jaw, but he repaid the blow—with good measure—to the postman, whose nose happened to be nearest. That started the claret flowing. Before long they were all four blooded.

While Terhune was still holding his own, two men emerged from the public-house. Despite the comparatively early hour they had already had more alcohol than was good for them. The sight of the scrap that was taking place round about the letter-box inflamed their own artificially inspired belligerence. The fight was apparently anybody's, so they lurched forward, and joined in the fun. Fortunately, with quite unconscious humour, they took opposite sides. Before the unhappy postman could properly realize what had happened a stunning blow on the side of his head spun him round, to face a new pair of milling, toughened fists.

With the odds against him still three to one, Terhune began to flag with fatigue. He warded off two blows at his face, then two more, and still another, but then one of his opponents let drive a heavy blow to his stomach which he was unable to divert. He grunted loudly as breath was temporarily driven from his lungs, and doubled up with excruciating agony. As his guard relaxed, a blow caught him neatly on the temple, which jerked his head back against the solid letter-box, and he saw far more stars than he had ever seen in the heavens.

At this critical moment a newcomer arrived.

"Hey! What's this? Break it up, now. Break it up, can't you?"

The fighting stopped abruptly as a large figure dressed in familiar blue uniform pushed his way between the combatants. The policeman glanced down at the letters and postcards which had been kicked out of the postman's sack, and were strewn about the pavement, gutter and road.

After a preliminary whistle of surprise he addressed himself to the postman. "What's been going on 'ere, Tom?" he demanded.

"Hullo, Bill! It's a good job you've arrived." The postman pointed an unsteady hand at Terhune. "It's all his fault. He tried to stop me collecting the mail. Said he was something to do with the police, he did. Then he started to fight me, so these other chaps came to my help."

The policeman grasped Terhune's arm—Bill had a big hand, and a hard one, and his fingers pinched into Terhune's flesh and hurt. "You'd better come along o' me. You've got some explaining to do—"

"Wait here and you'll see," Terhune gasped with an effort. "Detective-Sergeant Murphy asked me to keep an eye on this box. There's a letter inside which he wants to examine."

Bill did not relax his grip. "Tell that cock-and-bull story to the sergeant. Murphy! Never heard the name. Come along, now." He began to drag Terhune away from the letter-box.

Terhune glanced desperately up and down the street: there was no sign of a car. With a struggle he inserted his hand in the opening of the box, then doubled it up as much as he could so that his arm was anchored to the letter-box.

"I've got to stay here until the police arrive," he gasped hoarsely. "They'll be here any moment now."

"He's barmy!" exclaimed one of the men standing by. "Why don't you pull him away?"

The policeman pulled. Hard. He nearly wrenched Terhune's arm out of its socket. The pain, both to his muscles, and to his knuckles inside the box, was torturing. But he wasn't to be dislodged from his hold, and Bill began to feel annoyed.

"Unloosen his hand, Tom. Dig your nails into his wrist. That ought to do the trick."

The postman was only too pleased to oblige. "Leave it to me, Bill."

Tom's nails were sharp and jagged. Terhune straightened his hand and pulled it away from the letter-box slit. He had a feeling he had done enough on Detective-Sergeant Murphy's account, and that Murphy could do the rest of his dirty work himself.

"Come along, me lad——" the policeman began, without any real malice. But Murphy chose that moment to arrive. Brakes squealed as he rounded a nearby corner, and brought the car to a rocking halt by the side of the letter-box.

"What the devil's happening here?" he called out angrily as he clambered hurriedly out of the car, followed by a local police sergeant and a postman. "Hey, you!" This to the policeman. "What are you holding Mr. Terhune for? Let him go."

Bill was too bemused to obey. He stared at Murphy; and slowly his lower lip drooped. "You mean this—this bloke——"

"Let him go, Stokes," the sergeant ordered sharply. "Didn't you hear what you was told?"

This time Bill let go: if someone had just announced the end of the world to him his expression could not have been more completely flabbergasted. The postman's face was equally expressive. The surrounding men began discreetly to vanish into the nearby shadows—even the two drunks.

"What happened, sir?" the sergeant asked.

Terhune straightened his collar and tie. "Just as I arrived here the postman came to collect the letters. I tried to persuade him to wait, but he didn't believe my story. I can't blame him," Terhune added hastily. "It was rather an impossible story, but I couldn't think what to say. At any rate, he wanted to get on with his duty, so I tried to stop him by force, hoping you would be arriving at any moment. But Bill here arrived first."

"How was I to know——" Bill rumbled.

"Of course you weren't," Terhune assured the policeman. "Honestly, Sergeant, Bill was only doing what I would have done in the same circumstances."

"Thank 'ee, sir. You're a real gent."

"All right, Stokes, we'll take Mr. Terhune's word for what happened." The local police sergeant turned towards the postman who had accompanied him in Murphy's car. "Will you carry on?"

"I'll collect the letters from this box, Tom," the man said to his fellow postman. "The police want to examine them at the sorting-office."

"Suffering catfish!" Tom exclaimed feelingly, as he began to collect the contents of his bag.

The words were innocent enough, but they were full of meaning, and Terhune grinned. He sympathized with Tom.

Chapter Fourteen

"How do you feel?" Murphy asked Terhune as they entered the car; there was more than a suspicion of amusement in his voice.

Terhune tenderly felt his ear and his chin. "A bit, knocked about," he admitted. "One of them has a fist like a young sledge-hammer."

"You don't seem to have done too badly yourself." This time Murphy chuckled openly. "Poor old Tom's face—was that his name?"

"Tom Purvis," came from the postman in the seat behind.

"Well, his face didn't look any too good. I'll bet he won't want to blow his nose in a hurry." The chuckle became laughter. "By golly! I wish we had arrived half a minute earlier. I would have given a year's pay to have seen the scrap at its height."

"It was fine while it lasted," Terhune had to admit. He began to echo Murphy's laughter, but the effort was too painful, so he choked it down. "But I wouldn't thank you for an encore."

Presently they reached the sorting-office, which all four men entered, the postman carrying in a bag the letters he had collected from the letter-box opposite *The Pig's Ears*. In the presence of the head sorter the letters were tipped out on to a large table.

"What is the next move?" Murphy asked.

"Can you give me any hint to help me in identifying the letter you want?"

"Not one."

"Pity! Anyway, we can make the first move by winnowing the wheat from the chaff."

"How?"

"We can put on one side all envelopes with sender's name and address printed on the outside."

The sorter began separating the letters into two bundles, so Murphy gave a hand. Terhune stood just behind, watching. As soon as the job was finished the sorter shuffled through the pile of printed envelopes.

"Nothing here from Jenkinson," he announced. He placed the pile down, and picked up the other.

"You've no idea where or who the letter is addressed to?"

"Maybe to somebody in Farthing Toll."

The sorter ran quickly through the pile. "Nothing here." He passed the letters across to the sergeant. "Would you like to look through them yourself?"

"Thanks, though I don't suppose it will help."

While Terhune watched from one side, Murphy slowly examined the envelopes, one by one. Some of these he discarded as unlikely, such as letters addressed to firms in London, Folkestone, Northampton, Luton, and so on. Also letters to banks, income-tax officials, and other people in official positions.

He had almost run through the pile when Terhune touched his arm. "Look!"

Murphy glanced down at the next envelope. It was addressed to:

> *Mr. Guy Heather,*
> *Lavender Cottage,*
> *Bracken Hill Road,*
> *Bray-in-the-Marsh.*

"Well?" he queried.

"The name, Sergeant! Guy Heather! You remember—the initials—G.H.!"

Murphy whistled, and flicked the letter over to the head sorter. "Make a start with this one, old man."

The head sorter took the letter away. Terhune said to Murphy:

"For a moment I was startled by the significance of the initials, but I am sure Heather is not our man. I know him slightly. He is a schoolmaster, at the local Council School. He is a pacifist and wouldn't kill a living thing."

The detective was not impressed. "I've no time for pacifists. They may not be keen to fight for other people, but when it comes to protecting themselves, or their own property, they soon become aggressive. In many cases pacifism is merely another name for damned selfishness."

"Heather has always impressed me as being sincere."

"We shall soon see."

They had not long to wait. The sorter returned, with the envelope in one hand, the letter in the other.

"This looks like your man, Sergeant."

Murphy all but snatched the letter.

Dear Guy,

I don't know what you been up to, but just now a couple of plain clothes coppers arrived to know what I done with them poetry books Ive sent you from time to time. I didnt tell them nothing for I dont want you and Lil to get into no trouble, but if I was you I should burn the books and swear you dont know anything of them specially one called Rosymund. And what ever you been up to if you takes my advise youll watch your step. The police aint fools by a long chork.

Hoping this finds you in the pink as it leaves me,
Your affectionate brother-in-law

Harry.

Murphy glanced at the sorter. "This is the letter we're after, right enough. How long can you hold it back?"

"Will the first outgoing tomorrow morning suit you?"

"As long as it gives me time to make arrangements for the letter to be photographed before then. What time will it reach Heather?"

"During the afternoon delivery."

"Fine! I'll call upon him in the morning." Murphy passed the letter back to the head sorter. "Thanks for your co-operation."

"Glad to be of help, Sergeant. About what time shall we expect the photographer?"

"Can't say, for the moment. Some time before midnight, I expect."

"Then I'll see that everything is ready for him here."

From the sorting-office Murphy and Terhune proceeded to the police-station, where the sergeant sat himself down before a telephone. Very soon he was making arrangements for the official police photographer to visit the Hythe sorting-office to photograph Jenkinson's letter.

Not much later the two men were on their way back to Bray.

"A fairly satisfactory night's work," Murphy commented presently.

Terhune agreed. "Although I still do not believe Heather killed Smallwood," he added.

"Because Heather is a pacifist?"

"No. But I can think of no reason why Heather should be carrying the book *away* from Bray—"

Murphy interrupted with a sharp laugh. "I can give you half a dozen explanations. Here's one. He might have been on his way to visit friends in Farthing Toll, and was carrying the book with him to lend to somebody there."

"When a married man visits friends for the evening he usually takes his wife with him."

"There's no evidence that he was not accompanied by his wife. But, if you don't mind me saying so, Mr. Terhune, you seem convinced that the murderer of Smallwood was walking *away* from the direction of Bray, and not towards it."

"That is so. We have definite evidence that Smallwood was walking towards Bray, therefore I have assumed that his murderer was proceeding in the opposite direction."

"Probably you are right, but isn't it possible that Smallwood may have *overtaken* the man who murdered him?"

"Yes," Terhune was compelled to admit. Then, eagerly: "If that were so, it's a point in favour of Heather."

"Why?"

"Presumably Heather had had the copy of *Rosamund* for some months, hadn't he?"

"Yes."

"Then what would he have been doing with it, walking *towards* Bray? Of course, he might have taken it with him, while he rambled through the country, but I don't think that explanation a likely one."

"Nor do I."

"On the other hand, if he had previously lent it to somebody, say in Farthing Toll, that person might have been on his way to spend the evening with the Heathers, and was taking advantage of the opportunity to return the borrowed book."

Murphy chuckled. "Or Heather might have visited a friend, to whom, as you suggest, he had previously lent the book, have had the book returned to him, and was carrying it home."

Terhune could find no immediate flaw in this reasoning. "We could continue these theories all night," he murmured ungraciously.

"Of course we could, and that is why it is safer to leave theories to themselves, and stick to facts."

Following this remark Terhune was silent for nearly half a minute. Then he said to Murphy: "Facts or no facts, Sergeant, I am willing to make a very small bet with you that the man who murdered Smallwood had only just borrowed the copy of *Rosamund*, and was not returning it."

The detective rose innocently to the bait. "What makes you so certain?"

"Because the majority of people never dream of *returning* borrowed books," Terhune replied drily.

II

Just before one o'clock p.m. the next day Detective-Sergeant Murphy entered the bookshop. As only Terhune was present Murphy said: "I've just left Heather, Mr. Terhune."

"Did you have any luck?" Terhune had no real need to voice the question, for the detective's expression had already supplied the answer, but he realized that the enquiry was expected of him.

Murphy laughed that pleasure. "I did an' all," he exclaimed triumphantly.

An idea occurred to Terhune. "Have you had lunch?"

"No."

"I am just about to have mine. Will you share it?"

"Thanks a lot, Mr. Terhune, but I couldn't do that."

"Why not?"

"Well—"

Terhune appreciated the reason for the awkward pause. "There's enough for the two of us. Besides, smell it." He opened the door into the tiny private hall attached by a staircase to the living-rooms upstairs.

Murphy smelled, was tempted, and succumbed, so Terhune shut up the shop, led the way upstairs, and asked Mrs. Mann to set a second place. While the surprised Mrs. Mann was doing so Terhune took the detective into the study, and waved his hand at a small collection of bottles which occupied a section of bookshelves.

"Gin, whisky, or beer, Sergeant?"

"Beer, please," Murphy answered promptly. "Here's to you," he toasted some seconds later. And having emptied the glass with one gloriously satisfying draught: "Now you'd like to know what Heather had to say, I shouldn't wonder?"

Terhune nodded.

"Well, I called upon his wife about ten minutes before I knew Heather was due home for the midday meal. I said I wanted to see her husband on a matter of some urgency, so she asked me into the parlour, saying he wouldn't be long. Before she could leave I said to her: 'I saw your brother last night, Mrs. Heather.'

"That caught her interest. 'Which one?' she asked, in a friendly fashion.

"I told her: 'Harry Jenkinson, of Hythe.' Then I added, casually: 'I was talking to him about some books I was making enquiries about—I am a police officer, by the way.'

"She was too interested in her brother to worry about the mention of police. 'How is he? I haven't seen him for months.'"

Murphy grinned slyly. "I am afraid I drew the long bow, but she took it all in, so presently I brought the subject round to the books Harry was in the habit of sending her husband.

"'Harry's a dear, generous man,' she said. 'He knows how mad Guy is on poetry, and that he can't afford to buy books, so any book of poetry he gets hold of he sends to Guy for nothing. Then, if the books is suitable—are suitable, I mean—Guy reads them to the children in school.'

"She's a nice little woman," Murphy continued reflectively. "She is so proud of her husband, and does her best to hide the fact that she is not of his class. Anyway, for her sake she made me hope that her precious Guy didn't have anything to do with the murder."

"Well, and did he?"

"I don't think so. And by the way, Mr. Terhune, I agree with you about his sincerity. If he's a pacifist, then it's from genuine conviction. To continue. After Heather had come in, and I had introduced myself to him, I asked him whether he had ever received from his brother-in-law, Harry Jenkinson, a book of poetry by Swinburne, called *Rosamund*."

"Did he admit that he had?"

"At once. Said he had had it more than three months, so I asked him if I might take a look at it."

"What did he say?"

"Agreed quite readily, and began looking for it among all his other books, which he keeps in one of those glass-covered book-cases which you can add on to others whenever you have the money to buy another." Terhune had several, which Murphy suddenly spotted. "Like those."

"And then?"

"I was watching his face pretty closely. I must admit that it looked genuinely surprised when he failed to see the book. He took a second look, and then called for Lil—she had disappeared as soon as he came into the room. To get the meal, I suppose. Anyway, she came running in, and he asked her what had happened to the copy of *Rosamund* Harry had sent him a short time back.

"'Didn't you take it to school?' she asked him.

"'No,' he replied. 'I kept it with two other Swinburnes at the end of the middle case.'

"For a few moments her face remained as puzzled as his. Then it cleared. 'Now, I remember. We lent it to Vivian Harrison.'"

Terhune raised a protesting hand. "Harrison! I remember that name. Harrison! Harrison! Ah! Now I know. He has a small chicken farm in—" He stopped abruptly.

"In Farthing Toll! That's the man."

"But Harrison... Good Lord! He couldn't be Smallwood's murderer, Sergeant. Why, he's grey-haired, and frail."

"Maybe, but that is the man to whom Heather lent his copy of *Rosamund*. What is more, the day on which this lending took place was Tuesday, the eighth of this month."

"The eighth! The day Smallwood was murdered! Then—then Harrison is the murderer?" Terhune glanced at the detective's face. "Or am I jumping to conclusions too quickly?"

"You are, sir, like all amateurs, if you don't mind me saying so. We know that Harrison was in Bray the day Smallwood was killed, and as he lives in Farthing Toll we've every reason for believing that he proceeded home by way of Windmill Wood, for that is the way nearly all Farthing Toll people go home. We also know that the book which was found near the dead body of Smallwood was one which was lent to Harrison. That makes Harrison our present Suspect Number One—but there is a lot of ground to be covered before we can put him in the dock with any hope of a conviction.

"First of all, there is the time element to be investigated. On the day he borrowed *Rosamund* Harrison had lunched with the Heathers, but he left the cottage, together with Guy Heather, and the book, just before two o'clock. That book, there is good reason to believe, was not dropped in the woods until some time after five-thirty.

"What was Harrison doing between the hours of two and five-thirty p.m.? To prove a case against him we shall have to produce evidence that he was still in Bray at, say, four-forty-five. Otherwise he may assert that he went straight back to Farthing Toll after leaving Heather at the school, and we shall not be in a position to contradict him.

"Then we shall have to prove that he arrived back at Farthing Toll not earlier than six p.m. Also, that when he left Bray he still had the copy of *Rosamund* with him. If we fail to produce that evidence he may maintain that he lost the book, and that it must have been picked up by the murderer.

"Even if we can produce reliable corroborative evidence that he was definitely in Windmill Wood about the time of the crime, we shall have to bring out evidence of motive. Otherwise the accused will merely say he didn't kill Smallwood, and why should he have done so, anyway? And if he doesn't his lordship will. Specially old Snuffle-Nose—"

"Old Snuffle-Nose!"

"Mr. Justice Lovelace! He suffers from catarrh. And he's hot stuff, I can tell you. Still, he's not a bad old bloke. But as I was saying, even if we become convinced that Harrison is the murderer, it's still going to take a lot of time and trouble to put him in the dock. In the meantime—"

"Lunch is ready," Mrs. Mann announced.

Chapter Fifteen

Three days passed by, during which Terhune heard nothing further concerning the crime. He was not surprised. During the past two years he had seen Sampson, of the C.I.D., quite often—Sampson had fallen into the habit of dropping in upon Terhune at infrequent intervals; on a Sunday, usually. Murphy occasionally dropped in, too, and in the course of their conversation he had learned much of police procedure; in particular, something of the patient, systematic, monotonous and entirely undramatic spade-work which is the backbone of police investigation.

On the Wednesday Julia 'phoned again. "Feel like coming to Folkestone this afternoon, Theo?"

"Well—"

She was quick to hear the note of hesitation in his voice. "You don't want to come," she snapped.

"I did not say so."

"You did not need to."

He feared she might hang up before he had a chance to explain. "I rather wanted to go for a walk this afternoon, Julie." He knew she detested walking for its own sake, but he added: "Come with me: we can have tea at *Toll Inn*." *Toll Inn* was at Farthing Toll: it was a typical Kentish inn, small, cosy, raftered, mellow with antiquity: unusually, it was patronized equally for its teas, served in a low-ceilinged sitting-room with ingle-nook fireplace, as for its stronger drinks, served in the two bars private and saloon. Mrs. Brooks' teas were served with lashings of cream, home-made marmalades and jams, and cakes as light as thistledown.

After a pause Julia said: "I'll come, Theo. About three o'clock?"

"Fine."

Julia's car pulled up outside the bookshop dead on time—she prided herself on punctuality. Aware of this trait, Terhune was waiting for her. He joined her, and they set off for Farthing Toll. As they crossed Market Square she said abruptly:

"Still sleuthing, Theo?"

He was startled. "Sleuthing!"

"Yes, my sweet. That is the word I used."

He was puzzled to account for her perspicacity, but he did not deny the charge.

"What makes you think so, Julie?"

"My dear Theo, I know you are fond of walking, but I am sure you are equally aware that it is not a favourite pastime of mine. On the other hand, you love dancing as much—almost as much—as I do. It doesn't require a great mind to realize that you must have some reason for wanting to visit Farthing Toll, or the optimistic imagination of an amateur detective to connect that visit with the death of Frank Smallwood."

Terhune winced at her reference to the optimistic imagination of an amateur detective. "One of these days, my girl, someone will slice that tongue of yours in half."

"Halves!" she corrected bitingly. "As a budding author you should know your grammar better."

"You're very sweet this afternoon. Had another row with Mother, I suppose."

"Theodore, if you dare to lecture me—" Unexpectedly she relented. "You are wrong. I haven't rowed with Mother for more than a week. She has been too busy planning the Rector's Christmas Party. It is you I am really annoyed with—"

"With whom I am really annoyed," he murmured sweetly.

"Beast!" She laughed, and there was a gayer note in her voice. "I am feeling disappointed. I had so wanted to go dancing again today."

He was contrite. "I am sorry, Julie. If I had realized that—"

"Don't be silly. We can dance any time. But you haven't told me anything about the Smallwood affair." Then the familiar rasp returned to her voice. "This time you don't need my help evidently."

"That's mean!" he retorted sharply. "You know very well that if you could have helped I should have asked you. As a matter of fact, this time *I* haven't anything to do with the business, although I did find the body. But I'll tell you what has happened to date." And because he knew she was thoroughly to be trusted, he told her of everything that had so far happened.

She listened interestedly, and when he had finished said: "Why are you so keen to visit Farthing Toll?"

"In the hope of seeing something more of Harrison, Julie. I haven't seen much of him, but from the little I have I find it hard to believe that he could deliberately kill anyone."

"Does he sell eggs?"

"Probably. Why?"

"Couldn't we buy some from him?"

"Julie! You callous little devil!"

"Nonsense! A murderer deserves to be punished for his crime—" She stopped abruptly. He believed he knew the thought which had occurred to her. She might, by now, have been Mrs. Gregory Belcher had he not been directly responsible for exposing the man as an unsuspected murderer.

They walked in silence awhile, and when next Julie spoke she changed the subject: they did not speak again of crimes and murders until they turned into Windmill Wood. There, she asked:

"Where did you find the book, Theo?"

"I'll show you." Presently he did so, at the same time indicating the spot where the body had been laid.

"Was Smallwood a large man?"

"Not really large, but probably larger than the average."

"Heavy?"

"I should say, yes. Every part of him was solid and hard."

"Then could a frail, middle-aged man have dragged a heavy, lifeless body as far as that tree?"

"Murphy and I discussed that point on Saturday. We agreed in believing that a desperate man wanting to hide the evidence of his crime might have summoned a sufficient reserve of strength. Desperate men are rather like madmen; they seem to develop extraordinary and unsuspected strength at moments of crises."

"Why did Harrison—if he were the murderer—kill Smallwood?"

"Heaven alone knows! Unless—"

"Well?"

"A possible motive has just occurred to me. We know that Smallwood had a wild, impetuous character. Also, that he was almost penniless at the time of his death. I wonder if it so happened that, as he was passing through the woods, he saw, in the partial twilight, a frail-looking, middle-aged man coming towards him. Realizing that nobody else was near, and hoping that the gathering darkness might enable him to avoid future recognition, he might have held up Harrison in order to rob him. Or perhaps he meant to do no more than beg, menacingly. Anyway, whatever his intention the encounter resulted in panic on Harrison's part. To defend himself Harrison stooped, picked up a fallen branch, and struck out at Smallwood. The blow killed Smallwood. Made still more panic-stricken by this unexpected climax, perhaps Harrison then dragged the corpse over to that tree, covered it with fallen leaves, and fled, forgetting, in his fright, the book of poetry which had fallen from his hand when first accosted by Smallwood."

Julia remained silent.

Terhune laughed somewhat crossly. "You think I am spouting nonsense?"

"No, I don't, Theo. I was hoping that you are absolutely right." Her remark surprised him. "Why?"

"Because then Harrison would not have committed murder: he would have killed only in self-defence."

"Have you a soft spot for him?"

"I do not believe I have ever met him. Probably it is stupid on my part, but I should prefer to hear that the death was manslaughter and not cold-blooded murder. We are all of us so peaceful—we have had so much war, with its deliberate killing—its massacres and mass murders—"

Terhune dared not speak as he realized that Julia was revealing an unexpected side of her character. A word from him, however carefully chosen, might make her self-conscious, then, just as likely as not, she would turn upon him with her caustic, cynical tongue, and the afternoon would be spoiled.

"Isn't it silly, Theo, to shut one's eyes to the obvious, and to try to believe that everyone is as nearly perfect as the surroundings in which one lives, but that is how I am feeling at this moment. It is so beautiful in this wood, so peaceful and serene, I feel that nobody with a spark of decency in him could stand here by this lovely old tree, and deliberately, with malice aforethought, plan to kill another man."

Julia was still in this mood as they passed out of the wood and turned right on to Toll Road. Like the official Rye Road they had recently left, Toll Road also led to Rye, *via* Lydd, but whereas Rye Road went there by an inland route, Toll Road went due south as far as the seashore, which it followed for some distance until it lost its name, and mingled its identity with a more important main road.

Half-way through the village they saw Harrison's smallholding, which was opposite Toll House, and adjoining their destination, *Toll Inn*. Harrison was not to be seen, but a quick glance at the inn confirmed Terhune's recollection that the side window of the inn's famous tea-room overlooked the small chicken farm.

They entered *Toll Inn*. Welcomed by the beaming smile of the red-cheeked, matronly bosomed Mrs. Brooks, they passed through a narrow, flagged passage into the room in which teas were served. They were fortunate in finding it empty, but even so, a large fire of logs the size of small tree-trunks was blazing merrily in the ingle-nook, making music with its popping and crackling.

The room was too small to hold more than three tables, and then only by an ingenious placing of the small-sized chairs. One table stood partly in the small bay window overlooking Toll Road, the second, by the side window overlooking Baytree Farm (Harrison's); the third, midway between the other two, in the centre of the room, and close to the fire. In ordinary circumstances Terhune would have chosen the table nearest the fire; like most men he was always happy when roasting in front of a fire, gazing dreamily into its glowing red heart. But having a definite purpose, he chose the side window.

Mrs. Brooks re-entered to take their order—if they were in no hurry she would make them some of her special scones...

"Scones undoubtedly," Julia ordered.

And honey? Or lemon marmalade? Or blackcurrant jelly?

Julia chose the blackcurrant jelly; Terhune, the marmalade.

And rich, thick cream?

"I shall make myself ill, if it is brought in."

Mrs. Brooks was shocked. "But you could not have tea at *Toll Inn* without a serving of cream."

"Of course not."

A gratified smile from Mrs. Brooks; from Terhune a chuckle and a mischievous, significant glance at Julia's seductively slim waist.

As soon as Mrs. Brooks had gone to make the scones Julia asked: "What do you know about Harrison?"

"Very little. I am hoping to find out more from Mrs. Brooks later on. All I do know is, that he is a bachelor, that he has lived at Farthing Toll for two years, and that his appearance suggests his age as being round about fifty."

"Then you don't know where he came from—" She checked herself as she saw the mischievous sparkle in his eyes. "From where he came—" she corrected. "Or shall I be thoroughly pedantic, and say; whence he came?"

"However you put it the answer remains, no. Were you wondering whether he came here from one of the ports?"

She nodded. "Yes. If your theory of thirty minutes ago is not the true one, surely the only explanation of the murder must be that the two men must have met in the past."

"If they did I'll bet Murphy will have found out that fact by now— he hasn't let me know."

Her sharp eyes noticed a man coming out of the small cottage at the far end of the adjoining field. "Is that Harrison?"

Terhune glanced out of the window. "Yes."

They inspected the man who, carrying a large pail in either hand, was crossing the field towards one of the nearer chicken runs. For his part, a further inspection gave Terhune no cause to change his previous impression of the other man.

Harrison appeared to be little more than five feet eight inches in height. He wore trousers of dark brown tweed, a matching pullover, and wellington boots. He wore no hat, so the two people in the inn were able to see that, although his hair had turned an iron grey, it was still thick and plentiful. He had a rounded face, burnished brick-red by the weather. His body was slim, his shoulders were slightly rounded.

"He doesn't look like a murderer," Julia whispered. "There is not much character in his face, but what is there is not vicious or mean. To me he looks just a kindly nonentity. Besides, physically, he does not look muscular or strong. I am sure he is no murderer."

In his heart Terhune agreed with her, but he knew what Murphy's or Sampson's reaction would be were he rash enough to voice such an opinion.

They were still regarding Harrison when Mrs. Brooks came back to tell them that the scones had just gone into the oven, and did they want China or Indian tea.

"China, please," said Julia.

Terhune nodded. "We'll both have China, please, Mrs. Brooks." He nodded towards the window. "We were watching the chickens being fed. What are they? Light Sussex crossed with Rhode Island Reds?"

"Lord love you! sir, I don't know nothing about the breed of hens. I keep chickens, but all I asks of them is to lay well."

"Whatever they are, they look healthy."

"And so they are. Mr. Harrison sees to that. He is very partickler about his birds." She scented gossip, and opened with a neat gambit. "Perhaps you know him, sir?"

"Only by sight. I live in Bray."

"Bless my soul! You don't have to tell me that. Everybody knows you, Mr. Terhune. Many's the time I've seen you at work in your shop, and even if I hadn't I recognize you from your likeness in the newspapers. Why, it's only the other day Mrs. Rankin was telling me that you writes books." Mrs. Brooks's voice became awed.

"In the singular only, Mrs. Brooks."

She had not the slightest idea what that remark meant, but she carried on, quite unconcerned: "Now you being a writer, sir, I should have thought Mr. Harrison is the kind of man you would like to meet."

"Indeed! And why?"

"On account of his being a traveller all his life. Now, the things he could tell you about furrin' parts, why you could write a dozen books about them. And especially about Australia—"

Terhune dared not glance at Julia. "Why especially Australia?"

"On account of him being born there. Why, the things he tells us all in the bar about Australia, you wouldn't believe them. What I always says to myself after hearing Mr. Harrison speak of his adventuring all over the world: 'Truth is stranger than fiction, Rosy, my gal, so you don't need paying good money for books, or listening to that pesky radio, while you sit listening in comfort to Mr. Harrison telling one of his adventures.' And there's more than me of that opinion in Farthing Toll, I can tell you."

"Does he look after all those chickens himself, or does he have *any* help?"

"Well, you might say as how he does practically all the work himself, an' well he might do, after the huge farm in Australia which he once owned. But there is times when a certain party—not to mention names—gives him a helping hand."

She looked so pleased with herself that her audience had no difficulty in guessing that the certain party was none other than herself.

"You mean, in feeding his chickens, when he goes to Bray?"

"That is just what I do mean. Mr. Harrison insists upon them chickens being fed regular like, never mind what happens. Makes good layers of 'em, he says. So whenever he goes off for the day he says to that certain party: 'Mrs. Brooks,' he says, 'would you be an angel today, and feed my chickens for me while I am gone?'"

Terhune warmed with interest, as he saw an opportunity of manoeuvring the conversation along likely channels.

"And do you?"

"I'm always glad to offer a nice gentleman like Mr. Harrison a neighbourly hand."

Terhune smiled at her—one of those attractively winning smiles of which he was so supremely unaware. Like many another woman before her, Mrs. Brooks was suddenly afflicted with a wistful desire to mother the overgrown schoolboy before her, whose face was so pleasantly plain, with its ruffled, untidy hair, and eyes which danced cheerfully behind the misleadingly severe, horn-rimmed glasses.

"I am sure of that, Mrs. Brooks. Mr. Harrison is a lucky man to have you living so near."

Her red cheeks dimpled. "I wouldn't say that. But there, a hard-working man like Mr. Harrison deserves a little relaxation now and again even if it does mean only a visit to Bray to visit friends there."

"The Heathers?"

"You know them, sir?"

"Slightly."

She nodded. "Yes, Mr. Harrison often visits the Heathers. A nice couple they are. My boy Jim is one of Mr. Heather's scholars. He thinks the world of him, does Jim. My! I wouldn't dare to say a word agin him, not in Jim's hearing, I wouldn't."

"I haven't seen Mr. Harrison in Bray lately."

"He hasn't been for the past three weeks—not since the day of The Murder. Fair horrible it is, to think of a man being murdered not half a mile from here. Fair horrible for you, too, wasn't it, Mr. Terhune, to find a body so unexpected-like?"

"It wasn't pleasant."

"And the young lady—" She glanced with scarcely concealed excitement at Julia. "Was you the young lady with Mr. Terhune when he found the body?"

"I was not," Julia snapped.

"Oh!" With unexpected tact the kindly soul quickly changed the conversation. "Do you know, sir, it was only by the grace of God, as I've told Mr. Harrison several times since, that he wasn't killed as well as that other poor man what you found."

"Why?" Terhune asked, unsteadily.

"Because he must have passed the scene of the crime not ten to fifteen minutes afore it happened, one way and another. It was just about six-fifteen when he arrived back here, and when I read, two days later, that the crime was probably committed between five-thirty and six-thirty, well, as I says to him—Mr. Harrison, I mean—'If you had been ten minutes earlier, or later, as the case might be, there's no knowing but what that cruel murderer mightn't have hit you on the head with that same bit of branch.'"

"And what did—did Mr. Harrison say to—to that?" Terhune stammered.

A strange expression passed over Mrs. Brooks's glowing face. "Well, sir," she continued slowly, and perhaps a little unwillingly, as though regretting an indiscretion, "Mr. Harrison he said: 'Nothing of the sort, Mrs. Brooks. Just as it happened, for once I came back from Bray by way of Wickford and Toll Road, instead of through Windmill Wood, so I could call upon Mr. Jellicoe about some eggs'—Mr. Jellicoe lives on Toll Road just this side of Wickford church," she explained in parentheses. Then she sighed wistfully. "Poor Mr. Harrison! I think the idea of being nearly murdered frightened him."

"Why do you say that?"

"Well, sir, it's this way. I happen to know he come home by way of Windmill Wood."

"How do you know?"

"Because I saw him coming out of the wood, with my own eyes," she explained in a puzzled voice.

Chapter Sixteen

S oon after 11 a.m. rumours of the arrest of Vivian Harrison began to circulate in Market Square. The day being market day the Square was crowded, so the rumour spread with the rapidity of a heath fire fanned by a strong wind. Before thirty minutes had passed, everybody had heard that somebody else had heard that Harrison had been arrested, but there was not a soul who could have claimed personal knowledge of the arrest. This was so because Brooks, of *Toll Inn*, who had brought the news to Bray, and had mentioned it to Adams of the *Three Tuns*, had left on the local omnibus to Ashford, where he had to order next week's requirements from the brewers.

For once rumour was true. Early that morning Murphy had arrested Harrison, and conveyed him to Ashford, where he was charged with the murder of Frank Hugh Smallwood. Asked whether he had any statement to make Harrison had replied simply: "I have nothing to say. I should like to consult a solicitor." One hour later, he was closeted with Crawford, a junior partner in Howard and Howard, who handled all criminal proceedings undertaken by the firm. These were, in fact, few and far between, for Howard and Howard, being essentially family solicitors, tried, whenever possible, to avoid being concerned with criminal matters.

The next morning, Friday, Harrison appeared before the Justices of the Peace. The Court was crowded to suffocation, but the proceedings were exceedingly short, for the prosecution, having offered evidence of arrest, then applied for one week's remand, which was promptly granted.

On Saturday night Murphy once more called upon Terhune.

"Many thanks for the telephone call last Wednesday," he said, as he lowered himself into the usual easy chair. "Mrs. Brooks's evidence was ail we wanted—well, not quite all," he added reflectively. "As a matter of fact, we are still damnably weak, and if the newspapers hadn't been hounding us we should have preferred to have postponed arrest for the time being.

"It's the question of motive which is worrying us," he continued. "As yet we haven't the faintest idea why Harrison wanted to kill Smallwood, and I can't say that Harrison is proving much help to us. He won't say a damn' thing, and with Crawford looking after the defence we have to watch our step pretty carefully. Crawford's hot stuff, I can tell you. We can't afford to take chances."

Evidently Murphy was in a conversational mood, for he went on without a pause: "How did you get Ma Brooks talking? One of our chaps was at *Toll Inn* earlier in the week, but he couldn't get a word out of anyone. Of course, he didn't mention Harrison by name, but all the same, you would have thought Farthing Toll was a colony of archangels."

Terhune's face reddened. "She trusted me, Sergeant. I felt a swine, passing on that conversation—"

"Nonsense! It was your duty to do so; if you want to know you could have been charged with not doing so. Of course, I realize what you must be feeling, but Smallwood didn't ask to be murdered—or did he, I wonder? But that's not the point. What you must remember is this: a man who has committed one murder and retains his liberty is free to commit a second. And he often does, let me tell you. And here is another point. Every crime which remains unpunished is a direct encouragement for another person to commit a similar crime."

"I realize all that, but I shall never be able to face Mrs. Brooks again."

Murphy shook his head. "Don't you worry, Mr. Terhune. I give you my word that Mrs. Brooks will never suspect that our information came from you."

Terhune was relieved. "It is one of my favourite jaunts—to go to *Toll Inn* for tea."

"And mine, for that matter. And not always for tea. But now, I suppose, you would like to hear how the case goes against Harrison. You know, of course, that he is an Australian—yes, of course, you do. I remember you mentioning the fact when you 'phoned me up.

"It seems that Harrison was born in Australia, but at a very early age he ran away from home to become a sailor." The sergeant chuckled. "That makes you think, doesn't it? That's his first link with Smallwood. Maybe they once served on the same ship. Anyway, on the outbreak of the First World War, Harrison joined the A.I.F. and served in the Middle East with some distinction—was twice mentioned in despatches, I understand.

"After the war he went back to Australia, and tried sheep-ranching for a time. Nor for long, though. After a row with the boss he returned to his first love, and went roaming about the world again, sometimes as a sailor, but more often than not taking on any job which offered itself, from street-car driver in New York to a tea-planter's assistant in Ceylon.

"As far as I have been able to ascertain, he continued this sort of life until the outbreak of the Second World War, which found him in some outlandish place in South Africa. By that time he was beyond his prime, but he managed to find some sort of a war job in Egypt— quite what, I haven't found out. After the war he came to England for a change, and liked the country so much that he decided to settle down and spend the rest of his life here. During the following weeks he studied advertisements of smallholdings for sale, and eventually settled upon Baytree Farm. There he began chicken-farming, which he has been doing ever since."

"Has he never married?"

"Yes, in nineteen-twenty-two, but his wife was killed less than a year later, in a railway accident. He did not marry a second time."

"No children?"

"No. And no near relatives. He was one of three sons. Both brothers were killed in Mesopotamia, and died childless. In fact, only the elder had married, and he at the beginning of embarkation leave. Of the parents, the mother died in nineteen-eleven; the father, in nineteen-thirty. An only uncle died in nineteen-thirty-two, and left him a thousand pounds. He went on the loose with this money, leading a riotous life for as long as funds held out—which was just short of six months. As soon as he was penniless again he resumed his world hitch-hiking."

"From where did all this information come?"

Murphy grinned. "From the *Toll Inn* Regulars. Some of it before the arrest, but most of it in the last two days. Apparently Harrison spent many of his evenings in the saloon bar. He was by no means a heavy drinker: about the only time he was ever the worse for drink was at holiday times, but he used to keep his cronies amused for hours on end relating his past history, and stories of his travels round the world. Quite a favourite he was at *Toll Inn*. The Regulars won't believe that he killed Smallwood. 'The durned police are cock-eyed' is what is being said by most of the people in Farthing Toll."

Murphy sucked at his pipe. "Can't say I blame 'em," he mused. "Strictly between you and me, Mr. Terhune, Harrison doesn't strike me as being a murderer. He looks about as harmless as a well-fed kitten—well, no, not a kitten exactly, but, say, an old tom-cat; the kind that sits by the fireside all day long, and purrs every time anyone enters the room."

"That was much my impression of him. I suppose..." Terhune's words tailed off into an embarrassed silence.

"You suppose I haven't made a mistake?"

Terhune nodded.

The sergeant laughed somewhat bitterly. "For Pete's sake! I hope not. It won't do me any good if I have. Yet we've got him fairly well sewn up. Listen. The Heathers lent him that copy of *Rosamund* round about lunch-time. That means two witnesses to testify that he had it when he left their house, and walked with Heather as far as the school. After leaving Heather he caught the two-twenty bus into Ashford. George was the driver, and remembers Harrison getting into the bus, but nothing of any book. While he was in Ashford he entered Hall's and gave an order for two rolls of wire-netting and other sundry items— I've seen the counterfoil. He left Ashford by the four-thirty-five. This time Arthur was the driver, and Arthur has made a statement that, on getting out of the bus at Bray, Harrison was carrying a book of some sort under his arm because an elderly woman by the name of Wesley—"

"Mrs. Ralph Wesley, of Winchester House?"

"That's her! Well, she accidentally knocked the book from under his arm on to the pavement. So we have two more witnesses that he had the book about five-ten. From the *Wheatsheaf* to Farthing Toll, *via* Windmill Wood would have taken him to walk about how long?"

"Say forty minutes—I usually take that to *Toll Inn* from my place here, walking at average speed."

"Right! Knock off a minute or so, to allow for the difference between the end of the footpath and *Toll Inn*, and that brings the time to, say, five-forty-five. But Mrs. Brooks saw him emerging from the wood about six-fifteen. Allow a few odd minutes for error on her part, and a few more for his rate of walking being possibly slower than yours, and there's only about fifteen minutes still unaccounted for. Just about time enough in which to commit a crime.

"On the other hand, the time element knocks his story of having called upon Jellicoe sky high, for to reach Farthing Toll, *via* Jellicoe's house at Wickford, by six-fifteen, after having alighted from the bus at the *Wheatsheaf* at five-ten, would have meant his covering a distance of more than three and a half miles in just about the hour."

"A quick walker could have done that."

"And still have wasted precious minutes calling upon Jellicoe?"

"That would have taken some doing!" Terhune agreed. "Besides, if he intended calling upon Jellicoe at Wickford, why didn't he remain on the bus which passes quite close to Jellicoe's house on its way to Dymchurch?"

"Exactly!" the sergeant exclaimed drily. "Besides, Jellicoe says that Harrison did not call upon him. No, Harrison will find it very hard to persuade a jury, first, that he did not pass through Windmill Wood between five-thirty and six o'clock, and, second, that he didn't have the copy of *Rosamund* with him at that time."

"But even if you satisfy the jury that Harrison was in the wood at the time of Smallwood's murder, that doesn't make him the murderer."

"Not by a long chalk, it doesn't!" Murphy confirmed testily. "It's that part of our case which worries me. It worries the Chief Constable too: he almost refused to permit my application to the Justice for the warrant of arrest, but Harrison's remark about walking to Farthing Toll *via* Wickford tipped the scales in favour of the application. If Harrison hadn't a guilty conscience why did he lie to Mrs. Brooks?"

Murphy scraped the bowl of his pipe. "I was hoping that his arrest would surprise him into letting something out, but as I have told you, he kept as cool as a cucumber and wouldn't be tempted into saying a ruddy word." Unexpectedly, the sergeant's attitude became lighter; perhaps a trifle histrionic. "Fortunately, since the arrest one trump card has come into our possession."

"And that?"

"There's half a finger-print on one of Smallwood's overcoat buttons which corresponds exactly with the markings on the third finger of Harrison's left hand."

Terhune raised his eyebrows. "Won't that decide the case for the prosecution?"

"It'll help!" Murphy said cheerfully. "It'll help!"

II

On the following Friday morning the proceedings against Vivian Harrison were resumed. Terhune arrived at the Court well before time. As he entered the main door of the building he saw Murphy talking to another man, whose formal attire prompted Terhune to classify him as a lawyer.

Murphy waved Terhune to approach. "Good morning, Mr. Terhune." He turned to his companion. "I should like you to meet Mr. St. John Sinclair."

Terhune identified the name with that of a well-known counsel working for the Director of Public Prosecutions.

"Mr. Terhune discovered the body," Murphy explained.

The keen, alert face of the barrister crinkled as he held out his hand. "You are becoming quite a famous person, Terhune. Isn't this the second case of murder with which you have been connected?"

Terhune nodded.

Murphy broke in with: "The Chief Constable was suggesting yesterday that we should appoint him our local murder diviner."

Terhune grinned with embarrassment. "By the way the newspapers talk one would think I went about looking for murders. I don't do anything of the sort. It's just coincidence, really, that three have come my way."

"Did you say—three?"

Murphy glanced round to make sure that nobody was within earshot.

"You remember the affair of the House-on-the-Hill, sir?"

"Of course I do." Sinclair looked astonished. "Are you telling me that young Andrés Salvaterra's death wasn't accidental?"

"We didn't have enough proof to prosecute, but we hadn't much doubt about how he was killed, why, and who killed him."

"Indeed! Then no wonder the Chief Constable suggested what he did. But I must say that I wish you would unearth murders with more water-tight evidence. Between ourselves—I take it, I can speak in confidence—"

Before Terhune could speak for himself Murphy chipped in with: "Undoubtedly, sir. I am ready to vouch for Mr. Terhune."

"Well then, Terhune, I don't mind admitting that I am not too happy about this case. Of course, I think we have enough evidence to send it to the Assizes—although Sir Roger's a peppery old boy who doesn't stand for any nonsense. But if it should reach there, with somebody like Neville defending, and without more evidence than we have at the moment, I should say the chances of a conviction are about equal with those of an acquittal."

Murphy turned to Terhune. "By the way, Mr. Terhune, I have arranged with Mr. Sinclair for you to be among the first witnesses to be called."

"Thank you, both."

Sinclair laughed. "Not at all. I can quite understand, in the circumstances, your desire to see as much of the proceedings as possible."

For a time Terhune stood just inside the Court, watching the scene gradually change from austere melancholy to bustling activity. At first, besides Terhune, the cheerless Court-room was occupied by only three other people, laughing together. Two were uniformed policemen; the third was in civilian clothes, but Terhune took him to be—rightly—a plain-clothes policeman. In a very short while, however, a young man appeared, carrying a small pile of books. The clerk's assistant carried these books to the table below the magistrates' bench, and carefully arranged them in some sort of order. The assistant was quickly followed by the Clerk of the Court himself.

Then Crawford appeared, carrying a brief-case, and accompanied by one of his clerks. Having placed the brief-case down upon one of the benches reserved for counsel and solicitors, Crawford exchanged a few words with a uniformed policeman, then disappeared through a door leading to the cells—evidently the solicitor wanted one last conversation with the accused before the proceedings began. Meanwhile, his clerk brushed back a lock of dark hair from his forehead, spread some papers around in front of him, and began to study them with an air of gravity and importance calculated to impress all with the fact that, although his employer, Mr. Crawford, might do all the talking, he, the clerk, was really conducting the defence.

Quickly now the Court began to fill. St. John Sinclair came in, accompanied by a uniformed superintendent of police. Then the Warrant Officer. And the Probation Officer, who had no personal connection with the case, but meant, if possible, not to miss a word of it. Two or three plain-clothes men. Then, at the back of the Court, the eager, scrambling public. And lastly, Murphy.

"The magistrates will soon be entering, Mr. Terhune. We must leave now."

Terhune accompanied the detective out of the Court. The doors were closed behind them. As they walked away the two men heard the muffled echo of a knock, followed by the shuffling of feet.

"There they are."

III

Nearly thirty minutes later Terhune's name was called. He entered the Court-room, then the witness-stand. He took the oath, and looked across at Sinclair, who was rising to his feet.

"Are you Theodore Terhune, of 1, Market Square, Bray-in-the-Marsh, Kent?"

"I am."

"Are you the owner of a retail business concern dealing with books?"

"I buy and sell new and second-hand books, and run a lending library."

"Are you not also a writer?"

"In my spare time, yes. I have sold a few short stories from time to time."

"Do you also dabble in what, for want of a better term, I shall call amateur detection?"

"I do not," Terhune answered firmly. "I believe one or two of the daily newspapers have suggested that I do, but I am not an amateur detective. I do not pretend to be one, and I have no wish to be one."

"But in the past two years have you not been connected with one or two notorious affairs, involving a murder in one case, and—er—a case of accidental death in the other?"

"Yes, but—"

"But what, Mr. Terhune?"

"I find it hard to explain. It was just good luck on my part which supplied the police with a clue which enabled them to identify a murderer. It is nothing more than coincidence which has connected me with another alleged case of murder."

Sinclair smiled. "Not an alleged case of murder: the coroner's jury brought in a definite verdict of murder against some person or persons unknown. However, Mr. Terhune, we will leave the matter of your so-called amateur detection, and pass on to the events of Wednesday, October the ninth. On that day did a Miss Helena Armstrong suggest your accompanying her to Farthing Toll?"

"That is so. Sometime before lunch Miss Armstrong telephoned to say that her employer, Lady Kylstone, had asked her to visit Miss Agnes Hamilton, after lunch, and would I care to accompany her. I said I should be glad to—we both of us like walking," Terhune added unnecessarily.

"Miss Hamilton, I take it, lives in Farthing Toll?"

"Yes."

"There are two routes to Farthing Toll from Bray-in-the-Marsh, I believe?"

"Yes. There is one route, which the local omnibus takes for most of the way, from Bray to Wickford along the Ashford-Hythe road, and thence to Farthing Toll along the Toll Road. The bus diverges from this route at a point half a mile north of Farthing Toll, where it turns left into the Dymchurch Road. For walkers, however, there is a much shorter route, *via* Rye Road as far as Windmill Wood, thence through the wood to the northern boundary of Farthing Toll."

"Which route did you and Miss Armstrong take on the afternoon of October the ninth?"

"The one *via* Windmill Wood."

"Will you please tell their Worships, in your own words, what subsequently happened?"

In the fewest possible words, Terhune retold the story of the discovery, first of the book (produced, and inspected by the Justices with considerable curiosity), then of Smallwood's body; of his telephone message to Murphy, and, lastly, of Murphy's arrival at the scene of the crime.

Then, upon being further questioned by Sinclair, Terhune gave his reasons for believing that the book was probably dropped in the wood between the hours of five-thirty and six-thirty p.m.; produced proof of the purchase from the estate of Doctor William Knight, of Willesborough, of a copy of Swinburne's *Rosamund*, and identified it as the copy of *Rosamund* already produced.

That was all Sinclair wanted, so the man from London sat down, whereupon Crawford rose quickly to his feet, in the manner of a terrier scenting a rat. For two seconds witness and solicitor stared at each other—on Crawford's part with a deliberate aggressiveness which warned Terhune that the solicitor intended to fight the case tooth and nail, in the hope of securing his client's acquittal before the case went to the higher Court. Crawford had the reputation of being a fighter.

As Terhune inspected the solicitor's rather broad, handsome face, with its orderly, dark hair, its blue, emotionless eyes, its straight, Grecian nose, and its thin, firm lips, he believed that the other man's reputation was probably not unjustified. That is, if appearances were a reliable guide to character.

He prepared for an unpleasant few minutes.

Chapter Seventeen

"You have quite a good knowledge of books, I believe?" Crawford began, casually.

"I do not claim to possess more than is sufficient for the purpose of conducting my business."

"But enough to tell their Worship whether or no one might expect to find few, or many copies, of that particular edition of *Rosamund*?"

"If you mean, was that particular edition a limited one, the answer is no. But whether there are still many copies about or not I cannot say."

"Would not the price at which the copy was sold be an indication of its availability or otherwise to book collectors?"

"No. Generally speaking, the demand for books of verse is insufficient for the price of an individual copy to be affected by the number of copies still existing."

"I see. But would you agree that there may still be in existence many copies of that particular title in that particular edition?"

"There may be. I cannot affirm or deny that supposition."

Crawford looked annoyed. "Let me rephrase the question. Apart from the two letters D/T in the top left-hand corner of the flyleaf, is there anything about the copy of the book in Court by which you can positively identify it as the one which you bought, among others, from the estate of the late Doctor Knight?"

"No."

"You have informed their Worships that the letters D/T are symbols, representing in your private code the price two shillings and threepence, at which you were prepared to sell the book."

"That is so."

"You have further revealed that your code is based upon the French language."

"Yes."

"Good. Now, I am sure you will admit that the French language is known to many hundreds of thousands of people in this country. Do you not agree that it is quite likely that some other ingenious bookseller may have adopted the simple expedient of using the French language as a private code?"

"I should not care to deny that possibility."

"Then, can you be sure, beyond any doubt whatsoever, that the letters D/T were written on that flyleaf by you, and none other? Wait, Mr. Terhune, before you reply. Of course, I do not need to point out to you that a man's life may depend in part upon your evidence. You have shewn their Worships that you are a man of keen intelligence. But I do want you to reexamine those initials. Would you do so, please?"

The copy of *Rosamund* was passed to Terhune. He opened it at the flyleaf, and closely inspected the vitally important letters.

"You are examining that symbol, are you not, Mr. Terhune?"

"Yes."

"It was originally pencilled in, was it not?"

"Yes."

"And, in the course of time, the pencil marks have become faded and slightly smudged, have they not?"

"Slightly."

"In view of the fact that the letters are no longer as clear as they once were, I repeat my question: are you prepared to state, in unequivocal language, that those two letters are in your handwriting?"

Terhune stared at the tiny symbol: it danced before his eyes, mockingly. Could he swear, knowing that his answer might help to send a man to his execution, that he had written it? True, the D was very like his usual D. And surely nobody else had written that T? And yet...

It was not as if the letters were in script. They were in small, block capitals; the kind of capital letters, lacking all characterization, that anyone might have made.

"No," he replied in a low voice. "The letters are very much as I usually make them, but I cannot swear that nobody else but I wrote them."

Crawford sat down. Terhune glanced at Sinclair, who smiled, but did not rise to his feet, so Terhune listened to the Clerk of the Court reading out his (Terhune's) depositions, heard himself being bound over in the sum of £40 to attend the Court of Assizes, if called upon, signed the depositions, and sat down behind Sinclair, beside Murphy, who had already given evidence.

"Crawford means to fight the case here instead of letting it go to the Assizes," he whispered to Terhune. "I wonder why?"

Terhune did not attempt to answer the question; he knew he was not meant to, anyway; besides, Sinclair turned round again, so while the next witness was being called—probably Helena, he thought—he inspected the bench of magistrates. There were five in all, under the chairmanship of Sir Roger Johnson, a peppery gentleman of some sixty-odd years who, the police were convinced, had a secret grudge against them, for he never allowed them the slightest liberty in Court, and appeared far more suspicious of their evidence than of the most bare-faced lies told by accused people while trying to wriggle out of receiving just punishment. Still, the police had to admit, when tackled, that Sir Roger reserved that right to himself, and rarely allowed counsel a similar liberty.

On the left of the Chairman sat Mrs. Redwood. Mrs. Redwood was a local character of notoriety. She sat on—and ran—almost every local committee within a radius of approximately five miles, from linen leagues to library committees, or Church bazaars to the local Conservative Association. On her left was Colonel Seed, who was slightly deaf, missed a good tenth of the evidence, and invariably voted with the Chairman.

On Sir Roger's right was the tiny little figure of Doctor Enock Atwell. In Sir Roger's absence, Doctor Atwell acted as Chairman. He was so small that, in Court, he had to sit upon a special hassock, so that he should not look too ridiculously tiny in comparison with his fellow Justices. For all that, he was one of the best doctors in the neighbourhood, and possessed a keenly analytical, and well-balanced brain which made him a first-class magistrate. Sometimes he had to keep Sir Roger in order—for the Chairman could easily lose his temper—but he did so with discretion and patience, and the purpose of his quiet whispering was never suspected by the people on the public benches. The police always liked to see Doctor Atwell sitting on the bench.

Lastly, Mr. Alfred Bennett, who sat on Atwell's right. Bennett managed to lose, on an average, four hundred pounds per annum running a two-hundred-acre farm, but as he had inherited an income of more than five times that amount he was quite well able to carry on. He was a jolly man, extremely affable and good tempered. Everybody liked him, but he was no more efficient as a magistrate than a farmer. But as he never sat in the chair, justice did not suffer unduly from his presence on the bench.

These, then, were the five people who, in the course of time, would either pronounce Harrison's innocence, or find that there was enough evidence against him to send him for trial at Maidstone Assizes. But Helena was stepping up towards the witness-stand, so Terhune lost interest in the justices.

Helena looked, and was, nervous. She took the oath in a low voice which nobody heard save the officer who held up the finger-marked square of cardboard on which the oath was printed. When Sinclair said: "Are you Miss Helena Frances Armstrong?" her reply was likewise unheard.

"Speak a little louder, please, Miss Armstrong," Sinclair suggested affably. "Their Worships would like to hear you."

"I am," Helena repeated, jerkily, louder.

Helena's evidence was most undramatic, and merely confirmed everything Terhune had said. Sinclair did not waste much time upon her. Neither did Crawford, probably because he was a sufficiently good cross-examiner to know when, and when not, to press a witness. Or possibly, thought Terhune crossly, because he knew Helena. She had many times accompanied Lady Kylstone to the offices of Howard and Howard, who handled Lady Kylstone's legal interests.

As Helena left the stand, Terhune asked Murphy: "Did you have much trouble from Crawford?"

Murphy chuckled grimly. "He all but inferred that I was a direct descendant of Ananias. You should have seen the way Sir Roger glared at me! At one time I thought the old boy was going to explode."

"Why?"

But Murphy's opportunity to reply was gone, for Helena pushed her way past him to sit next to Terhune, and the next witness entered the box.

A tall, thin man this witness, with drooping shoulders, which made Terhune think of him as a human query mark. His face was lined, and cadaverous; most of the hair had disappeared from his temples; his nose was prominently large—a real beak of a nose; his sunken eyes gleamed with what appeared to be a fanatical glare.

"Who the devil—" Terhune whispered.

"Detective-Sergeant Dixon, of Headquarters—Finger-Print Bureau—looks like a ruddy skeleton, doesn't he? Yet, I'm told he eats enough for three men. He has a reputation for being efficient."

As soon as Dixon had established his identity and status, Sinclair said:

"As a result of a request from the Chief Constable of the Kent County Constabulary to the proper department, did you visit a mortuary in Ashford, on the morning of Thursday, October the tenth, and there examine the body and belongings of a corpse, subsequently identified as Frank Hugh Smallwood?"

"I did," Dixon replied in his deep, sepulchral voice.

"Would you please give their Worships, in your own words, the results of your examination?"

Dixon obligingly turned towards the justices.

"First of all, your Worships, I took the finger-prints of the deceased man for the purpose of re-checking them with the records of those which we still possess of Frank Hugh Smallwood. Then—"

Sir Roger interrupted. "Was that necessary, Sergeant?"

"Well, you see, your Worship, I felt that we couldn't be too careful in the circumstances, seeing that the deceased man was supposed to have been murdered nearly twenty years ago. It took some believing that the two men could be the same."

"Quite! Quite! And did your re-check satisfy you that the deceased man was, in fact, Frank Hugh Smallwood?"

"There isn't the faintest shadow of doubt about it. Would your Worship care for me to explain the points of similarity between the two sets of prints?"

"Not for the time being. We are prepared to accept your considered opinion."

"Thank you, your Worship. Well, next I began to examine all the personal belongings of the deceased which had been found in his pockets. There was always the chance that the purpose of the crime had been robbery, and that the murderer had been through the pockets of the deceased. I found plenty of prints on a number of those articles, but they all belonged to the deceased.

"After that I examined the deceased's clothes. In the course of this work I examined a bone button which I produce. Upon proper treatment being applied to the surface of the button a print became visible. I produce a copy of the photograph of the print, enlarged twelve times."

The sergeant handed the photograph to the Warrant Officer, who passed it on to the clerk's assistant. This young man then gave the photograph an Exhibit number—Three—entered its details on the requisite form, and afterwards handed it up to Sir Roger.

The Chairman carefully fitted a monocle to his left eye, and examined the photograph with an air of profound wisdom which hinted that most, if not all the secrets of the science of finger-prints were part of his vast store of wisdom. His fellow magistrates craned forward, and tried to obtain a simultaneous glimpse of the exhibit. Meanwhile, both Sinclair and Crawford had produced and were examining copies of the photograph with which they had been previously supplied.

Murphy murmured: "This is the most important piece of evidence in the entire case. The photograph is a poor one. Look out for fireworks."

Presently, with an air of condescension, Sir Roger gallantly passed the photograph on to Mrs. Redwood, then leaned back in his chair and glared belligerently at the witness.

"The photograph is not very good. Is it the best one obtainable?"

"It is the best of four negatives, your Worship."

"The best of four! Who photographed the impression?"

"Detective-Constable Bristow, of Headquarters. He will give evidence later."

"Is Detective Bristow a good photographer?"

"One of the best at New Scotland Yard, if I may say so, your Worship."

"Then I cannot say that the photograph of the button is a good testimonial of your photographic bureau. I should have thought any amateur could have produced a better print—a better photographic print, I mean—than the one which has just been handed up to me."

Sinclair interrupted impatiently: "With deep respect, your Worship, I suggest that the photographer is not to be blamed, but the object photographed."

"I do not agree with you, Mr. Sinclair. A really first-class photographer could have arranged his lighting better, so as to have produced a sharper impression. The print is quite blurred. I speak, modestly, with the experience of thirty years' amateur photography behind me."

"I think Sergeant Dixon will be able to explain to your Worships that the impression of the finger-print, being smeared, is to be blamed, not the photographic print."

"Of course, I am only an *amateur* photographer—" the Chairman retorted with ponderous sarcasm. He turned once more towards the witness.

"Is it your opinion, Sergeant, that the impression is a bad one?"

"Damn the old boy!" Murphy murmured. "One would think he was counsel for the defence!"

The question left the cadaverous witness unmoved. "The impression could have been better, but it is both distinguishable and identifiable, if your Worship will allow me to prove it so."

"I shall *require* you to prove it to be so before accepting it as reliable evidence," Sir Roger commented sharply.

"Very well, your Worship. As a photographer your Worship will know what kind of a photograph results from the subject moving during an exposure."

"Of course."

"That is what has happened in the case of this finger-print impression, your Worship. If the finger which left the impression upon the button had been lifted immediately afterwards, doubtless a satisfactorily sharp impression would have been left. Unfortunately, the finger shifted while pressing on the button, so leaving the impression an imperfect one."

"Very well. I accept that explanation," Sir Roger consented grudgingly.

Sinclair said quickly:

"Sergeant, have you studied the official impressions of the accused's fingers and thumbs?"

"I have."

"I ask for the official impressions of the accused's fingers and thumbs to be produced."

The Police Superintendent produced a series of photographs, which were passed on to the Clerk of the Court and entered as exhibits, while duplicates were handed to the opposing lawyers, and the witness, who examined a set.

"Sergeant, would you please examine Exhibit Five?"

"I have it before me, sir."

"Is it a photograph of the impression of the forefinger of the accused's left hand?"

"It is."

Sinclair glanced at the Chairman, who was shuffling through the photographs.

"Have you Exhibit Five, your Worship?"

"Yes, yes. Go on, Mr. Sinclair."

Sinclair, to the witness: "Are there any points of similarity between the impression of the accused's left forefinger, and the impression found upon the bone button?"

"Yes."

"Would you please point them out to their Worships."

The next part of Dixon's evidence was technical. He identified certain loops and whorls, or parts of them, first on the one print, then on the other. Terhune followed the evidence on copies of the prints which Murphy had, and which the sergeant generously pushed between them. Sir Roger, meanwhile, glared through his monocle at his copy of the photograph.

It was not easy to follow Dixon's explanation. "If you count ten ridges from the topmost ridge of Exhibit Three, your Worship, this will bring you, on the left-hand side of the print, to the arch of a right-inclined loop—the angle of this loop corresponds exactly with that which you will find in the same position in Exhibit Five, by counting ten ridges from the red line—"

The Chairman counted industriously—Sinclair counted—Crawford counted—Murphy counted.

"The topmost ridge of the loop is the eleventh from the top," Sir Roger presently announced.

"I make it the ninth, Sir Roger," contradicted Mrs. Redwood.

"The eleventh," the Chairman growled irritably.

"Perhaps you are not making allowances for the smear," the sergeant suggested, not very diplomatically.

"Of course I am," Sir Roger barked back. Nevertheless, he recounted. "It is the ninth," he admitted ungraciously.

"No, the eleventh," contradicted Mrs. Redwood firmly, she also having recounted.

"Sergeant Dixon suggests that the topmost ridge of the loop is the tenth from the top of the photograph," Sinclair interposed.

"Inclusive or exclusive of the ridge which touches the side of the button?" Doctor Atwell asked unexpectedly.

"Inclusive, I believe, your Worships." Sinclair turned towards the sergeant.

"Yes, sir. Inclusive."

"Why didn't the witness say so at first?" Sir Roger growled.

For thirty minutes the witness remained in the stand, patiently pointing out the alleged resemblance between Exhibits Three and Five until the Chairman admitted, finally, that he was satisfied. Sinclair sat down, with a sigh of relief. Crawford rose to his feet. Probably it was Terhune's imagination, but it seemed to him that the tip of Crawford's nose was twitching with eagerness.

"Sergeant Dixon," he began suavely, "how long have you been working in the Finger-Print Bureau?"

"The best part of fourteen years, sir."

"Can you tell me the probable chances of the finger-prints of any two people being identically the same?"

A faint smile passed across the long, thin face of the witness. To see the solemn face relax was something of a shock to the people in Court.

"Millions to one against, sir. Possibly billions," Dixon replied with satisfaction.

"Quite. But when you say that no one person has ever been known to have finger-prints identical with those of another person, are you referring to any one finger or thumb separately, or to the complete set of ten?"

The sergeant hesitated. "May I put it this way, sir?" he said presently. "My answer just now referred to any one separate finger or thumb. The chances of any two complete sets of ten prints being identical are astronomical."

"Then you would not agree that it is barely possible for one person's little finger to resemble, say, another person's index finger?"

"In the light of many years' experience, I should not agree that such a resemblance was at all possible," Dixon affirmed stolidly.

"Now be so kind as to answer me this question, Sergeant. Your previous answer, I take it, refers to a complete finger-print. But can you assure me with equal—and may I say, commendable—conviction that no two segments of any two prints are sufficiently alike as to be mistaken for each other?"

The question obviously shook the witness. "I don't follow you, sir," he stated slowly.

"If you were to mark a five millimetre square on any one finger-print—particularly at the top or on one side—are you prepared to state on oath your conviction that on no other print would you find comparable markings?"

The witness tried to prevaricate. "I have not heard of any test being made on those lines, sir."

Crawford metaphorically pounced on the sergeant's words.

"Then, if no such test has, to your knowledge, been made, you cannot deny the possibility of two small segments of two different prints being alike."

"No, sir. I cannot deny that possibility," the witness agreed heavily.

Chapter Eighteen

"That's a ruddy awful question to have had put to one," Murphy commented in an angry whisper. "And look at the old boy: he's beaming with satisfaction."

The sergeant was exaggerating, of course: the Chairman was merely nodding his head as if agreeing that the question was rightly asked, and correctly answered. Then he bent over his notebook, and made some notes.

"I wonder if it would interest you, Sergeant, to know what prompted me to put that last question to you?"

A humorous expression passed over the long, gaunt face. "Questions of that sort are put to me nearly every time I give evidence," the witness said drily.

A sighing titter echoed across the Court. Crawford pressed his lips together.

"Indeed!" he exclaimed acidly. "Yesterday afternoon I conducted a series of experiments at my office and in my home, by persuading more than twenty-five people in all to give me the impressions of all their fingers and thumbs. Afterwards I examined all these impressions carefully. Let me admit at once that no two impressions even vaguely resembled each other in their entirety. But—and mark this well—there was a small segment of one impression—that of the third finger of the left hand of our Chief Clerk—which could have been mistaken, if looked at upside down, for an equally small segment of the impression of the forefinger of my daughter's right hand." Crawford paused enquiringly.

"An expert eye could probably distinguish many differences, especially if the prints were enlarged on to a cinematograph screen," Dixon answered imperturbably.

"Even if one of the impressions were smeared or blurred?" Crawford asked swiftly—it seemed as though he had anticipated the witness's reply.

"That depends on how badly the impression was smeared," was the cautious rejoinder.

"As badly smeared as Exhibit Three, for instance?"

Dixon smiled confidently. "We frequently have to identify prints smeared as badly as that found on the button."

Crawford appealed to the justices. "Would your Worships please examine the button on which the finger-print was found?"

The button, which had been produced and numbered with the photographs, was mounted in a special box, which stood on Sir Roger's blotting-pad. At the solicitor's invitation the Chairman picked up the box and examined it.

"Well, Mr. Crawford?"

"Can your Worship see the actual finger-print?"

"Vaguely."

"What proportion of one of your own finger-prints would you estimate the impression on the button represents?"

"Approximately one-quarter."

"Exactly, your Worship. The impression which the Prosecution is asking you to accept as evidence against the accused is not only smeared, but rather less than one-quarter of a complete finger-print." Crawford sat down abruptly. There was in his attitude a suspicion of indignation with the Majesty of the Law for offering such unreliable evidence. He was a good fighter, was Crawford.

Sinclair rose. Very quietly he said: "Sergeant Dixon, just now, in answer to a question put to you on behalf of the accused, you informed their Worships that you would not care to deny the possibility of segments of two separate finger-prints containing ridge characteristics similar to both segments."

"That is so, sir."

"But in your long experience have you ever seen, or heard of any record of any two such segments containing identical ridge characteristics?"

"No, sir."

Sinclair sat down again.

11

The proceedings dragged on, were adjourned to the following Friday, and resumed. In company with all the other witnesses, called and still to be called, Terhune attended the resumed hearing.

One by one the witnesses gave their evidence: the detective-constable from New Scotland Yard who had photographed the button; the doctors who had performed the autopsy on Smallwood's body; then two seamen who had sailed aboard the s.s. *Cilicia*.

The first of these witnesses gave his name as Tom Carson.

"On the eighteenth day of October did Detective Miles call upon you at your home in Hove, Sussex, and ask you whether you would accompany him to the mortuary in this town for the purpose of identifying a body?"

"Yus, sir, he did."

"And did you agree so to accompany him?"

"I said, yus I would, if all me expenses was paid."

"Quite. And did you accompany him?"

"I did."

"And see the body?"

"Yus."

"Did you recognize it?"

"Yus."

"As whom?"

"Tom Wheeler."

"Had Tom Wheeler served with you aboard the Cunard s.s. *Cilicia*?"

"Yus, him and me was in the same watch."

"Did you know that that was not his baptismal name?"

"No, but it wouldn't have surprised me if I had 've known."

"Why not?"

"Blimey! There's more'n one bloke at sea what wouldn't want nobody to know 'is real name."

"Thank you, Mr. Carson."

"Pleased, I'm sure," said Carson as Sinclair sat down. He began to leave the box, but an officer waved him back. "Blimey! but he's sat down," Carson remonstrated, as he resumed his original position in the witness-stand and pointed at Sinclair.

Crawford waved his hand. "No questions."

"All right, you can go," the officer said.

"Can't you never make up your mind?" Carson muttered in an undertone as he stepped down from the box.

Carson was succeeded by another seaman from s.s. *Cilicia*, but Alfred Phillips merely corroborated the evidence of the previous witness.

Phillips was followed by Guy Heather, who, most unwillingly, first identified the copy of *Rosamund*, produced, as the one he had received from Jenkinson, and then went on to testify that it was the same which he had lent to the accused on the day of the murder.

"At what time did Harrison leave your home?"

"About one-forty."

"Was he alone when he left?"

"No. He left when I did. He walked with me to the school."

"Did he have the copy of *Rosamund* with him when he left your house?"

"Yes. He carried it under his arm."

"You are quite sure of that fact?"

"I—I—" The witness paused.

"Come, come, you heard the question," the Chairman barked.

"I—I am sure," Heather replied reluctantly.

Mrs. Heather confirmed her husband's evidence, but was unable to add anything to it. She was followed by George Binks.

George Binks was a driver, employed by the local omnibus company. After a few simple questions Sinclair finished with him, but this time Crawford took over.

"Mr. Binks, what is today's date?"

Binks's mouth opened as he stared at the solicitor with undisguised amazement. "November the fifteenth."

"Thank you, Mr. Binks. Now, touching upon the events which you have just described to my learned friend from London, you have testified that Harrison caught the bus which leaves Bray-in-the-Marsh for Ashford at two-twenty p.m."

"That is right, I did," Binks agreed perkily: he wasn't going to have anyone try to make out that he didn't know what he was talking about!

"Let me see, did not Mrs. Pain catch that same bus?"

"Mrs. Pain!" Binks looked blank. "I don't know. Did she?"

"I am asking the questions; you are here to answer them. You don't remember whether or no Mrs. Pain was on the two-twenty bus that day?"

"No."

"Was Mr. Lluellyn?"

"I—I don't know."

"Did anyone else get on the bus at the same time as Mr. Harrison?"

"Yes. About six or seven people, I suppose."

"Who were those people?"

"I don't know that I can remember all the names."

"Then give me just one or two."

The witness screwed up his face as though he were making a painful effort to think, but in the end he did not answer.

"Well?"

"I can't remember anyone in pertickler."

"Then how do you know there were about six or seven people?"

"That's about the number of people what usually catches the two-twenty into Ashford."

"Oh! I see. You were not speaking from memory. You were just making a rough guess."

"Yes."

"Well, never mind," Crawford purred. "Can you tell me the name of any one person who was on the bus that day—I mean, of course, from your *positive* knowledge, so that, if necessary, he or she can confirm your statement?"

After a long pause Binks shook his head. "No, I can't," he replied sullenly.

"You mean you cannot remember."

"It's a long time ago now," the bus driver excused himself.

This was what Crawford had been angling for, and he interjected swiftly: "Naturally. I quite understand. People travel on your bus every day of the week and you cannot remember who travelled on it on that one particular day, more than five weeks ago?"

Binks was relieved. "That's about it, sir."

"Then how can you be so positive that Harrison caught the two-twenty on Tuesday, the eighth of October, and not on Wednesday, the ninth?"

"I—well, it's just that I do remember *him* in particular."

"Why?"

"I—I don't know why, but I do."

"Perhaps I can help you to amplify your answer. When did you first remember having seen Harrison on the Tuesday, the eighth of October—before or after Harrison's arrest?"

"Well—er—"

"It was *after* the arrest, was it not?"

"I—I suppose so, but that was because I hadn't troubled to think on it before then. If I had've done, no doubt I should have remembered it before the arrest."

"In short, Mr. Binks, the news of the arrest prompted your memory—or perhaps prodded would be the better word?"

"Yes."

"You can remember Harrison travelling on your bus on that particular day, but you cannot remember one other person who did so?"

"No."

"Thank you, Mr. Binks. I think their Worships will be able to assess your evidence at its true value." Crawford sat down, apparently not unsatisfied with himself.

"No doubt we shall, Mr. Crawford," the Chairman confirmed drily.

Binks was followed by Arthur Wood. Wood was another driver employed by the local omnibus service. He gave evidence to the effect that on Tuesday, the eighth day of October, he had been the driver of the bus scheduled to leave Ashford at four-thirty-five p.m. He did not remember Harrison's getting into the bus, but he did remember, very clearly, his getting out.

"Why?" Sinclair asked.

"Because an elderly lady just behind him tripped over a bag and fell forward against Mr. Harrison. In doing so she knocked something from under his arm, which fell out on to the pavement."

"Did you know the lady concerned?"

"Yes, sir. She was Mrs. Ralph Wesley."

"What was it she knocked from under Harrison's arm?"

"Well, sir, I couldn't rightly *see* what it was because the passengers alighted from the near side of the bus, and I was sitting in the driver's seat on the off-side, but I think it was a book of some sort."

"Why?"

"Because when Mrs. Wesley began to apologize, and to say that she hoped the parcel contained nothing breakable, Mr. Harrison said that no harm had been done; it was only a book."

"I see. Now, Mr. Wood, I want you to be very careful about answering the next few questions. What time did the bus arrive at Bray?"

"The four-thirty-five from Ashford is scheduled to arrive at the *Wheatsheaf* at five-eight. I don't think I was late, but if I was it weren't no more than a couple of minutes at the most."

"Were you driving any other buses that day?"

"Yes, sir. I was on the second shift."

"The second shift?"

"Yes, sir. Whichever of us drives the early morning bus out of Ashford knocks off after three—"

"Would that be after the two-twenty from Bray has arrived in Ashford?"

"That's right, sir. We takes the bus into the garage for a fill of petrol, a check and a tidy-up, and then knocks off for the day. Then the next man on collects the bus at four-fifteen, drives it to the starting place, and carries on until the last bus home at night."

"How many journeys does each driver make?"

"That depends."

"On what?"

"Whether you are on the first or the second shift. We has three journeys to make on the first shift, and two in the second."

"By journeys, you mean return trips?"

"Yes, sir."

"From Ashford?"

"Yes, sir."

"Therefore, on the eighth of October you only drove your bus from Ashford to Hythe twice?"

"That's right."

"How can you be certain that both Harrison and Mrs. Wesley were not in the bus when you made the return trip for the second time?"

"You mean on the seven-fifty, from Ashford?"

"If that is the scheduled departure time of the last outward journey—yes."

"Because it would have been dark by then, and I know it was in the daylight when Mrs. Wesley knocked the book from under Mr. Harrison's arm."

Crawford wisely did not attempt to throw any doubt upon Wood's memory of Harrison's having had a book knocked from under his arm—after all, that minor affair was one of those insignificant but tangible things which a man might reasonably be expected to remember.

"No questions," he announced.

Wood was followed by Mrs. Wesley, who confirmed the bus-driver's evidence in every detail, while adding that she travelled into Ashford every Tuesday, so that the incident in question could only have taken place on a Tuesday.

Once again Crawford indicated that he did not wish to cross-examine.

Then came Sidney Jellicoe, of Wickford. Jellicoe testified, quite simply, that Harrison had not called upon him at any time during the afternoon of October the eighth; in fact, he went on positively, Harrison had not called upon him since the previous August. August the twenty-first, to be exact. He had the date noted in his diary.

Murphy chuckled. "Crawford won't be able to make much out of that," he whispered to Terhune.

Murphy was wrong.

"Tell me, Mr. Jellicoe," Crawford began, "have you any ground attached to your house at Wickford?"

"Yes. A little."

"How little?"

"About half an acre."

"Where is it situated? In front of the house, or behind?"

"Most of it behind."

"What do you do with the ground? Cultivate it?"

"Yes."

"Do you do the work yourself?"

"Every bit," Jellicoe answered proudly.

"Were you at home on Tuesday, October the eighth?"

"I was."

"How can you be so sure of that?"

"Because I had intended walking to Willingham to have tea with my sister."

"Didn't you go?"

"No."

"Why not?"

"Just as I was about to set off it started to rain cats and dogs, so I changed my mind and stayed at home. I went the next day instead."

"Quite. The rainstorm lasted about thirty minutes, I believe?"

"About that, but Doris always has tea punctually at four-thirty—"

"Quite, Mr. Jellicoe, we understand. What did you do when the rain stopped?"

"What I usually do when I am at home—some gardening. I did some digging, as a matter of fact."

"Some digging—in your kitchen garden?"

"Yes."

"I see. Whereabouts is your kitchen garden?"

"Practically all of it is a kitchen garden."

"But whereabouts were you digging—near the house, or some way away from it?"

"In the onion bed—about sixty or seventy yards from the back door, I suppose."

"Were you there long?"

"Till about dusk."

"Have you a front door as well as a back door?"

"Yes, of course."

"Do visitors usually knock at the front or the back door?"

"It all depends."

"Whenever Harrison visited you, upon which door did he usually knock?"

"The front."

"Is the front door within sight or sound of where you were digging?"

For the first time Jellicoe began to realize the reason for the series of strange questions.

"Well, no," he admitted.

"Then you were digging from—shall I say—five o'clock to about six-thirty?"

"About that time."

"Then is it not possible, Mr. Jellicoe, that Mr. Harrison did in fact, call at your house but, owing to your being some distance from the front door, you neither saw nor heard him?"

"Yes," the witness admitted, after giving some thought to the question.

Mrs. Brooks was Crawford's next victim. In answer to questions put to her by prosecuting counsel, she had testified, had she not, to having seen Harrison emerging from the footpath through Windmill Wood about six-fifteen on the evening of Tuesday, October the eighth.

"That is what I told the other gentleman, sir," Mrs. Brooks agreed, in a frightened voice.

"Your exact words were, Mrs. Brooks: 'about six-fifteen'. Now that loose expression may satisfy counsel for the prosecution, but not, I am sure, their Worships. Was it *exactly* six-fifteen when you saw a man emerge from the shadows of the wood?"

"I couldn't say exactly what the time was, sir. I didn't have it on me."

"How long before the encounter had you last been aware of the *exact* time?"

"At six o'clock, sir."

"How was that?"

"I heard the church clock strike the time, which reminded me to switch on the wireless to hear the news. I was just in time to hear the Greenwich time signal."

"Did you listen to the news?"

"Only the first few minutes of it. Then I left to call upon Mrs. White, as I've already told the other gentleman."

"Yes, and on the way to Mrs. White's you stopped at the gate of Mrs. Morgan's cottage, to exchange a few words with her?"

"Yes, sir."

"You arrived at Mrs. White's at what time?"

"I don't know exactly."

"How long were you with Mrs. White?"

"About ten minutes."

"*About!* You do not know for certain that it was not more or less than ten minutes?"

"It didn't seem more than ten minutes."

"You arrived back at the inn precisely at six-forty, I think you said?"

"Yes, sir."

"How long does it take you, normally, to walk from *Toll Inn* to Mrs. White's cottage?"

"About four minutes."

"*About! About!* Can you not get away from that word, Mrs. Brooks?"

"No, sir. But it couldn't take me more than four minutes."

"Very well, suppose we accept that estimate of four minutes as being reasonably correct? How long were you listening to the news?"

"Not more than five minutes, that I do know."

"How do you know?"

"Because just as I was leaving the house Bert Carley, who was in the bar, looked at the clock and said something about five past six being time for him to go home."

"I see. And you were talking to Mrs. Morgan for how long?"

"Just a few minutes."

"Just a few minutes!" Crawford gestured theatrically. "Listen, Mrs. Brooks: you left the inn at six-five: you arrived back at precisely six-forty. In all, therefore, you were away for thirty-five minutes. From that thirty-five minutes should be subtracted the eight minutes for the double journey to and from Mrs. White's cottage. That leaves twenty-seven minutes. You were with Mrs. White *about* ten minutes, which gives us the figure of seventeen minutes unaccounted for. You were with Mrs. Morgan just a few minutes. Three, four, five, for instance?"

"About five."

"Five! Five from seventeen leaves twelve. Twelve minutes unaccounted for. Now, might it not be possible that you were with Mrs. Morgan for only three minutes, instead of five?"

"I suppose it might," Mrs. Brooks agreed doubtfully.

"In which case you would have passed by the footpath through Windmill Wood not later than ten minutes past six, wouldn't you?"

"I suppose so."

"On the other hand, you might have spent the best part of ten, or twelve, or even more minutes with Mrs. Morgan, mightn" you?"

"It is so long ago now—"

"Mightn't you, Mrs. Brooks?"

"I might."

"In which case you could not have passed the footpath before twenty past six, could you?"

"No, sir. I couldn't."

Sinclair interrupted: "I do not know what my friend's cross-examination is supposed to be leading up to: surely five minutes one way or the other does not affect the issue?"

Crawford was not abashed. "At that time of the evening five minutes can change grey shadows to black; and dusk to darkness. A face which is just recognizable at six-fifteen may be shadowy and less distinct at six-twenty."

Sinclair could not object to this line of argument, so Crawford proceeded next to cross-examine Mrs. Brooks on her recognition of the accused. Before long she was so flustered that she was ready to admit that it was not Harrison's face which she had recognized, but only his general build, and walk.

Crawford fought tenaciously, brilliantly—afterwards, Sinclair congratulated him—but the unruffled, patient counsel from the Public Prosecutor's office had made out just enough of a case against Harrison for the magistrates to shirk the responsibility of finding the accused not guilty. When the magistrates announced their decision, towards the end of the fourth hearing, and asked Harrison whether he had anything to say in answer to the charge against him, Harrison replied calmly that he had nothing to say, so Crawford rose, and reserved the prisoner's defence. The prisoner was thereupon committed for trial at the next Assizes, and the proceedings were at an end. Harrison vanished, the justices began to converse with one another, the public shuffled towards the exit door, the witnesses formed into self-conscious groups, Crawford and Sinclair began to stroll out of Court together, while the uniformed police and the plain-clothes men joked together, and tried to forecast the afternoon's winners.

In a surprisingly short time the Court was empty.

III

With Christmas intervening, the Press temporarily lost interest in the Windmill Wood Crime. Once the Press had reported the fact that the accused had been committed for trial, the names of Harrison and everyone connected with the trial vanished from the newspapers. The lives of the witnesses became normal again—with the exception of Mrs. Brooks. In *Toll Inn* the subject of the murder remained the chief topic of conversation; again, and again, and yet again she was asked to repeat to her customers her experiences on the late afternoon of the crime, also her 'adventures' in Ashford police court.

Some weeks later Helena and Terhune stood on Ashford station waiting for the arrival of a train for Maidstone. Murphy saw, and joined them. He and Terhune had not met since the proceedings in the police court.

"Good morning, Miss Armstrong. Good morning, Mr. Terhune." He clapped his gloved hands together. "Bit parky this morning, isn't it? Sorry I haven't had an opportunity of visiting you lately, Mr. Terhune, to let you know what has been happening, but that post-office robbery has been keeping us all busy."

"What has been happening?"

Murphy grinned. "The murder or the robbery?"

"Which do you think?"

"Nothing new, I'm afraid. But from an outsider's point of view this case is likely to prove one of the most interesting for a good many years."

"Why?"

"Unless I'm mistaken, there's going to be a first-class fight. On our side the Treasury has appointed Sir Kenneth Griffiths, K.C., to lead—"

"That was more or less a foregone conclusion, wasn't it?"

"Well, yes. The point is, have you heard who is representing Harrison?"

"Yes. Douglas Bax, K.C."

"Perhaps you don't realize what happens when Griffiths and Bax oppose each other! Sparks usually fly. By golly! They are a couple of clever devils. Neither gets away with anything while the other is anywhere around, I can tell you. Of course, you have seen that Old Snuffle-Nose will be trying the case?"

"Yes."

While they still awaited the arrival of the train, other witnesses came on to the platform. Soon there were familiar faces to be seen on all sides.

"I don't think the Press will give the trial so much publicity as they did the police-court proceedings," Murphy remarked presently.

"Why not?" Helena asked.

"In the first place, the trial is no longer new, so it is, therefore, no longer sensational; secondly, the evidence at the trial will be mostly a rehash of the evidence given in Ashford; thirdly, the South American earthquake is using up all the headline space. Besides—"

The sight of the train interrupted the conclusion of Murphy's arguments. By the time it had steamed into the station and they were all settled in a carriage, they had forgotten what Murphy had been saying, and began speaking of other matters.

Later they arrived at Maidstone, and proceeded to the Court of Assize. The scene was a busy one, but the witnesses were not conscious of the bustle and commotion. Most of them were anxious to give their evidence, and so put an end to the worse ordeal of waiting. They wandered about, sometimes whispering to one another, but for the most part silent and disconsolate.

Murphy disappeared, leaving Helena and Terhune alone. They sat down, watched their fellow witnesses, and waited. So, through no fault of theirs—certainly no fault of *his*, Terhune reflected bitterly, that night—they missed being present at one of the most dramatic and sensational moments in legal history.

IV

The Court was in session. Mr. Justice Lovelace sniffed loudly, and gazed benignly at the people below. The Clerk of Assize rose to open the case. Facing the accused he read out in a dry, rather squeaky voice:

"Vivian Thomas Harrison, you stand charged upon this Indictment for that you, on the eighth day of October last, at Windmill Wood, in the Parish of Farthing in this county, murdered Frank Hugh Smallwood. Are you guilty or not guilty?"

Before the accused could answer Douglas Bax rose to his feet. Bax was squarely large, square-shouldered, square-faced, square-headed—a peach of a subject for the caricaturists, who invariably drew him as a cubistic figure composed of squares.

"My lord, I beg to plead a special plea in Bar."

The judge's wig twitched.

Bax went on: "My lord, we plead *autrefois convict*."

Autrefois convict! Already convicted of the specific offence for which the accused was being tried!

A gasp of amazement swept round the Court.

Chapter Nineteen

M r. Justice Lovelace cleared his throat.

"Did I hear you plead *autrefois CONVICT*, Mr. Bax?"

"Yes, my lord, *CONVICT*."

The judge pulled at the lobe of his left ear.

"Very well, Mr. Bax. The Court must deal with your plea." He addressed the jury. "Members of the jury, in answer to the Indictment for murder against the accused, which you have heard the Clerk of Assize read out, the accused, through his learned Counsel, has put in the Special Plea in Bar known as *Autrefois Convict*. For the benefit of those members of the jury who know neither the meaning of a special plea in Bar, nor that of *Autrefois Convict*, I will offer an explanation of both terms.

"When a person is placed in the dock, and charged with an offence against the established laws of this country, that person must choose one of several alternatives open to him. He may stand mute. Should he do this a jury is thereupon empanelled to enquire whether the accused is mute of malice—that is to say, although well able to speak, he is remaining silent for no other purpose than to obstruct the proceedings being taken against him. In the event of the jury's finding the accused mute of malice the Court will then order the plea of not guilty to be entered in his behalf. But if the accused be found mute *ex visitatione dei*, by visitation of God, then the Court may order all proceedings to be translated and made known to the accused by means of the deaf-and-dumb language, or by other means.

"The second course which an accused may adopt is that of pleading guilty to the offence of which he has been charged, whereupon proceedings are brought to an end by the accused being sentenced to just punishment. The third course is that of raising a legal objection to the Indictment itself, with which course I shall not now attempt to deal further.

"Lastly, he may, what is baldly known as, plead. But there are three pleas. One, a plea to the jurisdiction, which means simply that the accused claims that, on legal grounds, the Court has not the jurisdiction to try him. Two, a special plea in Bar, with which I shall deal lastly. And three, a general plea in Bar, which means, simply, that he pleads not guilty, whereupon the proceedings against him are opened, and the trial follows a normal course.

"To deal now with the special plea in Bar, this plea is further subdivided, for the accused may plead that he has received a pardon from the Crown, for the specific offence with which he is being tried, or he may plead, in the case of proceedings for criminal libel, that the libel complained of was justified, and that its publication benefited the public.

"Lastly, in this sub-section, he may plead *autrefois acquit*, or *autrefois convict*, The first means that he has already been tried for the offence for which he is again being tried, been found not guilty, and acquitted; the second, that he has been found guilty and convicted."

The judge paused: the members of the jury, for the first time realizing the significance of the judge's explanation, looked at the judge, at the accused, and at one another, in obviously puzzled astonishment.

Mr. Justice Lovelace continued:

"The pleas of *autrefois acquit* and *autrefois convict are* based on the wise and just maxim of common law—*Nemo debet bis vexari*—no man may be twice put in jeopardy of his life or liberty for the same offence. Therefore, if he has been once found not guilty, the law insists that he may not subsequently be found guilty of that offence. Similarly, a man, rightly, may not be twice punished for the same offence. It follows, therefore, that any accused person who can substantiate and prove his plea of *autrefois acquit* or *autrefois convict* is entitled to demand the cessation of all proceedings against him, and immediate discharge from custody.

"Before either of these pleas may succeed the accused must be prepared with evidence in support of his plea, the onus of proving which lies upon him. When this special plea in Bar is raised, a jury must be sworn to try the issue. In the event of the plea failing, the accused is subsequently entitled to enter a general plea in Bar, which, as I have already explained, means that he pleads not guilty, whereupon the trial against him on the original Indictment proceeds.

"Members of the jury, you were assembled for the purpose of hearing the Indictment for murder against the accused, Vivian Thomas Harrison. Had he pleaded not guilty, the next step in these proceedings would have been to swear each of you separately well and truly to try and true deliverance, make between our Sovereign Lord the King and the prisoner at the Bar on the Indictment for murder. Instead, the Clerk of Assize will swear you to hear and make a true verdict on the special plea in Bar."

The dry, emotionless voice of the judge came to an end as he sniffed once or twice, but discreetly, so that the only evidence of his catarrhal condition was the twitching of his nostrils as he sought to clear his head.

With an enquiring glance at the judge the Clerk of Assize proceeded with the business of swearing in the members of the jury, the while the Court buzzed with a low undertone of excitement. Griffiths and Bax slid nearer to each other, and conversed together in low voices: it was apparent from Griffiths' expression that the prisoner's plea was as surprising to him as to everyone else in Court.

Presently the swearing-in of the jury was over. The noise of subdued conversation was succeeded by nervous shuffling. Bax rose majestically to his feet.

"My lord," he began suavely, "I must beg your lordship's indulgence for pleading verbally instead of properly reducing the plea to writing, and so giving your lordship warning of the course I proposed to take, but the truth of the matter is, my lord, that the accused did not acquaint me with the circumstances which allow the plea to be made until seven a.m. this morning."

"I had already assumed that so conscientious a counsel would be able to offer a satisfactory explanation," Mr. Justice Lovelace admitted graciously.

"I thank your lordship."

"But I am concerned to know whether you have the necessary evidence to place before the Court?"

"Your lordship will be pleased to hear that witnesses have arrived and are waiting to be called."

The judge nodded his satisfaction, then faced the jury again. "Members of the jury, the position is this: By his plea of *autrefois convict* the accused claims that he has previously been tried for the murder of the deceased, Frank Hugh Smallwood, and has been convicted. You will hear evidence in support of this plea, and if you are satisfied that the accused has proved his case, you will bring in a verdict to that effect, and the accused will be freed forthwith. If you are not satisfied that the prisoner has proved his case you will be discharged, and a fresh jury will be empanelled from other members of the public, called to the Assize for jury service, to try the accused on the Indictment which has already been read out in Court.

"Before the accused offers evidence in support of his plea, it is necessary for me to give you an outline of what he must prove to justify you in bringing in a verdict in his favour. He must first satisfy you that upon the occasion of the first trial he was, in fact, in jeopardy on the former Indictment. That is to say, that the Court was competent to try him, that the Indictment was valid, and that his conviction was not subsequently quashed on appeal, on the grounds of the incompetency of the Court, or the invalidity of the Indictment.

"He must also prove that the offence with which he is now charged is the same, or substantially the same, as the former offence. Sometimes, in pleas of this nature, it is a subtle problem to decide whether the two charges are substantially identical, and in considering the problem the jury must keep in mind the legal aspects involved. In this specific instance, however, you, members of the jury, will have to bear the added burden of having to make your decision in circumstances which, to the best of my knowledge, are without precedent in the history of this country. I know of no case in which a person, having been once convicted for the murder of another person, has been subsequently tried a second time for the same offence—that is, the murder of that same person. The reasons for this are twofold. Firstly, a person can only once be killed, so quite obviously the murderer cannot twice kill the same victim. Secondly, the murderer is usually executed, and a dead person can no more kill a live man than a live man can kill a dead person."

The judge faced the Court. "Mr. Bax, will you begin?"

"I thank your lordship." Bax hitched his gown over his shoulders.

"My lord, members of the jury, I shall begin by recapitulating, briefly, the events of a trial which began, on Wednesday, November the sixteenth, nineteen-hundred-and-twenty-seven, at the Central Criminal Court, London—more popularly known as Old Bailey.

"The trial arose from the discovery of a man's limb in the River Thames, which during the course of the trial was positively identified as belonging to one Frank Hugh Smallwood. In consequence of police enquiries, Charles Cockburn was arrested, and charged with the murder of Smallwood. Cockburn was found guilty, and sentenced to death. He appealed, but the appeal was dismissed. Before the day of execution arrived, Cockburn's sentence was commuted to one of imprisonment for life. According to the merciful custom of our country the maximum sentence of imprisonment which any man may serve is twenty years, less a maximum remission of one-fourth of the sentence for good conduct. At the end of fifteen years Cockburn, having earned the full remission, was discharged from prison.

"Members of the jury, the man who stands in the dock, charged, for the *second* time, with the murder of Frank Hugh Smallwood, is none other than Charles Cockburn, *alias* Vivian Harrison. I claim, therefore, that Cockburn, having been already convicted, in a properly competent Court, of the murder of Frank Smallwood, is entitled to immediate discharge on the plea of *autrefois convict*."

The silence in Court was absolute. Affected by the drama of the scene not a soul moved. The rustle of paper, as Bax turned over some sheets, sounded irreverently loud.

In a quiet, even voice Mr. Justice Lovelace said: "Will you proceed with the evidence, Mr. Bax?"

"With your lordship's permission. I call Detective-Sergeant Dixon."

Presently the cadaverous one appeared. In mournful tones he took the oath.

After the usual formal questions, Bax said:

"As a result of a telegram which I sent to New Scotland Yard this morning, Sergeant Dixon, did you look for and obtain the official record of the finger-prints of one Charles Cockburn, convicted in November, nineteen-twenty-seven, of the murder of Frank Hugh Smallwood?"

"Yes."

"Do you produce them?"

"I do, sir."

"Do you also produce the official records of the finger-prints of Vivian Thomas Harrison?"

"I do, sir."

"As a consequence of certain instructions, have you compared the prints of Cockburn with those of Harrison?"

"I have, sir."

"Are they in any way similar?"

"They are identical."

"Is it your opinion that the two sets of prints belong to one and the same man?"

"Yes, sir. That is my positive opinion."

Bax glanced enquiringly at the judge, who shook his head. Bax said: "I call upon Detective-Constable Smart."

Detective Smart entered the Court, and stepped into the witness-stand. His evidence was short; he formally testified to having taken the finger-prints, Exhibits Four and Five, and he identified the accused, Vivian Thomas Harrison, as the man whose impressions he had taken.

After Smart, one Henry Noakes entered the witness-stand. He was elderly, and grey-haired. He testified that he was a retired prison warder, and that he had been employed, as such, from 1930 to 1940 at Dartmoor prison.

"During your period of employment at Dartmoor prison, were you acquainted with a 'life' prisoner by the name of Charles Cockburn?"

"I knew him mostly by his number, sir."

"But you did know him by name as well?"

"Yes, sir."

"Do you think you could recognize him again?"

"Unless he has changed very much, sir. I've a pretty good memory for faces."

"Would you please look round the Court and tell his lordship whether or no you recognize the man known to you by Charles Cockburn's prison number?"

The ex-warder turned, and slowly surveyed the Court. His gaze rested for some time on the man in the dock. Then he faced counsel again.

"I think I do, sir."

"You *think?*"

"Well, sir, the man in the dock reminds me of Cockburn."

"Why does he only remind you of Cockburn? Are you not prepared to identify him as Cockburn?"

"Oh, yes, sir! I'm ready to do that. I haven't any doubts in me mind. But he's changed a bit."

"In what way?"

"His face is browner and healthier than when I used to see it; his hair wasn't grey in those days; his face has aged."

"How many years ago did you last see Cockburn?"

"I last saw him in nineteen-forty. I didn't see him after that 'cause I was pensioned off."

Once again the judge expressed no intention of questioning the witness.

"Thank you, Mr. Noakes." As Noakes left the box, Bax continued: "I call Mr. Fred Rigley."

Fred Rigley appeared, a young man with bright eyes and dark, sleek hair. Terhune would have recognized him as the clerk who had accompanied Crawford to the police-court proceedings.

"Are you Fred Rigley, of sixteen Primrose Villas, Ashford Road, Ashford, Kent?"

"Yes, sir."

"Are you employed as a clerk by Messrs. Howard and Howard, of Ashford, solicitors?"

"Yes, sir."

"Acting upon the instructions of your employers, did you visit the Central Criminal Court, London, early this morning, and apply for a certificate that Charles Cockburn, in November, nineteen-twenty-seven, had been convicted of murder and sentenced to death?"

"Yes, sir."

"Do you produce that certificate?"

"Yes, sir."

An usher carried the certificate to the Clerk of Assize, who presently handed it up to the judge. Mr. Justice Lovelace examined the certificate, laid it down upon the blotting-pad before him, and looked at Bax.

"My lord, the accused is prepared to give evidence in explanation of his becoming known as Vivian Harrison."

"I do not think his evidence is needed, Mr. Bax. I am satisfied that the accused is the man, Charles Cockburn. His reasons for changing his name may be surmised, but they do not concern the present issue. You have now to satisfy the Court that the offence for which the accused is being tried is the same as that for which he was previously sentenced to death."

"But surely, my lord, it must be the same? As a man can be only *once* murdered, that offence can be only *once* committed. The accused has been *once* convicted for that offence. It would be against all the principles of common law to argue otherwise. *Nemo debet bis vexari*—a man must not be put twice in peril for the same offence. To continue with this trial would be to put Charles Cockburn in peril the second time for the alleged murder of Frank Hugh Smallwood."

"Mr. Bax, I have indicated to the members of the jury that the accused must, in finding a verdict for the prisoner, satisfy themselves under three separate headings. Was the prisoner 'in jeopardy' on the first Indictment? I shall advise the jury that the prisoner was so in jeopardy, for no evidence has been given that the Court which tried the case was not competent so to do. Was there a final verdict? An authenticated certificate that there was a final verdict—namely, sentence of death—has been produced in Court, and I shall therefore advise the jury to accept the certificate as evidence that there was such a final verdict.

"But under the third heading it is now necessary to ask, as I asked just now: was the previous charge substantially the same as the present one? I have before me an official record of Rex *v.* Cockburn, nineteen-twenty-seven. For the benefit of members of the jury I shall read aloud the Indictment in that trial."

The judge glanced towards the jury, and read aloud: "'Charles Cockburn, you stand charged upon Indictment for that you on the night of April the fifteenth-sixteenth in this present year, in the county of Surrey, murdered Frank Hugh Smallwood. Charles Cockburn, how say you, do you plead guilty or not guilty?'" The judge laid down the records, and picked up a single sheet of paper.

"I shall now read the Indictment referring to these present proceedings which you heard read earlier on: 'Vivian Thomas Harrison, you stand charged upon this Indictment for that you, on the eighth day of October last, at Windmill Wood, in the Parish of Farthing Toll in this county, murdered Frank Hugh Smallwood.'

"Ignoring the difference in the names of the defendant, do you agree, Mr. Bax, that an Indictment which charges a man with murdering another in the county of Surrey, in the year nineteen-twenty-seven, is substantially the same charge as that contained in an Indictment which deals with a murder at Windmill Wood in the county of Kent, in the past year?"

"But, my lord, Smallwood was *not* murdered in nineteen twenty-seven, but Cockburn was convicted of a murder, which was never committed."

"You are not denying that a murder was committed at Windmill Wood last October?"

"Of course not, my lord; but the fact remains, that if this present trial should continue, Cockburn would be put in peril for the second time for the same offence, which would be to negative an otherwise jealously guarded maxim of our *common law*."

Mr. Justice Lovelace pulled at his ear, and addressed the jury.

"Members of the jury, you have heard the arguments of learned counsel, and my replies. You must now consider you; verdict. In so doing, you must not allow yourselves to be influenced by feelings of sympathy towards the accused, who has undoubtedly been the victim of a miscarriage of justice. At this present juncture you have one duty, and one duty alone, to perform. To decide, according to your conscience and the oath you have sworn, whether the charge of murder of which the accused was convicted in nineteen-twenty-seven is substantially the same as that with which he is now charged. You do not even have to consider whether or no the prisoner is in fact guilty or not guilty of the murder of Frank Hugh Smallwood. He has neither pleaded guilty, nor not guilty. He has pleaded *autrefois convict*, and demanded an immediate release. Will you now retire and consider your verdict."

Several of the jurymen—they were all men, as it so happened—rose, but one or two who were nearer to the foreman leaned forward towards that gentleman. For some seconds a whispered conversation interrupted the proceedings. Presently the foreman stood up.

"May I ask a question, my lord?"

"You may."

"If we find that the two indictments are not identical, will the prisoner be tried for the murder of Smallwood?"

"The trial will proceed in the normal manner."

"If he is found guilty will he be sentenced to death?"

"In the event of the jury's finding the accused guilty of Smallwood's murder it would become my unhappy duty to sentence him to death."

"Then he could be hanged for having killed a man for whose death he had already served life imprisonment?"

"The ultimate consequences of the trial, if it be continued, will become the concern of another jury. You may not anticipate possible events. Your duty now is to decide on the issue before you."

Amid a subdued silence the unhappy jury left the Court. They were absent thirty-five minutes. When they returned their faces were expressionless.

The Clerk of Assize rose to his feet. In a voice from which a note of excitement was not entirely absent, he asked them if they had arrived at a unanimous verdict.

They had.

The two Indictments were *not* identical.

Chapter Twenty

While the members of the jury were filing out of the jury-box and, at their own request, being squeezed into a few vacant seats on benches at the back of the Court, outside the Court-room a new jury was being collected. These presently entered: this time, there were three women among them. They took their seats in the jury-box, and the bustle in the Court-room subsided as the proceedings began anew.

Once more the Clerk of Assize read aloud the Indictment against the accused. Once more he pleaded not guilty. Then Sir Kenneth Griffiths rose to open the case for the prosecution.

His opening speech was not a long one, and the first witness was soon called: Theodore Terhune.

Terhune entered the witness-stand, puzzled by the long delay which had preceded the calling of the first witness. He sensed an atmosphere of drama and excitement, but when he glanced quickly round he noticed nothing particularly revealing on the faces of the judge, or the jury, or the line of counsel, or the prisoner.

Sir Kenneth rose. "Is your name Theodore Terhune…"

The examination proceeded very much along the course which it had taken at the police court. In between-while Terhune inspected the opposing King's Counsel. As far as Sir Kenneth was concerned, there seemed very little difference between him and St. John Sinclair, except that Sir Kenneth wore wig and gown, which Sinclair, naturally, had not. Both spoke in a quiet, subdued, almost an apologetic voice. Still, there was, no doubt, some reason for transferring the case to Sir

Kenneth, instead of allowing Sinclair to follow it through to the higher Court, Terhune surmised.

His examination of Douglas Bax was more critical. Lord! What a big man Bax was, to be sure. What a big head, and a big, slightly florid face! And how curiously square in shape. Like his shoulders. It was easy to see why the newspaper cartoonists drew him in straight lines! But his appearance suggested that he was as much a fighter as Crawford had been. Probably more dangerous, too, because he looked capable of more self-control, and had the perky expression of a man who knows just one more trick than his neighbour. He'll make the witnesses sorry that either Harrison or Smallwood was born, Terhune thought. It was a darn' good job his own evidence was straightforward and uncomplicated. Even Bax wasn't likely to upset it.

Sir Kenneth sat down. Now for it, thought Terhune. But Douglas Bax negligently waved a big, square hand.

"No questions."

Helena Armstrong entered the witness-stand, and gave her evidence with rather less nervousness than she had betrayed at the police court. Perhaps the mildness of Crawford's cross-examination had given her more assurance. It is to be hoped Bax doesn't jump down her throat, Terhune reflected uneasily. And unnecessarily.

"No questions."

No questions! The two words soon became familiar to the people in the Court-room, as counsel for the defence waved away witness after witness. In consequence, the case proceeded smoothly and quickly. Before long more than half the witnesses had been heard.

At this point Mr. Justice Lovelace put down his quill pen with a determined air.

"We will adjourn for luncheon until two o'clock," he remarked. Then he addressed himself to the jury.

"Members of the jury, circumstances make it necessary for me to give orders that you may speak to no persons other than yourselves during the luncheon adjournment. All arrangements have been made for luncheon to be served to you in comfortable if isolated surroundings."

"What's Old Snuffle-Nose talking about? What's happened, I wonder?" Murphy whispered to Terhune.

The judge continued: "I should also remind representatives of the Press here today that the proceedings which preceded the empanelling of the second jury are *sub judice*, and may not be published or otherwise revealed to the general public until a verdict has been reached in these present proceedings."

With those words Mr. Justice Lovelace rose majestically from his seat, and swept out of Court.

"*Second* jury! By crikey! No wonder we were so long being called. What the devil's been happening?" Murphy could scarcely speak coherently. "There's Mr. Crawford: I'll ask him." Murphy, closely followed by Terhune and Helena, pushed his way through a group of people towards Crawford, who was just coming away from a brief conference with Bax.

"Mr. Crawford!"

Crawford turned round. With a sombre smile embracing them all, he greeted the three people with a general "Good morning."

"In the name of Pete, Mr. Crawford, what happened in Court this morning before the witnesses were called?"

"Drama and sensation, Murphy, of the kind you would expect to find in one of our friend's books"—he smiled at Terhune—"rather than in a staid Law Court. In answer to the Indictment the accused pleaded *autrefois convict*."

"Begod!" Murphy was amazed. Then, stupefied: "But that isn't possible—"

Terhune was quicker than the sergeant to realize the significance of the plea. "Harrison is Cockburn?"

"Yes."

"But Cockburn is dead!" Murphy exclaimed, floundering.

"No deader than Smallwood was, until a few weeks ago."

The detective gestured uncertainly. "That beats cock-fighting!"

The other three were inclined to agree with him.

II

At two p.m. sharp the judge re-entered the Court. As soon as the shuffling and rustling had died away Sir Kenneth's junior rose and called for Detective-Sergeant Dixon.

Terhune's attention wandered as he listened to Dixon's evidence. He was sure that Bax would not allow Dixon to leave the witness-stand without severe cross-examination, for though Dixon's evidence was the strongest link in a weak chain of circumstantial evidence, yet it was, in itself, none too reliable. Crawford had very nearly succeeded in persuading the justices to discount the evidence of the smudged, incomplete finger-print. Had the ultimate responsibility of the prisoner's life or death rested with those magistrates, instead of with the higher Court, they might even have declared Harrison—or Cockburn!—not guilty. If Crawford had done so well, how much better might the cunning, clever K.C. do.

Once again Terhune was to learn that he was a bad prophet.

"No questions," Bax grunted.

As it had begun, so it continued, right through the case. No questions! No questions! No questions!

Members of the jury, and many members of the general public as well, gazed at the K.C. with eyes in which smouldered a suspicion of anger. To them Bax was not doing his duty. He did not seem to be trying to defend the prisoner. His neglect was contrary to the spirit of fair play. Whatever the accused had done, they felt that it was up to somebody or other to give a helping hand to him.

No questions! No questions! No questions! And at three twenty-seven p.m. precisely, Sir Kenneth said: "That is the case for the prosecution, my lord," as he sat down.

Bax rose slowly—Terhune wondered whether he would ever stop rising. But when he had reached his full height, one realized there was something comforting about so much bulk, A man of that size wasn't to be defeated without some sort of a fight. Ten to one he had a trump card which he would play at the critical moment.

"My lord—"

Bax had a loud, bass voice. Even when the last echo of it had ceased travelling round the Court, one seemed to sense an aftermath of deep, unheard reverberations.

"I call the prisoner."

Accompanied by a warder, the accused man left the dock and moved across the Court to the witness-stand, where he took the oath in an even voice. His face was drawn and worried, Terhune thought; he even looked shrunken in size; small and insignificant —but perhaps this was in comparison with his counsel. He looked incapable of crime.

"Are you Charles Cockburn, otherwise known as Vivian Thomas Harrison?"

The members of the jury looked interested—it was possible to read from their expressions that they were reflecting that it was curious the prisoner should have two names—Cockburn! Cockburn! The name was vaguely familiar! Then the face of a fat man in the back row became startled. He whispered to his next-door neighbour. It was easy to guess what the fat man had said.

"I am."

"At the time of your arrest were you living, in the name of Harrison, at Baytree Farm, Farthing Toll, Kent?"

"Yes."

"How old are you?"

"Forty-nine."

"How long have you been calling yourself Vivian Thomas Harrison?"

"Since April, nineteen-forty-three."

"Is this the first time you have been a defendant in a murder trial?"

"No."

"When was the previous occasion?"

"November, nineteen-twenty-seven."

"Have those proceedings any direct bearing on this present trial?"

"Yes, they have. Indeed they have."

"Very well, I shall recapitulate, briefly, the events leading up to that trial, and its consequences."

In well-chosen phrases Bax retold the story of the first meeting between Cockburn and Smallwood. Skilfully he obtained a confession from the witness that Smallwood had been a bully of the worst type, that he, particularly, had been the butt of Smallwood's mean nature, and that he had always been afraid of Smallwood, because he had been weak and undersized, while Smallwood had been strong and burly.

"But you had several fights with Smallwood despite your fear of him?"

"Yes. He used to torment me so much that now and again I was not able to prevent myself hitting back at him."

"Why did you try to stop yourself hitting back at him?"

"Because that meant a fight."

"Did you not want to fight Smallwood?"

"Of course not. I always lost." A ripple of subdued laughter greeted this remark. Then Cockburn added impulsively: "I stood no more chance of beating him than I should of beating you."

More laughter.

The judge said: "But even a man of more than average size would, I think, hesitate to exchange blows with Mr. Bax. Do you not think so, Sir Kenneth?"

"Each time I meet my learned friend in Court I congratulate myself that we are to be mental and not physical opponents, my lord," Griffiths answered promptly.

The sly humour in this remark produced more smiles. Mr. Justice Lovelace's nostrils twitched.

Bax also smiled good-naturedly. He was sure that Cockburn had spoken ingenuously, but the comparison of the dead Smallwood with himself he believed to be a stroke of genius, the effect of which would be to cause the jury mentally to visualize the corpse as being as immense as himself. Nothing could be better! Nothing!

The story of Cockburn's schooldays told, Bax guided the prisoner forward, by stages, to the evening at the Chanticleer Restaurant, the renewal of his acquaintance with Smallwood, and the events of the ensuing weeks up to the moment of his journey to the houseboat on the afternoon of Thursday, the 14th of April, 1927.

Bax spoke to the judge. "My lord, I do not want to spend more time than is necessary in dwelling upon events which took place nearly twenty years ago, but I can assure your lordship that they have a direct bearing upon this present trial."

Mr. Justice Lovelace glanced at the time. "The afternoon is passing, Mr. Bax. Do you see any prospect of this trial being completed today?"

"No, my lord."

"In the circumstances, Mr. Bax, would it be convenient for you to have copies made of the official record of the previous trial for circulation among the members of the jury in time for them to read the evidence given at that trial, before the resumed hearing of these proceedings?"

"I am sure arrangements could be made."

The judge turned towards the jury. "Members of the jury, you will adjourn now until tomorrow morning. Before that time you will receive copies of Rex *v.* Cockburn, which I suggest you should read and digest before the hearing is resumed. In view of the fact that learned counsel for the prisoner has now, of his own accord, identified the accused with Charles Cockburn, this double identity need no longer be considered *sub judice*. From my knowledge of newspaper methods I am sure the news will be treated in a sensational manner. You will, however, not read newspapers containing accounts of this trial until its completion, nor will you discuss this trial with any person other than yourselves. In the meantime, I enjoin you to keep an open mind on the issue which you are sworn to try and true deliverance make, and not allow yourselves to be prejudiced by feelings for or against the accused.

"The Court is adjourned."

III

If the newspapers made the most of the sensational story which emerged at the Maidstone Assize Court, as Mr. Justice Lovelace had prophesied they would, their editors were scarcely to be blamed. The plot of an innocent man being charged with a murder, punished, and subsequently killing the 'victim' for whose alleged death he had suffered—this was a situation which for many years had formed a stock, hypothetical case for discussion among legal students. But now the incredible, the unbelievable, had happened!

Placards! Four, six, even seven, column spreads! Double column headlines! Leaders! Articles! Photographs! All other news had to give precedence to the Windmill Wood Crime.

As a consequence of this whipping up of public interest, the next morning the Assize Court was besieged by a vast crowd of curiosity-mongers who scrambled and jostled and fought one another for the chance of occupying one of the public seats. Police reserves had to be called to the scene to control the situation, and to clear a lane for people who had genuine business at the Court. The number of these latter was swollen by an influx of Press people: special correspondents, columnists, gossip writers, photographers, and others; and a contingent of Famous Personages who hoped their names would assist in squeezing them into Court.

Exactly on time Mr. Justice Lovelace entered the Court. As soon as quietness was restored, he addressed the jury.

"I understand from learned counsel that copies of the pertinent evidence in Rex *v.* Cockburn were duly delivered to you between nine and nine-thirty p.m. last night. May I take it that you have digested at least the gist of the proceedings?"

The members of the jury shuffled uneasily, and glanced uncertainly at one another. Each one of them carried a bundle of typescript. The fat man leaned forward and whispered to the man in front of him. The whisper passed along the line to the foreman, who presently stood up.

"Yes, my lord, I understand that all the members of the jury have read their copies of the previous trial."

"Good. Then we can proceed. Mr. Bax, will you begin?"

Cockburn was already in the witness-stand. Before him was a copy of the evidence, similar to that on the lap of every member of the jury. Sir Kenneth Griffiths also had a copy. Somebody must have performed a fast job of summarizing and typing! Terhune reflected.

"It had been my intention to examine you at short length upon your evidence-in-chief at the previous trial," Bax began. "Now that members of the jury have had an opportunity of reading that evidence for themselves it becomes necessary for me to do no more than touch upon one or two specific replies. Will you turn to page seventy-two of your typescript?"

"What page, Mr. Bax?" the judge asked.

"Page seventy-two of the abridged version, my lord. On the official records, page one hundred and twenty-five."

There was a momentary rustling of papers as people who had copies of the typescript turned to page 72.

"Mr. Cockburn, will you refer to your explanation of what you did immediately upon your return to the houseboat?"

"Do you mean where I say: 'I went first of all to my bedroom—'"

"That is the place. Now, I am going to refer to each paragraph in turn, by asking you whether there is anything in it which you wish to revise or correct."

"I do not follow you, Mr. Bax," the judge interposed. "Are we interested in having the accused revise his evidence of the previous trial?"

"I shall hope to make my reason clear to your lordship very soon."

"Very well, then."

Bax continued:

"Do you wish to revise the paragraph just referred to?"

"No."

"Or the next?"

"No."

"Or the answer beginning: 'Presently I left the bedroom—'?"

"No. Every word of what I said then was true of what happened."

"Then Smallwood walked into the kitchen?"

"Yes. Everything happened as I described until the answer beginning: 'He began to threaten me,' and so on. I should like to amend the rest of my reply."

"Mr. Bax, I still do not follow the reason for this part of your examination. I presume the prisoner took the oath to tell the truth, the whole truth, and nothing but the truth?"

Cockburn replied to the question. "Yes, my lord, I did; but my account of what happened subsequent to Smallwood's threatening me was not true."

"Mr. Bax, I hope you realize the serious consequences of the course you are proposing to take?"

"If you mean, my lord, the risk in allowing the prisoner to admit quite deliberately that he perjured himself, then I do realize the consequences."

"You are asking us to believe implicitly in the word of a man who, by his own confession, committed perjury at the last trial—"

"He was on trial for his life," Bax expostulated.

"He is still on trial for his life," the judge pointed out in a dry voice.

"I am prepared to let the prisoner's demeanour and evidence speak for themselves."

"Very well, then."

To Cockburn again: "What really happened?"

"Smallwood advanced towards me. I realized by his attitude that he intended to strike me. I picked up the meat-chopper, as I said in evidence, and warned him he would get hurt if he moved another step nearer to me."

"And then?"

"Well, sir, it isn't true that my words shook him, and that he was suddenly frightened of me. It was I who became frightened, for he laughed at my warning and came on at me."

"What did you do?"

"Nothing. I stood still, waiting to be hit, like a hypnotized rabbit facing a stoat."

"And then?"

"He raised his arms as if he intended to grip my throat with his strong fingers. At the same time he stepped towards me. As he did so his foot slipped on a piece of fat which had fallen to the floor. His feet slid away from him. He fell forward on to my right shoulder, forcing down the hand which held the chopper. The chopper grazed his scalp as he continued to fall towards the floor. Then his head cannoned against the corner of the electric stove. He doubled up and did not move."

Something of the horror which the prisoner had suffered upon that occasion was passed on to people in Court who were watching him at that moment, for his weak, timid face reflected his mental disturbance at having to relive, even temporarily, a past which had been so unhappy for him. With a shaky hand he pulled a coloured handkerchief from his breast pocket, mopped his glistening forehead with it, then tucked it back in the pocket again, only to repeat this complete performance every minute or so.

"Go on."

"At first I thought he was playing a trick upon me, tormenting me. I stood still, with the chopper in my hand, ready to strike him with it when he resumed the attack—at least, it was my intention to strike, but perhaps if he had gone for me I should have stood just as still as at first. You see," the witness pleaded wistfully, "Smallwood had always had that effect upon me; he had always made a coward of me. Perhaps it was something in his eyes. Or his superior height and strength."

"But there were some occasions when you both attended the same school that you had defended yourself by fighting him back?"

"Yes. In all those years, there had been three or four times when my mind had seemed to go blank, and when I came to, as it were, I found myself lying on the ground, once again a loser."

"We are dealing with the scene on the houseboat, Mr. Bax," the judge reminded counsel.

"As your lordship pleases. Mr. Cockburn, what happened when Smallwood did not rise from the floor and continue the attack upon you?"

"Presently I saw that a few drops of blood had dripped on to the floor from his scalp. I realized that he really was unconscious. I knelt down on the floor, and tried to make him come to. While I was trying to stop his head bleeding the idea occurred to me of dragging him to his punt, dropping him in it, and pushing it off, so that the current could carry him away from the houseboat."

"What eventual good did you hope to achieve by such a plan?"

"I don't know, really. I don't think I considered what might happen the next day. The only thing which affected me just then was the idea of getting rid of Smallwood, if only for a few hours. I dragged him to the punt, managed to heave him into it, then went back for his belongings.

I collected these together, pushed them into the case he had brought with him, and ran back to the punt."

"And then?"

"I saw that he was recovering consciousness, and stirring. Almost insane with fear that I should be unable to carry out my plan after all, I rushed back to the kitchen, picked up the chopper, and hurried back to the punt. I found him on the point of clambering back on to the landing stage of the houseboat. I threatened that if he tried to get back on the houseboat again I would kill him."

"What happened then?"

"I think he was still dazed from the knock on the head and the loss of blood. He stared at me, and stepped back from the houseboat. Before he could recover, I loosened the painter which secured the punt to the houseboat. Then the punt began to drift slowly downstream until it was out of sight."

"One moment. Was there a pole or paddles in the punt?"

"No. I had taken them out so that he should not have a chance of poling or paddling the punt back to the houseboat."

"Well, and then?"

"That was the last I saw of Frank Smallwood."

"You mean, as he disappeared into the darkness of the night?"

"Yes."

"Why did you not tell the full story of what happened at your previous trial?"

"Because I believed that, although I was not directly responsible for his death, I was, indirectly."

"Will you explain that reply?"

"I accepted as a fact that the part of a limb produced at the trial really was Smallwood's. I believed that while he was still dazed he must have fallen out of the punt, and that some accident or other must have befallen him which severed the leg from the rest of the body."

"What kind of an accident?"

"I don't know. I was afraid to give the matter too much thought."

"Why?"

"Because of my—my conscience."

"I see. Now, what of the rest of your evidence at the previous trial? Was any more of it not quite true?"

"Yes, the part where I said I accidentally cut my wrist on the chopper. I did it purposely."

"Why?"

"To account for any bloodstains which might be found."

The judge spoke to the witness. "Just now you were trying to make the Court believe that you were so beside yourself with fear of one sort or another that all your actions that night were the result of panic."

"That is so, my lord."

"The deliberate wounding of yourself to account for the presence of bloodstains resembles more the cunning precautions of a deliberate murderer than the act of a panic-stricken man."

"I don't know what to say, my lord. I can only report what actually happened."

"But you are supposed already to have reported all that at your previous trial. Now you tell us that you were perjuring yourself then. How can we be sure that you are not perjuring yourself now?"

"I don't know, my lord."

"Not a very helpful answer."

"Nor a cunning one, my lord," Bax interposed hastily.

"That is a matter for the jury to infer for themselves, Mr. Bax." To the prisoner again: "Instead of cutting your own wrist with the meat-chopper to account for bloodstains, would it not have been easier for you to have cleaned up the stains of Smallwood's blood?"

"But I did, my lord."

"You did! Then why did you take the precaution of wounding yourself as an alibi?"

"In case there were some bloodstains which I had overlooked. As a matter of fact, the next morning I found I had forgotten to clean up several bloodstains. They were the ones which Philip Shakespeare saw when he went into the kitchen to make tea for his wife, and the ones which I later cleaned up at six-thirty."

The judge remained silent, so Bax continued: "So you went to prison knowing that you had not directly killed Smallwood, and dismembered his corpse, but believing that he had accidentally died as a result of your casting him adrift in his punt?"

"Yes."

"And when was the first occasion thereafter that you realized you had served a term of life imprisonment for a crime you had not committed?"

"Tuesday, last October the eighth, when I met him face to face in Windmill Wood."

The intense silence in Court was disturbed by a faint shuffling noise as the people there realized the significance of the prisoner's admission.

Chapter Twenty-One

"Before we touch upon the events of October the eighth, I should like you briefly to inform the members of the jury how you came to be masquerading in the name of Vivian Thomas Harrison. You were released from prison, I believe, towards the end of nineteen-forty-two. What was your first act upon becoming a free man again?"

"I went to a hotel in Bournemouth for three weeks to celebrate my freedom. And how I celebrated!"

The people in Court were glad to relax temporarily from tension. Subdued laughter came from all quarters.

Bax smiled contentedly. The human touch! Good! Very good!

"And after that?"

"I volunteered to serve in any one of the Services, but my physical condition was not good enough. Eventually, I joined NAAFI, and was sent to the Middle East, where I was employed in canteen transport work. One day I became friendly with an Australian by the name of Vivian Harrison. We—"

"There is a real person by the name of Vivian Thomas Harrison?" the judge interrupted.

"There *was*, my lord."

"You mean, he is dead?"

"I am just about to speak of his death."

"Very well."

"Harrison and I worked on the same transport. We exchanged confidences. Harrison told me of his past history, I told him mine. He believed my story. One day we were both transferred from Egypt to

Tripolitania—this was early in January, nineteen-forty-three, soon after the Eighth Army had occupied the town of Tripoli. Driving our own transport we set off for Tripolitania. One day a German 'plane machine-gunned us. Harrison was killed. While I was awaiting the arrival of a transport which was following behind, the idea occurred to me of changing identities with the dead man—"

"Why?" the judge questioned sharply.

"So that I might make a fresh start in life when the war finished. I believed that the name of Charles Cockburn was too notorious in England for me ever to live there happily."

"Did you particularly want to live in England?"

"Yes, my lord, I did."

"Did you ask yourself whether or no the family of the dead man might resent your borrowing his identity?"

"I did, but Harrison had told me that he had no near relations, and had not returned to Australia for nearly ten years."

"Surely it is no simple matter to exchange identities with a dead man? Were you not likely to he recognized?"

"Well, my lord, I suppose that, normally, it would not be possible to become somebody else overnight, but in this particular instance there were circumstances which made it a risk worth taking. You see, in the first case we were *en route* to a neighbourhood where neither of us was known, and in the second, both of us had somewhat similar physical characteristics. Harrison was only an inch taller than I, and just a shade broader. The shape of our heads was alike, also the colour of our eyes."

"But were your faces alike?"

"Yes, and no, my lord."

"What do you mean by yes and no? Either your faces were alike, or they were not."

"We both had long, drawn faces, and both his skin and mine had been burned a dark brown by the sun. The chief difference between us was my moustache. I believed that without it I might possibly be mistaken for Harrison by anyone who had not seen us for a long time."

"It is inconceivable that such a preposterous plan could have had a successful conclusion. But continue."

"I exchanged identity discs with Harrison, and all my private papers with his. I also slipped on to his finger the ring which Miss Webb had returned to me. Then I quickly cut my moustache down to a stubble. Later, I shaved it off entirely. When we were eventually reached by army transports which had been travelling in the same direction two miles or so behind, the soldiers helped to bury Harrison. The officer in charge took possession of the dead man's identity disc and papers, and reported the death of Charles Cockburn. I went forward to the next base as Harrison, and Harrison I remained until this morning."

"Did you never return to Egypt?"

"No, my lord. I returned to England from Algiers, where I was later posted."

"Did you never meet any people who had known either yourself or Harrison in Egypt?"

"Yes, my lord, several."

"Did none of them suspect or note anything strange about you?"

"Only one young fellow, who had known Harrison fairly well. He stared at me in a strange way, and asked me if I hadn't altered a bit in the past year, but as by that time I was talking with an Australian accent, and using all Harrison's mannerisms, I didn't find it a very hard job to deceive him, and made him believe that his memory of Harrison in Egypt wasn't too clear. Of course, from the first I had realized that I should be running risks by adopting Harrison's identity, but for the sake of starting a new life I was prepared to take those risks. As for Harrison himself, his character was not one to resent a pal making use of it for a decent purpose."

The judge remained silent, so Bax went on: "So you came back to England as Vivian Harrison?"

"Yes, and eventually settled down in Farthing Toll, where I have been ever since."

"You have heard witnesses give evidence of the stories you used to tell in *Toll Inn* of your supposed travels. They were untruths?"

"Some of them were stories of Harrison's travels, which he had told to me from time to time during our journeys in Egypt. The other stories came from books which I had read while in prison. I was specially keen on books of travel and books about foreign countries because they carried me right away from the prison cell."

"Very well, we will now deal with the events of October the eighth. You have heard witnesses give evidence of your movements that day. Was that evidence approximately correct?"

"Yes. But I want to admit that I did walk home *via* Windmill Wood, and not *via* Wickford. When I learned from Mrs. Brooks that she had seen me coming out of Windmill Wood, I lost my head, and said the first thing which came into my mind."

"You are not a very truthful man," the judge accused.

"Normally, my lord, I think I am as truthful as any man. I am not fond of lying. But when one is in fear of one's life, lies come easily to the lips. They are out before one realizes one had any intention of speaking."

The judge waved his hand. Bax said: "You arrived at the western boundary of Windmill Wood about—when?"

"About five-forty p.m."

"And you entered the woods by way of the footpath leading to Farthing Toll?"

"Yes."

"Now tell the Court, in your own words, what happened next?"

"Just as I turned off the Rye road—"

II

Cockburn glanced up. Although the rain had stopped, the sky was heavily overcast; massive, black-lined banks of clouds were moving ponderously inland. No break in the gloomy, forbidding skyscape was anywhere to be seen.

He looked at his watch. Only twenty minutes to six. The fading light created the impression of approaching darkness, but evidently this was due to the clouds, for, properly, there should still be twenty minutes to go before approaching dusk became noticeable.

He turned off the road on to the well-defined footpath which meandered through Windmill Wood as far as Farthing Toll Road. Windmill Wood was private property, and belonged to Godfrey Hutton, of Wickford, but the public had used the footpath through it for so long they had long ago established a right of way along it; Cockburn smiled to himself as he reflected upon what would happen should Hutton, or any subsequent owner, attempt to close the path by placing an obstacle across it. The law would frown upon Hutton's temerity for using his own property as he willed, and order him forthwith to remove the obstruction to some other spot where it would be less offensive to the public.

A queer business, this question of right of way, he thought, as he avoided the puddles. Just because some distant ancestor had raised no objection to a handful of people's using the path as the quickest way home from market, his son's son, and all his descendants thereafter would no longer have the right to consider the path their own property—at least in so far as its assets were concerned, though its liabilities would remain. On the surface, it was a poor sort of a reward for a man who had been disposed kindly towards his neighbours.

A few more paces carried him well into the leafy tunnel of trees, where the depressing autumn chill became a subdued, green-tinged half-light. Underfoot, the path was deceptively covered by a thin carpet of fallen leaves, and as the leaves still retained their colours, the effect was not unbeautiful. But as his feet slithered in the oozing mud which the leaves concealed, Cockburn thought that a bare, dry path was preferable to one which would coat his boots and the ends of his trousers in thick, sticky mud.

He whistled loudly as he moved along the slippery footpath. He always whistled, or hummed, or sang unmusically when he passed through the wood at dusk. Was he nervous, or afraid? Scarcely. But as a man born a town-dweller, who had spent the first half of his life surrounded by brick buildings, he had the city dweller's instinctive shrinking from the brooding solitude and uncanny quietness of the country night. At first he had experienced this even when crossing his own few acres on a dark night, but time had accustomed him to the soothing silence, and he had even grown to appreciate it. But neither time nor many journeys through the wood had helped him entirely to ignore the eerie mystery of the thick belt of trees and undergrowth which stretched for nearly half a mile on either side.

Momentarily, the dance tune faded as he tried to reach a high note. It was precisely at that moment when he heard a snapping explosion from a short distance ahead. He had no doubt as to the cause—somebody had stepped upon a dead branch. He stared at the spot where the path curved to his right. Sure enough, as he approached it, another person appeared in sight, approaching from the opposite direction.

The stranger was a man, a burly, sizeable man, but in the uncertain light, and because the man's coat-collar was turned up, Cockburn was unable to recognize the newcomer by face. Nor by build, for that matter. Probably an Ashford man, he thought.

"Goodnight," he called out, as the two men neared each other.

The stranger grunted unintelligibly, then recoiled.

"Godalmighty!" he gabbled.

Cockburn halted abruptly, and peered at the other man. What was the matter with him?

"God Almighty!" the stranger repeated. "Charlie Cockburn!" Amazement became raucous laughter. "As I live and die—*Charlie Cockburn!*"

The mist of bitterness obscured Cockburn's vision. The ghost of his past, which he had thought laid for perpetuity, had risen to confront him. Charlie Cockburn! Somebody knew him as Charlie Cockburn!"

With a mocking gesture the other man thrust his hat back from the forehead so that he might be recognized more clearly.

Presently Cockburn shook his head, smiled deprecatingly, and blinked. Absurd, he thought, how lifelike an apparition could appear— he had often read of people who suffered from hallucinations, but he had never expected—and yet, why not? Out in the desert he had seen a mirage. Hallucinations—mirages—ghosts—they were all of one family, as it were—all tricks of the brain, or tricks of nature...

Smallwood found it easy to follow, from the expression on Cockburn's face, the trend of his reflections. The sailor's laughter increased.

"What is the matter, little man? Do you think you are looking at a ghost? Some ghost, eh?" He struck his chest with the flat of his hand; the hollow sound which resulted was flung back by the trees.

"Wake up out of your faint, little man! Wake up and listen to me. This is a moment I dreamed about for fifteen years, and I'm not going to be robbed of the pleasure of it now. Look alive, there, you little bastard, and listen to me."

Cockburn did not move. His pale blue eyes remained lifeless. This hallucination was too horrible—he would not be able to bear it for long. Why hadn't he taken the bus as far as Wickford, and walked home *via* Toll Road? Why hadn't he called upon Jellicoe to ask about the eggs—as had been his intention at one moment during the afternoon? He should have known better than to pass through the wood so late in the afternoon, when deepening shadows could play queer tricks upon the imagination.

Frank Smallwood! As if Smallwood, of all people, could be still alive! Smallwood had been dead twenty years. Why, hadn't he, Charlie, spent fifteen years in prison just on account of Smallwood's death? Well, then...

Smallwood continued to laugh and jeer.

"Do you remember the night when you threatened to strike me with that meat-chopper, Charlie, me boy? I'll bet you haven't forgotten." His face became bestial. "Nor have I. My God! I'll say I haven't. I'm not likely to have, neither. I went through hell because of you. Do you know why? I said, do you want to know why?"

Still Cockburn remained dumb. He thought: What can I do to stop this hellish nightmare? How does one stop nightmares? Try to make oneself realize one is only dreaming? I'll try it. I'm only dreaming. This is a nightmare. Wake up, Charlie, boy. Wake up. Oh, God! Wake up, you fool! Wake up! Don't you know that Smallwood is dead? You are a blasted fool, Charlie! Smallwood is dead.

But Smallwood went on:

"When you cast me adrift in that punt you thought you had got the better of me, didn't you, my little man! And all the time, you moon-faced rabbit, I was laughing at you, because I intended to make sure that you would soon be laughing on the other side of your face. Did you think I was going to let you put one across me as easily as that? Not me, by God! I had whacked you all my life, and I wasn't going to stand for the tables being turned. As soon as you were out of sight I meant to use my hands to paddle the punt to the bank, and return to the houseboat by way of the road. Do you hear me, you speechless fool?"

Cockburn stared at his tormentor. How could an hallucination appear so real? Could it be that he was not dreaming after all? That it was a living man who was shouting at him, and not a gibing spectre?

Smallwood laughed as he saw his victim begin to shrink back with fear. "That's the stuff, Charlie, me boy; that's what I want to see. Now you're beginning to realize what's coming to you. But not yet, Charlie. Not yet. All in good time. I'm going to make the most of this moment, and while I tell you the story of me travels, I'm going to enjoy watching you squirm in anticipation of what I'm going to do to you to make you suffer for what I've been through these last twenty years. Don't think you've any chance against me. I'm stronger than I ever was. Strong enough to twist you into knots, to wring your ruddy little neck if I want to. And maybe I shall, too, just to finish off with. But that won't be yet awhile. First you're going to listen to me."

Petrified by the coarse, sadistic voice, Cockburn did not move. The book which he was carrying under his right arm dropped unnoticed on to the soft footpath.

"As soon as I was out of sight I started paddling for the bank. I reached it, landed, and began to make me way back to the houseboat. And then—" A stream of vituperative oaths interrupted the thread of the story. The violence of his temper smacked of insanity.

"A drunken swine of a Finnish skipper, driving a hired car, ran bang into me, and knocked me cold. The son of a bitch! What did he do? Leave me there for someone else to find me? Drive me to the nearest hospital? Blast him! I'll tell you what he did, Mr. Blooming Charlie Cockburn. He pitched me into the back of his car, drove me to the coast where his ruddy hulk was being loaded, and carried me aboard. When I came to the damned ship was heading down Channel."

I I I

"Are you implying that Smallwood was abducted?" The judge interrupted incredulously.

"Shanghaied was the word he used, my lord. According to

Smallwood, the ship was a sailing vessel bound for a South American port, and due to sail by the outgoing tide early the following morning. Apparently the skipper was afraid that if he were to report the accident to a hospital or the police his departure would be delayed. Being short-handed, anyway, he decided to shanghai Smallwood in the hope that, by the time the ship reached port, he would have persuaded Smallwood to keep his mouth shut. If Smallwood should prove obstinate the skipper intended to see that one night he—Smallwood—accidentally fell overboard when there was no chance of picking him up. At least, that is what Smallwood told me." Seeing that the judge had no comment to make, the witness continued.

"As soon as he could, Smallwood deserted his ship, and managed to get a berth aboard a homeward-bound Dutch vessel. When the Dutchman reached an English port he deserted again. That night he read all about my trial in the newspapers."

The judge lifted his head sharply. "Do you allege that Smallwood read an account of your trial in the newspapers?"

"That is what he told me. I swear he did, my lord."

"Then why did he not announce to the authorities that an innocent man was being tried?"

"Because he wanted to revenge himself upon me for what I did to him aboard the houseboat."

The judge pursed his lips together, and continued writing.

Bax asked: "What did Smallwood do when he realized that your life was in danger?"

"Went to sea again the next day so that nobody should recognize him from the photographs in the papers."

"He went to sea with the deliberate intention of ensuring that you should suffer the consequences of a crime you did not commit?"

"Yes, sir. I can still hear him saying: 'I wasn't going to let you get off scot-free if I could help you to swing.'"

"Then he expected you to be executed?"

"That is what he told me in the woods."

"And then?"

"He went on to tell me of reading one day, in one of the South American ports, an old newspaper which reported that my sentence of death had been commuted to life imprisonment. 'That meant my staying away from England for twenty years or so,' he said. 'But I didn't mind that. Whenever I wanted to have a good laugh I had only to think of you sitting in a ruddy cell, and of me steaming round the world, and God! did I laugh. Many's the hour I've laughed away, thinking of you in a cell for something you wouldn't have had the nerve to do, even if you'd had the chance.'"

"Try not to be hysterical," the judge ordered sharply.

"I will try, my lord," Cockburn agreed submissively.

"Very well. Did Smallwood have anything more to say?"

"Yes, my lord. He went on to tell me that he read of my death in the Middle East, so what was I doing alive, and in England?"

"Did you tell him?"

"No, my lord. I was incapable of speaking. All I could think of was that I had spent fifteen years in prison for nothing, and that Smallwood could have saved my life from being ruined merely by calling in at any police-station. Then he demanded if I had any money on me, and if I had, I could damn' well pass it over.

"When I still didn't answer he lost his temper. He told me he was going to do to me what he had intended doing aboard the house-boat, and help himself to my money at the same time. With that he advanced towards me, laughing hoarsely, his eyes gleaming with fury——"

The judge's calm, even voice was in sharp contrast to the witness's pathetically weak, hysterical raving.

"Omitting these annoying melodramatic embellishments, what did you do?"

"I don't know, my lord."

"You don't know!"

"No, my lord. Everything seemed to go black, just as it used to happen when I was at school. For a moment it seemed to me that we were both back in the past, aboard the houseboat. I felt myself looking round for the meat-chopper. And then—"

"And then?"

"I found myself holding a heavy branch in my hand, and saw Smallwood lying at my feet."

"In fact, with certain changes, the scene was similar to that which took place twenty-five years ago? For the second time Smallwood had attacked you, and for the second time you came to from a momentary mental 'black-out', to see your powerful adversary lying, unconscious, at your feet?"

"Yes, my lord, that was the situation."

"Very well."

"I dropped the branch, and tried to bring Smallwood round—"

"You did not think of running?"

"I do not think I did, my lord. I am not quite sure what my real thoughts were. But presently I discovered he was dead. I became panic-stricken. I remembered the events of my trial, and the fifteen years' imprisonment I had suffered. I felt I could not bear to go through the terrible suspense and punishment all over again. I looked round, and seeing nobody about I dragged the body beneath a tree, covered it with leaves, and hurried off to Farthing Toll. That is the truth, my lord. I swear that is the truth."

I I

The trial dragged on. After the examination-in-chief followed the cross-examination, which very soon confounded the prisoner on minor details, but failed to shake his evidence about the major. Then came the speech for the prosecution: the speech for the defence, and lastly, the judge's charge to the jury.

"Members of the jury," the judge began, after a few preliminary sniffs, "the prisoner, Charles Cockburn, is charged with having murdered one Frank Hugh Smallwood, on the afternoon of October the eighth last, in Windmill Wood. In reply to this charge the prisoner, through his learned counsel, has put forward two alternative defences, with which I now propose to deal.

"The first defence was that of a special plea known as *autrefois convict*. I do not propose to deal fully with the legal aspects of that plea, because a properly qualified jury has already dismissed the plea before you were empanelled to try the prisoner on the present charge. Yet I must deal briefly with that plea, because it is my duty to instruct you not to be influenced by the knowledge that the prisoner has been tried and punished for a crime which he did not commit in nineteen-twenty-seven but which the prosecution alleges he did commit last October.

"The common law of this country—that precious heritage for which men have fought and died from the eleventh century onwards to protect and retain—that common, law justly and mercifully lays down that no man may twice suffer for the same offence. It is only human, not to say fascinating, to argue, therefore—as in effect learned counsel for the prisoner has argued in the course of his closing address—that, because the prisoner suffered unjustly for a crime which he did not commit, he should not again suffer similar penalties for that crime when, it is alleged, the prisoner did, in fact, commit it. Counsel has invited you to say that Smallwood's death last October at the hands of the prisoner is a reversal of the usual process of making the punishment fit the crime. For the first time in legal history, says counsel, the prisoner has made the crime fit the punishment. For the first time, he continues, the prisoner was punished before he committed the crime, instead of afterwards. But the fact remains, counsel argues ingeniously, the prisoner was punished for the crime of killing Smallwood, so that the law against the wilful taking of human life has been satisfied by the prisoner's having been declared guilty, and justice has been served by a sentence of death, which was afterwards commuted to one of life imprisonment.

"Counsel then went on, you will remember, to speak of his plea of *autrefois convict*. He said—I will quote his words: 'The learned judge properly advised the jury to dismiss the plea of *autrefois convict* on legal grounds. He drew the attention of the members of the first jury to the fact that, before they could bring in a verdict that the plea succeeded, it was necessary for the defence to prove that the two charges were identical. His lordship then instructed the jury that the two charges were not identical, because the first accused the prisoner of murdering Smallwood in the county of Surrey, in nineteen-twenty-seven, whereas the second accused the prisoner of murdering Smallwood in the county of Kent, in nineteen-forty-six. In consequence of his lordship's direction the jury dismissed the plea. But you, members of the second jury, need not, cannot dismiss the plea on just, on human, on merciful grounds.'

"So saith counsel for the defence. But it is my duty, members of the jury, to instruct you that, in arriving at your true verdict, you *must* dismiss the plea. The prisoner in the dock is being tried for having, on October the eighth last, killed Frank Hugh Smallwood in the county of Kent, and that is the simple issue which you must decide. Did Cockburn kill Smallwood on the day, and in the place alleged? If you find that he did, it is your duty—and you have taken an oath to do that duty faithfully and well—to bring in a verdict of guilty. If you find that he did not, then you will bring in a verdict of not guilty. What happened in the past must not concern you. You must not take into account the fact that the accused served fifteen years' imprisonment for a crime he did not commit. There is one issue and one issue only before you. Did, or did not, Cockburn kill Smallwood on October the eighth, nineteen-forty-six?

"So much for the first defence. Upon its dismissal counsel fell back upon the second, which was obvious to me from the first, and perhaps to you also, upon which he enlarged during his closing speech. Briefly, members of the jury, counsel invites you to say that the prisoner did, in fact, kill Smallwood, but in circumstances so provocative to the prisoner as to reduce the charge of murder to one of manslaughter.

"Let us examine, quite shortly, the essential qualifications of the two charges. What is the essence of murder? The crime of murder may be defined as the unlawful killing by a sane person of another person in being and under the King's peace with malice aforethought, either express or implied.

"How do these essentials apply in this present case? We have listened to incontrovertible evidence that there was a killing, also that that killing was unlawful. But is the prisoner sane? He has offered no evidence of insanity, so you are entitled to conclude him sane. 'A person in being.' The words need no further comment from me. 'Under the King's peace.' Only alien enemies are not under the King's Peace. Lastly: 'with malice aforethought, either express or implied.'

"Upon these seven words will depend your verdict. You have heard the evidence. From first to last was there any suggestion in it that the prisoner entered Windmill Wood on the afternoon of October the eighth with the prior knowledge that he would there meet the prisoner? I think not. So, in the absence of proof to the contrary, the prisoner is entitled to be believed when he asserts that, on recognizing the man whom he was supposed to have murdered nearly twenty years previously: 'I stared at him as if he were a ghost—at that moment I believe I thought he was a ghost.' I could enlarge upon the many reasons the prisoner must have had for believing the other man to be dead, but I do not think it necessary to do so; they are obvious to any normally intelligent person.

"So we arrive at the word 'malice'. Did the prisoner kill Smallwood with deliberate malice, or was he overtaken by one of those mental blackouts which he would have you believe he has sometimes suffered when tormented by the hectoring bully? It is possible that the prisoner knew the elementary rudiments of law—and we all know that a little knowledge is a dangerous thing. Perhaps he saw a man coming towards him whom he suddenly recognized as Smallwood. In the recollection of all he had suffered on account of his supposed murder of the man in front of him; in the recollection, also, of what he may once have read concerning the common law of England which lays down that a man may not be punished twice for the same offence, it is possible that he picked up the fallen oak branch with the deliberate intention of striking the oncoming Smallwood. If this is what you conscientiously believe did actually occur, you do not need to ask yourself if the prisoner really intended to kill Smallwood, or only intended hurt or injury. Even if the prisoner intended no more than minor hurt upon the other man, in making a hurtful blow at Smallwood's head the prisoner is none the less guilty of homicide if it should so happen that his blow is a direct cause of death.

"It is for you, members of the jury, to believe or disbelieve the prisoner's story, for upon that story rests his only defence. He has offered no evidence other than that story. He has said, in effect: 'Yes, I killed Smallwood. I was in fear of my life, so I picked up a handy branch of a tree in the hope of defending myself.' He has also said, in effect: 'I did not know how or when I hit him; I was temporarily unconscious of my actions.'

"These two separate explanations are contradictory. If the prisoner was in fear of his life then that fear supplied, most understandably, the impulse which prompted him to defend himself, but the impulse was one which I conceive to be very, and humanly, conscious. Nevertheless, either explanation, if you believe it, entitles you to say that the prisoner did not kill with malice, and is not, therefore, guilty of culpable homicide, but only of manslaughter.

"Do you believe the prisoner's story? Do you believe his bare word in explanation of what took place in Windmill Wood upon the occasion of that tragic meeting one early October afternoon? You have seen the prisoner give his evidence. You have heard him confess, quite unashamed, that he perjured himself at his first trial. Perhaps you might wish to excuse this perjury on the grounds that his life was in jeopardy, and that the man who would not utter a simple lie to save his life must be a saint. I cannot prevent your regarding his previous perjury with an understanding forgiveness, but I must remind you, as I have reminded the prisoner, that he is still in jeopardy of his life, and that a man who had previously perjured himself in the hope of saving his life is not likely to hesitate to do so again.

"Is the prisoner's story an improbable one? Certainly, it is less improbable than the amazing truth that the same man should be twice tried for murdering the same man. Moreover, it is, I suggest, consistent. You have read the evidence given at the previous trial, and are aware that Smallwood's character was, to say the least, unenviable. He was a despicable man who might well have acted in a manner described by the prisoner. But was Smallwood so despicable?—could any human being have been so despicable?—so deliberately to have exiled himself from his own country for the sole satisfaction of revenging himself upon a victim who, for once, had dared to defend himself and fight back. On this point I will say no more than that I did not form an unfavourable opinion of the witness while he was giving evidence on his own behalf.

"Members of the jury, will you now retire and consider your verdict."

III

The jury retired. Before they had been gone fifteen minutes, Helena said to Terhune:

"This suspense is unbearable, Tommy. Why are they so long absent? Isn't it obvious that poor Mr. Harrison—I mean Cockburn—didn't mean to kill Smallwood?"

"I wonder!"

"Tommy!" Helena was shocked. "Do you meen to sit there calmly and admit that you think that that poor harmless man picked up that branch with the intention of killing his tormentor?"

"Would you have blamed him if he had, Helena?"

"I—I don't know—"

"Think! If you had served fifteen years in prison on account of supposedly killing someone who had always bullied you, and if, suddenly, you met that person again, and learned that a word from him would have saved you from serving that sentence, wouldn't you have felt like killing the other man?"

"I suppose so. But do you really—honestly and truthfully—think that Cockburn *meant* to kill Smallwood?"

"N-no," he admitted slowly. "Personally, I believe the truth is, that with one thing and another, hatred of the other man, fear of being attacked, and so on, Cockburn didn't know what he was doing."

"Well, then!" she exclaimed triumphantly. "If you can believe that, why can't the jury?"

Just then Murphy nudged Terhune. "Do you know who is in Court?"

"Who?"

"Romance, in the name of Miss Patricia Webb!"

"Good Lord! Poor Miss Webb! I should have thought her presence at this trial would have re-opened too many old sores for her."

"Don't you believe it! She told Inspector Street that she's convinced the jury will bring in a verdict of not guilty, and if so, this time she means to marry Cockburn even if she has to use Street's handcuffs to chain him up to her while she carries him off to church."

"They deserve each other."

"They do," the sergeant agreed, as the bailiff in charge of the jury re-entered the Court. "Here they come."

As soon as the Court was ready, the Clerk of Assize addressed the jury.

"Members of the jury, are you agreed upon your verdict?"

"We are," said the Foreman in a husky voice that was warm with the Kentish burr.

"Do you find the prisoner at the Bar, Charles Cockburn, known as Vivian Thomas Harrison, guilty or not guilty?"

"Not guilty of murder, but guilty of manslaughter."

A storm of handclapping broke out in the public benches, but this was quickly hushed.

The judge addressed the prisoner.

"Charles Cockburn, otherwise Vivian Thomas Harrison, you have been tried, for the second time, for the wilful murder of Frank Hugh Smallwood, and a jury of your fellow men and women have found you not guilty of murder but guilty of manslaughter. With that decision I heartily concur.

"You have been the victim, in the past, of a grave miscarriage of justice, which I would consider even graver than it was had you not, in some small measure, contributed to your own subsequent misfortune by the manner in which you cast Smallwood adrift from the houseboat without pole or paddles. It is not for me or anyone else to censure you for that foolish, though understandable, gesture, particularly as you suffered for it by serving a sentence, which, but for God's mercy, might have been even worse.

"I have now to sentence you for your crime of manslaughter, of which the jury properly found you guilty. In deciding what sentence I should impose upon you I am conscious of your previous sentence. Although I instructed the members of the jury not to be prejudiced by that sentence in arriving at a verdict, because the wilful taking of another's life is a crime which a properly constituted Court of Law cannot and will not excuse, whatever the circumstances, nevertheless, it remains a fact, which I propose to take into consideration, that you have already served fifteen years' imprisonment for the killing of Frank Hugh Smallwood.

"Since your arrest you have been in custody for more than three months. I therefore sentence you to three months' imprisonment in the second division, sentence to be retrospective from the date of your arrest."

"I thank your lordship," Cockburn said in a trembling voice.

Mr. Justice Lovelace rose to his feet.

The trial of Charles Cockburn was over.

"How about something to eat?" Terhune suggested to Murphy and Helena.

"Come to think of it, I could do with a bite. I'm peckish," the sergeant agreed enthusiastically.

The trial of Charles Cockburn was indeed finished!

THE END